IN THE FLESH

JUSTIN HERZOG

ORPHIC BOOKS

USA

IN THE FLESH published by Orphic Books, 2011

Cover Design by Dauntelle

http://www.orphicbooks.com

ISBN 978-0-615-37123-8

The novel depicts actual people, living and dead, in fictional settings, events, and behaviors. This is for entertainment purposes and does not suggest any actual similarities to the persons referenced.

The novel depicts actual events in world history in a fictionalized manner and is not intended to be an accurate description of those events.

All other characters and events in the novel are fictional.

Cover includes elements of historical art works in the public domain.

PRINTED IN THE UNITED STATES OF AMERICA

1

I am older than I look. My name, if such words apply, is Nathan Sorren. Who can say what I am? I can only tell you how I came to be. It was so long ago.

Preceding the elixir, the Forbidden Knowledge, and centuries before I became a movie star bells sounded for a condemned man. The rusty chain cries between each toll were mine. They still wail today.

Father was there with me. We stood upon the eroded cobblestone brick commons. Ahead was an altar of black iron and jagged timber. On the platform, grim hooded figures watched upward. Father wanted to show me, but I did not want to see.

I looked downward to the pooled waters at my feet. There was a crimson band beneath the water, old anonymous blood. Shimmering on the surface was the masked boy. The painted porcelain covers me from forehead to chin. I wore Father's gift since the first day I remember.

Behind was the ruin of my original face. There had been no trauma or tragic cause, only an accident of birth. A gaping void hung where my top lip should have been. The snaggle of teeth and gum was a nasty sight. He called me the little beast, a godless wonder.

"Look now, boy! They bring the prisoner!" shouted Father over the rumblings of the vengeful crowd.

Father brought my three brothers and I to the beheading of England's Chancellor. The soliciter defied the King and found himself locked away in the great tower of London. At that tender age Father believed me ready to witness a human slaughter. This would be the first of two deaths that day.

"There is no better understanding of the King's authority over England than what you will see here," he told us as we readied for the deadly axe swing.

Father seized my hand in an agonizing grip. A smile filled his face. He pleasured in cruelties against his hated son. Father was an angry, hulking figure. His hands were chiseled mallets. He was matted in thick brown hair; his eyes a merciless black.

Through the pain of his crushing hold, I surveyed the gathered crowd. Some heads hung in guilt and prayer. Others held fists skyward, threw rotted fruit, and ranted in hateful anticipation. Merchants sold beverages, linens, and woven rugs. Street performers entertained the crowds with painted faces, acrobatics, and deeds of trickery.

"The bastard!" Father shouted.

Hooded men forced the man forward across a twisted, descending wooden walkway. The prisoner's tightly tied hands upset his balance at their pace. The condemned one was thin, hunched, and weak. His hair was thinning and gray. They brought him to us within a rod.

Father's dealings with the King placed us only feet away from the cleaved wood block where More would rest his neck. As the prisoner neared his final earthly posture he uttered, "See me safe up. For my coming down I can shift for myself." Then he declared, "I die the King's good servant, and God's first."

With the swing of a jewel-encrusted axe he was gone. His silver-haired head dropped free from his emaciated body. I saw the lackluster paste death had rubbed over his open eyes. The animate became the inanimate. Life receded to death and its tangible subtraction. The transformation was complete.

Father laughed along with others in the crowd, mocking the head dropping in the basket.

"Long live the King!" exclaimed the many of them.

The kind ones wept and prayed. They made religious motions and signs through their tears. A few men held their women tightly as they turned and walked from the capital penalty. Most cheered the bloodshed.

This was my first memory of death, but not my first encounter. I once defeated a grave illness as Mother surrendered to it. My brothers told me of her demise. Their lesson comforted me. Life was not eternal. Life's end would one day rescue me. The beheading reminded me of this.

Hours after the execution I sat on the floor of the parlor. I played with the wooden men Stephen fashioned from driftwood. A rumbling arose from the entryway. It was the snarl of clashing metal and stone, of vicious words and hateful contempt.

"Where is that cruel bastard? Sorren!" the trespasser hissed into the vacant air.

He smelled of manure and spoiled earth. He was a peasant, a nameless and faceless farmer evicted from one of Father's lots. The high rents made no guarantee of the dirt and green fields within its domain. A spoiled grain crop and disease-plagued swine left the man ruined. Arrears accumulated for the months of the crisis and Father proved unforgiving.

Stephen, my kind and eldest brother, set out to ask what it was the man wanted done. I remember him there, his hair and skin brilliantly fair, standing so gently. Lacking in the cold cruelty that came first nature to Father, Stephen asked in tranquil concern, "He is not here in this moment, but perhaps I could be of some aid?"

The farmer's visit was not about what he wanted done, but what he intended to do. His arm pulled back over his shoulder. He plunged a rusted ore spike through the chest of my brother. Stephen's wide eyes turned lifeless as he fell into his own pooling blood.

There was in that second a change as his spirit, or what I would later come to call his "essence," departed from his physical body. Stasis set. Stephen had been handsome and charmed. I envied him in every way. Even then when he was dead and free.

Where had Stephen gone? His body was there before me, but it was no longer him. I imagined him a faint facsimile drifting about in his pressed nightshirt. From there he would float up and away through the second and third floors into the night. Tripping through the air, free from mortal bondage, he would no doubt find the place I knew loosely as heaven. Through the mist was a conglomerate of gold and cloud, a phantom palace in the sky. Within its ethereal walls the risen dead would await his glorious appearing. No doubt Mother was there to receive him.

The murderous farmer ran from our home covered in my brother's blood. He was captured, tried, and executed the following day. Being of no special relation or interest to Henry VIII, he knew a death far worse than simple beheading. The man had been hanged, drawn, and quartered. I was disappointed Father did not bring us to the execution. True, I wanted justice for my murdered brother, but I equally sought to view the travel of the enraged farmer's essence as it left him. I wanted to bear witness to the change again.

The reception after Stephen's secular funeral became a business meeting for Father once his tears dried. He spoke of rents and ousters. Then he was drunk and foul. By the end he had dismissed the mourners and us with harsh insults.

He believed in no spiritual element to the world, his case furthered by the senseless murder of his favored son. Life moved on and I went about the drab existence of being ignored, blamed, or abused by Father. His contempt for me knew neither ends nor bounds. Deep into the night he cursed the heavens and hell for taking his wife and then his son from him.

Eventually Arthur, my second eldest brother, entered into Father's business affairs. Over some years this became necessity as Father now indulged in drunkenness daily. Arthur, like Stephen, was handsome and articulate. He pleased Father with his quick study and natural talent for business dealings.

"You are good, but not so good as to be like your brother," I heard Father say to him. Arthur accepted this as an unequivocal compliment with a gentle nod of his head.

I did my best to stay clear of Father when he was home. Arthur's competence relit Father's vigor for his works. My avoidance of Father was made easier by this for a time. Then one day Father appeared in the doorway of my room as I read discarded pages secretly taken from his burn pile.

"You will join us in our travels tomorrow. Make us all a lunch for the coach ride as it will take us much of the morning to arrive. We will leave at daylight, so sleep soon."

I was in awe. Father never included me in his business affairs, in anything really, and now I would be given a chance to take part. I was eager to impress Father and Arthur with my knowledge of the common law of English realty learned from my secret collection of discarded pages. For one sleepless night I knew what it was to have the love and acceptance of my father.

Strong horses pulled the coach before the main entrance to the manor. Behind loomed a red, angry sun creeping over the rolling greens to the east. I clutched the satchel holding loaves of bread and cheese to my chest in excitement. I climbed in to Arthur and Father. Father looked out the open window of the coach at the sun while Arthur looked at me. There was something troubled in his expression, but I was too eager to consider it. During the ride I would learn only that Father was selling a tract of his land and I would be participating in the transaction.

In the noon of that day I learned of the Livery of Seisen. I stood there on an open patch of land. A filth and dirt-covered man looked and laughed as he counted the money in his hand. Father stood before the man clenching a fistful of earth pulled from the ground.

"Let it be known by those present that I, Emerson Rand Sorren, hereby convey in absolute fee this land upon which I now stand," said Father. he next offered dimensions and landmarks measured in rods while passing the gripped earth to the filthy laughing man.

The crude transfer completed, or so I thought. With the clump of soil exchanged I rested back on my heels. Two men grabbed me and threw me to the ground. The men there, Father and Arthur included, gave me successive kicks and punches. My heart broke with consciousness. As there were no deeds of public record, my beating would ensure I would never forget the transaction. This was the Livery of Seisen.

I awoke in my bedroom covered in blood and dirt. I felt sharp pains in my mouth and upon inspection found missing a fair number of teeth. I washed in a filled basin next to me. Nobody in our home ever said a word. Nobody in history ever came inquiring about ownership of the property.

Father fell forever deeper into alcoholic oblivion. When he lost Stephen, Father lost his remaining soul. In time, Arthur tired of the relentless anger and criticism. He fell in love with a girl named Anna whom my family never met. He ran away with her. I heard nothing of him ever again.

My remaining brother, Aaron, and I became invisible to Father unless targeted for his violence. Aaron was put to the menial tasks of Father's enterprise. He was used for type copying and deliveries rather than taught. After a year Aaron left, too.

Father liquidated real estate interests, building with the proceeds a rudimentary mortgage bank and general investment company. He funded sugar expeditions paying tenfold when the sweet rivaled gold in value. In his misery he vaulted to be amongst the wealthiest of England in even greater standing with Henry VIII.

Father spent his time in a tavern built on his cherished piece of Thames waterfront. This was one of the first parcels he bought as a young man. He drank day and night at the pub: inebriated, gambling, and carousing. With my brothers aged and gone, I was left largely alone. This I preferred.

Father's fall from the world was not absolute. Through the camaraderie of the drink, he found the gossips and the tales they tell. Their tongues filled the spaces in Father's life that could not compete with money and business. He sat alone, waiting.

One such night Father was approached by a man and woman who knew Father and our home. They asked him of the ugly, unkempt boy playing about in the adjacent pasture. They reported the boy was covered head to toe with filth; his clothes were but tattered rags. All of these things they considered odd, but unworthy of troubling the constable.

Father came home rageful.

"I tell you to hide!" he shouted as he whipped me with a leather strap. "My friends should not have to look upon you! Look at you!"

I placed my arms over my head and crouched to the floor. I could take his beating, but he ceased. He left me for a moment and returned with a bucket of rainwater. Father threw it over me.

"Take off those rags."

Somewhere in the violence his shame bloomed.

2

Her brilliant beauty lit our doorway in the cold dark of night. She came to us with a humble manner and glistening reference. It was the first I would know of caring regularity and order. It was the first I would know of love.

Rosetta would be my new caretaker. To write the name swells my cruel, old heart. She was sixteen years of age when Father found her. Rosetta was born and lived in the countryside with a mother some took as an elder sister. The conception of her mother's liaison with a nobleman, the beauty never left England yet spoke the telltale accent of English as a secondary tongue.

The impetuous nobleman lost himself within Rosetta's mother. Rampant rumor told him the object of his desire was a gypsy witch. Villagers spoke of her dark practices and rituals. It was the things that turned the men of his generation away from such a woman he found irresistible. Her sins created in him an insatiable thirst.

He ignored the turning heads and provided ample financial support. The man sometimes spent weeks and months with his concubine, returning to aristocracy only after his monies were depleted. Finally a threat from most high led him to abandon his relationship with the witch and, as some rumored, their precocious daughter.

Rosetta's heritage provided her with an absorbing bronze skin. Her eyes were dark, nearly black, as was her long curled hair. She held a kind smile which was offered unsparingly. She was eternally scented in sweet citrus as she passed by. Within her I found great solace.

We were alone the first time, standing in the foyer. She reached out with elegant fingers and pulled the mask from my face.

"This is better," she said.

I felt the heat of embarrassment in my naked face. Panic and shame erupted. I wanted to run from her sight.

"You are too beautiful to hide away," she said. She placed her hands on each side of my head and held me that way. She looked into my eyes and I could only believe her.

She told me tales of the world and all of the beautiful and mysterious things that happened throughout. She took to me, tickling and holding me. The pain of Father's rejection had been alleviated because Rosetta loved me so. With nearly unlimited resource she scrubbed me clean and dressed me in the finest clothing. Father insisted that she look as aristocratic as his child. To her came the newest and richest dresses, hats, and shoes. She took me almost everywhere with her and I was happy to accompany.

Over the next months I was not the only one smitten by Rosetta. I noticed his leering as she served us dinner and made certain I had time at the piano before retiring. Father, still deep in drink, watched as she moved throughout our home. It was not in his nature to romance her. He began grabbing at her and using an innuendo shocking to our time. I never did resent her capitalization on his obsession, especially since he may have taken her without the benefit of consent. She had lived in the embrace of privilege and lost it. Father offered her a refuge from bleak peasantry.

Father brought her to his bedroom. He knew no discretion. My room was across the hall left me the witness to his beastly grunts and moans. When I listened with all attentions I might have caught her sighing along with him. Usually I clutched a blanket over my ears until he ceased.

Jealousy burned hotter in my twelve-year-old heart when the two married. To see her wed Father in the simple legal ceremony tore me from within. Beautiful music and all other elegance were deprived. She received only a simple ring in the dingy office of Father's shiftless solicitor. She truly was his property.

After the ceremony Father returned to his business ventures which required extensive travels. This gave us a great deal of time alone and she took me everywhere. I schooled at home with my soft spoken instructor Doctor Morinth, but was otherwise with her. She encouraged me to run and play with other children wherever we went, but I was content to be by her side. She never made any extraordinary effort to change this.

Heads turned wherever we walked. She was a fairy tale queen and I was her ugly-loved prince. I needed only tolerate her romps with Father when he was home. For all other intents and purposes she was mine. These are the things I told myself.

One day this closeness brought with it a new dimension. I was to discover this as an unwitting voyeur. Rosetta called me to her room. I opened the door. She wore nothing save the exquisite string of pearls Father gave to her weeks earlier. Her breasts were full and fleshy. Her body was toned and slender. I instinctively covered my deformed mouth with my hand in shame.

Rosetta slowly reached and partially covered herself with a sheepskin blanket. "Please run to Benson's and get me a pint of goat's milk," she directed. Her voice was peppered with smoke and fire.

I told her I would be happy to oblige, walking from the room backwards. As she went from my site I saw a seductive smile expand across her beautiful face. Her eyes ignited. My heart arrested.

The petty errand took only half of an hour. I always walked briskly to return home to her. Today I ran. When I returned my heart sank. Father's men surrounded his carriage unloading luggage. Father had returned early from his venture.

I placed the goat's milk on an entry table and receded to my bedroom. I lay in my bed glaring at the cold stone ceiling. Jealousy and envy consumed me. I hated my father. I wanted Rosetta, all of our worldly riches, and the very manor where we resided. I wanted to be handsome or dead as my brother Stephen. I cursed myself and my love for her.

Over the course of the next few days I encountered Rosetta throughout our home. Her eyes held that same searing invitation.

The time came when Father was required to travel across Europe for a series of meetings, inspections, and prospecting. As was the norm, Father did not inquire as to whether Rosetta wished to travel with him.

I was again gleeful. I hoped that all of the staring and looks we shared with one another could evolve with this opportunity. Father would be gone for over a month and I would return to my status as her companion.

In the first days of Father's sabbatical, Rosetta said, "There is a place that I go and I want to bring you there, but you can tell nobody. You cannot tell your father or anyone. It is my secret. I want it to be our secret. Can you swear this to me?"

"I will never tell," I said. My eyes watered as I looked up at her. I loved her so deeply and here again she made effort to return my affections. That she wanted to create something which was just ours shattered, if only briefly, all the horrible things I thought about myself. I could be loved.

Days passed. I was eager to know her secret place, but did not dare inquire. Perhaps I feared I would run her off with my childish poking and prodding. She controlled our relationship and I enjoyed it that way.

We shopped and strolled and ate at fine cafés. She made me laugh and she laughed at everything I did. Many of the townspeople projected their condemnations as we walked by holding hands. I cared not if God himself disapproved of our affections.

One day while walking in a public garden of flowers she stopped abruptly and asked, "How do you feel about your father?"

Nobody ever asked how I felt about anything. I knew how I felt but was too filled with fear and shame to answer honestly.

"Please Nathan, tell me. It will be our secret, like the place I will soon show you."

I was aroused by her resuscitation of the place, and now she wanted us to have another secret. I trusted her absolutely and believed her when she said it would be between only us. This trust was imperfect. There remained the fear of Father's omniscience as if he would know if I were to dishonor him.

"I hate him," I said plainly. I expected the roof of the world to fall upon us or the stones on the garden path to give way, dropping me into the depths of hell.

She said, "He is cruel to you. I cannot bear it. There is no position for me from which to stop him and his hitting of you. I have tried to talk to him, but…"

"But what?"

"He strikes at me, too."

Tears filled my eyes. I hugged her tightly.

She continued, "There is no action for us to take now, but someday, maybe someday we will run away from him. Maybe his drinks will take him early for us to be alone. Are these terrible things to say?"

"No," I said flatly.

We walked from the garden speaking of lighter things and enjoying the sun that shone down upon our special union. We forgot Father then for he was gone for a long spell.

3

"Awaken my love," she said one morning.

Rosetta led me to her secret place. The stone cathedral was burnt and abandoned. Covered in a vibrant moss, it slumped from the earth. A brisk chill accosted us when we went inside. Creeping fear filled me, but she made me brave.

The vaulted ceiling arced over the half dozen occupants of the building. The ancient church sat stripped of all remnants Christian or otherwise religious. The altar, cracked in two, was fallen into itself. Lying before the broken table rested a large wooden crate. I sensed raging life inside of it. Paralyzed in fear, Rosetta led me through the congregation surrounding the box.

Rosetta left me in the front pew before she approached the box. I feared for my love, but was unable to act. In horror, I saw a man covered in strange engravings pry open the wooden crate. As he did this, Rosetta slipped out from her bright red dress.

I was incapable of looking off. The tattooed man and another began to paw at my beauty as the *thing* emerged from the case. For a moment, the ugly brilliance of the creature drew my attentions away from the nudity of Rosetta. The thing had a man-like face, two blazing green eyes, small ears, a gaping mouth, and weakened chin. Its body was feline, long and lanky with human-like hands extended from each leg. The creature was covered with swatches of grey-green scales that allowed sickly dark hairs to grow through with no pattern or consistency.

Seeing Rosetta nude and engaging in unspeakable acts with the two men paled to this monstrosity that emerged. It moved slowly, hindered by old age or infirmity, but approaching me. After a pause to consider the trio, it continued its progress. Rosetta and the two men also stopped. Everything stopped.

The thing reached with its left claw-hand toward me. The motion was perverse in its elegance, yet hindered by the obvious weakness of the creature. With something so uniquely ugly one cannot be certain, but the creature seemed to smile as it ran the talon nail of its index finger over my youthful right hand. Blood ceased flowing as quickly as it began. The open wound was sealed, leaving only the faintest white line of a scar. The monster retreated from me, never releasing the menacing grin from its face. Rosetta and the two men were nearly finished with their ritual indulgence.

The creature, which turned nearly inanimate waiting, sprung to life upon cue and took its turn with my love. The crowd was ecstatic rather than repulsed. I wanted to die.

****

"Do not be troubled," she said as we began our long walk home. "I know what you saw was unusual, but you were in no danger. I was in no danger."

I retorted, "It was not that... thing. It was you. I could not bear to watch those filthy men do those things to you. Then to see that creature know you in that way . . . it was just more than I could bear."

"Would you like to do such things to me?" she asked.

I was silent, embarrassed, yet completely aroused. She understood my assent and squeezed my hand even tighter. Today, I thought, I would truly know my precious queen. I would become a man with the woman I loved.

My heart crashed again. When we arrived at the manor, Father had again returned premature. He sat in the parlor drinking an amber-colored whiskey directly from the bottle. My blood heated at the sight of him, but he acknowledged me in no way. He whisked her away up the stairs and I was alone, save the bottle left behind.

I refused to abate into my tomb. I endured too much that day to have my most intimate dream ripped away moments before consummation. I never had tasted alcohol. With stone bravery I reached for the encased spirits.

I drank the entirety of the bottle as I listened to the sickening goings on above me. I was drunk and invincible at thirteen years of age. My thoughts raced. I wanted to stop Father from any further defiling of my Rosetta. I wanted to kill him.

The largest knife in our kitchen gleamed. It whispered softly to me.

Salvation rested within its razor-sharp blade. This weapon would end the terror of Father. His death would free me. Rosetta and I could be together forever.

I crept up the stone staircase toward Father's bedroom. I was set to spill his blood and innards. I wanted to see the miracle of death as his essence passed from his body into the hell he belonged.

Reaching the room, I noticed the door. They had been careless before but today was paramount. The door to the room was left completely open. I set the shank on a small table atop the stairs and peered into the bedroom. I watched agape for what seemed an eternity.

His blow crashed hard upon my head. I closed my eyes for the briefest of moments. This allotted Father enough time to traverse his bedroom floor and strike me with all his drunken might. My world went black as I crashed across the hall, striking the table upon which I laid the blade destined for his blood. My eyes opened.

Father struck me again and again. He kicked me and stomped me into the floor. I groped for the knife and he laughed as he threw me down the staircase. Head over broken heel I tumbled hard onto the stone entryway floor. The light of the world extinguished.

I awoke in the cellar. Whether days or weeks later, I will never know. This incident was never spoken of, so I can never be certain how long I was tied down there. It was long enough.

The basement of our manor was dirty and rancid. There was no source of natural light and nobody saw fit to set a torch for me. I only knew where I was from the familiarity of the smell. It was a musty and putrid odor. I reeked from soiling myself. Had the room been lit, I probably could not have seen much. The entirety of my head was swollen. A cursory search with my hand revealed a featureless melon of hurt.

I rendered myself unconscious by adjusting my body on the dirt floor. I drifted in and out. I awoke again, wet, to the familiar smell of lamp oil. Whatever the reason, he failed to ignite me.

The pain was too great, the chain that held me too strong, and my body weakened by denied sustenance. I prayed for death. I wanted my essence to leave my battered body. I did not care where it went. The agony transcended even my love for Rosetta. I asked myself where she was as I laid in that dismal black hole. And then, like a dark angel, she appeared.

Her face held the telltale remnants of Father's anger. She lifted a small torch over me and took a long look. I attempted to speak but it was fruitless. She said nothing to me. He probably sent her down to see if I was still alive.

She leaned in and placed an ear to my chest. She stood and dropped a piece of bread. It bounced into the dried blood pool where my face laid. She turned and left me there.

I was unable to reach for the bread even if I had wanted it. I fell under again for a spell, but awakened. There was a crushing pressure over my chest. And there it could have ended.

Weightless, I drifted upward slowly. I was traveling towards the beams and aperture supporting the home over me. The pain was gone as was the swelling. I was warmed, as if sitting by a pleasant fireplace on the cold nights of fall. There had been no light, but now embers of brilliant illumination appeared directly above me. They burned brighter and brighter upon my approach. Feet away, I could see embers had formed before the dirtied wood. It was the way from this world.

I turned back in horror to my beaten and bloody body. I was dead. I was certain. I looked at my hand where that creature made its mark. The faint white scar was gone. It was all I ever wanted, an end or out. But I was scared of the light. It felt wrong. Some intangible purpose steered me away. I willed myself back to my own body. First I found resistance, then momentum. The air around me turned ice cold as I plummeted for what seemed to be a lifetime. Then there was more of the blackness.

My eyes opened to Rosetta washing my face with a warmed cloth. Her wounds were healed. Inexplicably back in my damaged shell, I laid in agony, but felt happy to again be with Rosetta. I could not move my broken-jaw mouth to tell her of my magical, terrifying experience. I was confident I could recover and escape from our home with her if I could only tell her.

"Sleep, my precious child." She whispered prayers in some unknown tongue as she continued to wipe the warm cloth over me. She did this until I slept.

I was brought to my bedroom. I did not see Father. I did occasionally hear his acid-anger spewing. Rosetta nursed me back to health and I loved her more for it.

My legs were forever damaged by his brutality. There was a limited range of motion and much pain, but I was able to walk. The severe limp resulting was but another dead flower in the potpourri of my defects. I needed to escape the wrath of Father. I desperately needed Rosetta to run with me. I was not the only one to conclude this.

My teacher, Doctor Morinth, learned of the severity of the beating from loose-lipped house servants and observation. He was a decent and respectful man. He remained silent to the inferior cuts and bruises over his tenure. This he could not ignore.

"Nathan, you are a special and gifted child. Your mind is brilliant and should not be used as a battering ram," he said. In his delivery I saw that he, too, feared Father. Looking over each shoulder he continued, "There are opportunities abroad for you; things that I could arrange."

He spoke of an esteemed scientist of whom I had read. The man chartered a small school and offered positions for personal lab assistants. This man was well advanced in a number of areas of medicine, chemistry, and human biology. Dr. Morinth said his research was defining the outward bounds of scientific pursuit in the era.

"With the right presentation, I believe I could convince your father that such schooling would be in the best interest of all," Morinth said, "and this shall be done post haste."

I agreed without thought or question. The unbearable thought of leaving my Rosetta caused deep hurt, but I feared that neither she nor I would live if I stayed. Father was blind with rage and alcohol. After my beating, he perpetuated a several months-long drunk, destroying our home and the temple that was Rosetta's body. I schemed to steal her from him once situated abroad, yet her fate had already been sealed.

Dr. Morinth worked quickly indeed. He made immediate arrangements for me to meet a traveling salesman of sorts. The man Cruikshank was in England but would be traveling to greater Europe. The sales route would ultimately land him on the outskirts of Heidelberg, Germany where I would be schooled. Dr. Morinth assured Father I would be gainfully employed and put to hard, grueling work. Success under the scientist would bring great pride to our family name. He assured me I would be accepted first by Cruikshank and then the scientist Faustus. This all for a generous endowment, of course, but I was more than capable of any academic challenge once inside.

Father took no time to consider. He was eager to have me from his home, as eager as I was to leave. The offer also provided him fodder for boasting to his drunken comrades. Within days, he provided significant funds to the school and its laboratory.

As the day approached for me to leave on my journey, I rehearsed my plea to Rosetta. I would clear the path for her to run to me. I knew her life was in grave danger, particularly since she would be the only person remaining to suffer the wrath of Father. As I built the nerve to approach her, I heard the eruption.

I ran down the stairs to the sound of the crash. I saw her there in the parlor, bloodied and lifeless. Father beat her badly. He threw her into a stacking of glass jars, the shards of which she laid upon. She likely was already dead. There was much blood.

Father sat on the floor beside her staring blankly at the wall. His hands were covered in guilty crimson as he held them out before himself oblivious to my observation. His mouth gaped open. Tears seeped from his eyes, the only movement in the kitchen in that moment.

Father would suffer no penalty for his action. He was a wealthy and accomplished man with favors owed to him from the highest perches of justice. Rosetta had been a mere gypsy bastard with no living family member to exact revenge. I thought of attacking him yet again, but swelling fear pushed the thoughts from my mind. I was impotent in his presence.

True to the coward I was, I returned to my room and finished bundling the few belongings I decided to bring. I wanted little from that house. Any object taken would only carry with it ugly sentiment. I looked at this forecoming journey as a new beginning as much as it was an escape.

I closed my eyes tightly, but could not find sleep. I dared not move, as I feared a single sound could awaken further rage in Father. He truly loved Rosetta in his own toxic way and if he could kill her, I had not a chance against his senseless brutality.

In that next morning, the sun lifted slightly over the far eastern hills. I mourned Rosetta's violent passing then gathered my remaining baggage. Father continued to sleep as I carried my parcels down to the front door so they could be efficiently loaded to hasten my departure.

As the carriage approached, Father stood at the door blocking my reentry to the home. He stood there, mighty and powerful, sneering at me. A blast of hatred and sadness danced inside of me before he spoke. I greeted Dr. Morinth who sat inside the coach as he took the extended parcels from my hands. I turned back to Father.

"Boy, I did not want you. I never wanted you here in this house. You were a mistake and an embarrassment to me. Why you were spared from that vile sickness and your mother was not I will never know, but it will forever remind me that there is no God above or below us. You are never to return here," he said. But something was missing. The raging fire of hatred was dampened.

The dysfunctional farewell only reverberated what I knew about his feelings toward me my whole life. The words still carried an acidic sting. There was nothing he said that I had not already come to believe myself. I simply nodded in concession and climbed into the coach. I sought only survival with my new and vacant heart.

4

I did not look back. If only it could all have been forgotten. It never would be. I closed my eyes and listened to the click-clack of slave horses pulling the old wooden coach on its rusted iron wheels.

I found some hope in the road ahead. There was a future in its distance. In a day's time I was to arrive into the employ of Mr. Cruikshank. He planned to expand his sales route into central Europe and would pass near Heidelberg, Germany within the year.

I was brought to a small camp on the meadows many miles northeast of Father's home. There were a number of large burlap tents raised and the crackling heat of a bonfire. Some were dancing and drinking while others wailed on string instruments and skin drums. Their community sprung forth from the green grass as if it had always been.

It was a pleasant, inviting atmosphere. There were only smiles and glee and laughter. Everybody danced and held each other in hand. It was a place to which I could be accepted. A member of the group, Herky, came to me first. He was drunk, but friendly.

"Hello there! Are you our new boy?" he asked.

I nodded my head, too shy to speak to a stranger.

"Well then, great to have you aboard!" Herky said and placed a relaxed arm over my narrow shoulders. This sent a quick blast of terror through me. The only man that ever touched me before was Father and that was exclusively an act of violence. "Mr. Cruikshank is, well… Cruikshank is occupied this moment here so let me get you a bit to drink. A man must know what it is he is trying to sell," he said. He poured from a large glass container into a tin handled cup.

The chattel was a magic tonic, billed as nothing less. The rich and poor purchased the beverage in bottles, jugs, and barrels. Cruikshank claimed himself a great and respected healer. I soon learned the powerful concoction was an earthly thing. Its ingredients were some mystical combination of herbs and spice, vegetation, and wild beast things. At its center: a lie. The potion healed nothing and only deluded away ailment.

Before I drank from the offered cup, a tall man emerged from the master tent. Behind came a youthful male and a teenage girl. The three shared a secret smile as their oily skin gleamed in the light of the fire. The tall man was radiant in his appearance and command. Instantly I knew him to be Cruikshank.

He approached me with an extended hand. He took firm hold of mine and pumped up and down twice. He brimmed with a contagious confidence.

He was towering and well proportioned. His tanned skin contrasted sharply with his bright white teeth displayed through his inviting smile. Cruickshank's wardrobe reflected the wealth he enjoyed since sharing his discovery with the world. Frocked ruffles of fine linen broke free from the red satin coat. Rings of gold and silver encircled each finger.

"Welcome. Enjoy," he said and walked away. I was his instant disciple. I had much to learn. Cruikshank was a pioneer in marketing. He was as much part of the product as the elixir he sold.

The six of our sales troupe traveled in two separate wagons drawn by powerful, handsome Clydesdales. The first wagon was large with a flat base supporting a three-sided black wooden box. Its innards stored thousands of single-serving bottles of Cruikshank's magic water.

When this wagon was set up for the pitch, four chairs would sit face forward toward the audience while Cruikshank flanked them in a large cushioned leather chair. The four seats were always filled with persons suffering from varying maladies in the localities Cruikshank seized. In a booming, compassionate voice he inquired of the seated persons' aches and pains of the body and mind.

"What if I told the each of you that I have devised a potion, a magic serum, to relieve each and every of the complaints you set forth here today?" he asked with a blistering intensity. His eyes would dart over the seated four and then the crowd.

On this cue, uniform everywhere we went, the crowd would mumble and murmur. Some would outwardly mock. At that moment he would pull from its shielded position the intricately designed bottle of smoky red glass. Eclectic patterns masterfully etched in the glass displayed the great pyramids of Egypt, column-laden Roman structures, and mystical symbols of ancient gods long passed.

The bottle would be passed amongst the maligned. Each swallowed a healthy drink as Cruikshank spoke of his journeys to dark and strange lands. He explained the fusion of the science of the new age and principles as old as time itself. Without these things, he said, his concoction was not possible.

Then came the testimonials. The man with chronic knee pain would spring from his seat and run about the stage. The woman with a blood-spewing lung disease would belt out in song. The elderly couple, each crippled with grinding arthritis, would dance. After this bolt, the "healed" would give praise to Cruikshank and his magic beverage.

Cruikshank would then boast even more. Not only would his serum cure these nagging aches and pains, the potion greatly benefited those suffering from a variety of emotional and mental disorders. He would prove this point, too.

There was always a recently widowed woman. She was no doubt buried in the grips of desolate depression, raising her fatherless, starving children in the world of her limited resource. Her struggle was not unique. She was in every town.

"I challenge any of you before me, any here troubled in mind or spirit or the both, to drink from my cup. I defy you to drink and continue in your sadness and misery, for my elixir cures all ailments of the body and the mind!"

At this juncture, the hopeless woman would step forward, reaching out to take the bottle from his hands. The lines of her face told her woeful tale. Cruikshank would pull the woman up onto the wagon stage into his supportive embrace. The sadness of each would fade with one drink and then transform into euphoria. The lines would rise out and the eyes would widen in luster. This was not drunkenness as the mind was crisp and decisive, the body decadently warm.

Then came the hook. The crowd was afforded a small taste, a trial-sized sample, if you will. They lined up to be served a small ladleful of elixir from tin pails. We would pour the precious liquid into every open mouth. None of the flock was denied.

This was all that was necessary. After the small drink they approached, money extended from their eager hands. Cruikshank found they would pay all they had for the elixir after time. Many paid more than they had.

Soon the dangers would begin. But first, we swam in their artificial bliss. We planted ourselves in the given place, accepted invitation to lavish parties and meals, and danced the night away with the upper crusts. We were all popular until few could afford the elixir. Then we would steal away in the night to avoid the desperate bandits the process inevitably created. Terrible things had been done to perpetuate the consumption of Cruikshank's elixir.

I, with the caravan, took to drinking the potion throughout each day. I enjoyed the carefree euphoric peace it brought to me. I was able to laugh and love as they. It was easy to forget about my ugly face, Father, and my dead Rosetta.

Within a month of joining the troupe we traversed the English Channel headed for Paris. I had never been there, but my instructors over the years familiarized me with the grandiose architecture of the city. Everything was overdone in gold plating that could not cover the smell. It would be that ungodly odor of raw sewage that would impress upon me greater than any human design. It was as rank as the prison Father fashioned out of our dank old cellar.

Life with Cruikshank's band and the elixir created a manageable distance between myself and life with Father. Though I still desperately pained over my dear dead Rosetta this new family of mine made the days pass. And it went on like this.

In time I was charged with the duty of synthesizing the tonic from the ingredients provided by our runners. Bottled and capped, our potion proved a long shelf life, but we all acknowledged that the fresher the batch the more intense its wicked effects. Much of those days were spent sampling the brew.

Days turned to weeks and then into months as we traveled through the small French villages and into the German countryside. We traveled by moonlight, our camp rising for discovery with the sun. Cruikshank placed me under his wing, frequently bringing me out on the town after a day of unloading the magic elixir. Cruikshank was a king of the night.

The village girls took immediately to his rugged good looks and worldly charm. He told them stories of savages in Africa. He told them of black magic and human cruelty. They would be unable to draw their attention from him. He would lure two of the girls away with him together. He boasted how he seduced the most innocent ones. I envied Cruikshank.

Each step closer to Germany caused a stirring panic within me. I could not live without the elixir and shortly would be separated from my supply. Cruikshank had summarily rejected my suggestion I stay with his band.

"Though it has been a pleasure, we each must go away separate from here," he offered.

My sadness was apparent to Herky. He consoled me with a smile and a fresh cup. As I pondered a future without the elixir, he slid me a small key. The key was to Cruikshank's lockbox. No words were exchanged between us. Only a moment would be needed.

I waited for Cruikshank as we camped only a day from Heidelberg.

True to his nature, he ensnared a German girl with his charms and was off to dance and drink the elixir.

Cruikshank was my friend. Justified through compulsion I seized the moment. I would trespass upon his trade secret strictly for personal use. I turned the key in the simple metal box. There inside was the formula for the precious elixir. The reagents and processes where equally mine now. Ecstasy filled me. I would forever have the knowledge to create the most splendid concoction. I would never know the agony, desperation, or pain of being without the holiest of drinks. I could bury the rest of me inside of that.

I furiously copied the handwritten notes of Cruikshank into my own bound journal so that I was sure not to forget a single reagent or process. As my last day with the caravan was coming to its close, I took great comfort in knowing that Cruikshank's secret was then my secret as well. With my eager hands I gripped his newly scribed recipe for a last comparison. Though no Gutenberg duplicate, it was sufficient to satiate my needs.

5

Cruikshank provided a stout mare and generous rations for my cleaving journey. I made my way by the late sun and early moon to Dr. Faustus. Not one soul crossed my path. The dwelling was of aged gray stone blocks. The place towered over neighboring homes and the river running behind.

Faustus was not alone. The home was completed by Wagner, first apprentice to the good doctor, and two other students approximately the same age as I. The two left of their own accord my first months at his home and they bear no mark on this tale. Others, nameless and faceless servants, drifted in and out.

Dr. Faustus was an irregular man. His worldly eyes glowed like green emeralds. He studied and mastered the great disciplines of the world: law, biology, theology, chemistry, and political science. With all the knowledge there was also an absence within his eyes. Perhaps the void was apparent because I, too, harbored my own empty spaces.

He was very large, though not as big as Father. When I arrived, he sported a large bushy black beard concealing most of his face. It was tangled and matted, the result of long working hours rather than cosmetic choice. His hands were rough and scarred from infinite spills of chemicals and physical labor. He offered a jovial welcome. I was ensnared at our beginnings.

"Welcome, young master Sorren," he said with his bellowing voice. He took my hand and pumped it up and down. The man was shorter than Cruikshank by many inches, but clearly outweighed him in both charisma and character. Faustus, in his entirety, was more a man than any I have ever met.

The enormous house was kept simple, though it held elaborate objects of beauty here and there. It was clear Faustus wasted little energy on decorating the home. The furniture throughout was mostly plain and unfinished. The walls were unpainted and the floors worn and deeply etched. There were sparse, yet ornate, window treatments. There were other fine things of silver and gold about, but seemingly out of place. The home was half of a thought.

The laboratory below was fitted with the newest of scientific gadgetry. There was no experiment conceived that could not be carried out there. My sense of excitement peaked. I did not want to waste a moment placing my belongings away, but I was desperate for a drink of the elixir and used settling in as an excuse to sneak away for the moment.

Upon request he brought me to my sleeping quarters. He assured me little time would be spent in this, the simplest of rooms, as we would work both day and night. Only in complete exhaustion would I grace this sleeping place and its single bed with my presence.

That night of my arrival, Faustus put me to reading a text on basic elemental chemistry. I assured him I had read the very same book in its entirety twice and would gladly take an examination of any kind to prove my mastery. He laughed at my eagerness.

"Oh, Master Sorren, I know the extensive course of your studies. I could have guessed that you read the *unannotated* copy of this book. I do not accept just any pupil who finds his way to my doors with some tribute in hand." He offered the book to me. "In this book, however, I have made notes from my own research, things you will no doubt find interesting."

I opened the text and saw that the white space of each page was filled with his meticulous, perfect writing form. The characters were miniscule, but drawn in a proportion visible under the light of a single candle. Over the next several months, each of the books he gave me were similar, marked with his radical observations and insights, each comment seemingly more profound than the one preceding. I will not elaborate to the pedantries, as they are themselves elusive to most comprehension.

Faustus put me to cleaning glass instruments and preparing rudimentary suspensions in the lab as he and Wagner worked. In my first weeks I learned Faustus and Wagner were not engaged in conventional scientific pursuits. They were chasing some intangible heretical thing. They spoke in whispers and worked in shadows, but their unnatural quest was plain as the day. I suspected Dr. Faustus wanted me to draw such a conclusion from the pieces opened to me.

They studied metaphysics. They sought a "world beyond this one." That said it all. The pair believed there was another dimension reachable through our physical world. They thought they could go there, or bring something from the place. For a prior decade Faustus traveled the world, searching for some rift or wrinkle and found only more circumstantial evidence. He spoke to mystics, wizards, medicine men, and religious leaders. He studied ageless texts and places. In the end, he believed no one ever knew any more than he.

In his opinion Faustus learned all the knowledge in the world, able to practice any profession to perfection. Here lied his conundrum. Only through violating the most basic laws of the universe would he be able to move forward. That is what he intended to do. He wanted me to see.

Faustus left an old scroll authored in primitive, unreadable symbols on a lab table. Bizarre engravings filled a number of the pages. Some of them depicted ritual practices while others showed horrid means of torture and death. Then there were the images of the strange beasts not of this earth.

He believed if he could find entry into "the next realm" he could manipulate matter at some infinitely small level and would even be able to create matter. He thought he could defy gravity, breathe under the ocean for days at a time, and perform other great feats. He was grandiose, but spoke with such a learned intensity one would believe that he could already do the things to come.

Wagner, being his quiet, faithful counterpart, largely carried out the instructions of Faustus. He studied under the Doctor since he was my age and grew close to Faustus, electing to stay in the shadows of his brilliant teacher rather than lead his own research. Wagner offered little in the way of new insights, but he kept excellent records and could follow any direction to perfect execution.

The sense of mystery in his laboratory cannot be fully described. There was a palpable feeling of suspense and the macabre. Many of the experiments, some on living human beings, were illegal, unethical, and would no doubt be considered heretical above all else. They performed bizarre rituals Faustus studied in his travels throughout Africa and found in the pages of the ancient parchments. I heard the screams and saw the blood.

Ultimately Faustus abandoned his teaching position at the academy entirely. He worked day and night reciting old poems and mixing various roots with chemicals isolated in the laboratory. He invoked electric magnetic fields. There were sights brave and bold, but I saw no real progress towards his ends.

I was not privy to the underlying knowledge of any of these activities. I merely watched while cleaning and combining formulas for his later use. I took to brewing the elixir whenever time and Faustus would allow me unfettered access to the lab. One night I was working away on my potion when I heard Faustus muttering in a side storage room. It was dark and I made the dangerous assumption he was alone there in the pitch black. I thought perhaps he had grown mad.

6

Sipping from my breasted elixir, I crept toward his ravings. I was close enough to see a stark white figure, luminescent in the blackness. This creature lit the room. To a degree I could distinguish the figure of Faustus standing in reverence before the beast. I thought back to the thing in the crate. I sensed some eerie fraternity between the demon and this anthropomorphic ivory monster.

From the darkness the being conjured a large scroll and dry fountain pen. The items seemed to glow, as if they were connected to his body by that cold white light. The being provided the pen to Faustus. Faustus removed his shirt and plunged the pen into his own chest. He screamed out in agony as he pulled the pen from his ribs and reached out to the paper and signed it in his blood. He then fell to the ground clutching his heart.

The thing looked to me and I felt its unholy power. I was frightened, frozen in its eerie white stare. The thing dissolved into the air. It receded into nothingness. I ran to Faustus to aid him in his hopeless medical condition. I reached and tried to stand him up. As I lifted him, he was aiding me. He was lifting himself. He gently pushed me away to reveal only a small scar where the pen pierced his heart. He smiled at me.

"Oh, my good boy, I have achieved the greatest of scientific discovery. I have found that which I have sought!"

With that he went to the west wall. With two closed fists he smashed at the stone and blasted an orifice. He struck again, enlarging the hole to man-sized proportions. He looked back at me and then walked through the broken space.

I peered through the giant fissure to see him reach his arms outward. He then began to rise up, ensnared in some summoned wind, out and over the river that ran behind.

"I can do anything I desire, young Sorren! Anything!" With that he pumped his fists and illuminated himself in a brilliant white light. This was his transfiguration. He ignited the sky for something less than a moment and then whisked off into the sky and far out of my sight.

From the darkness again came the man-thing shrouded in its white, iridescent skin. The creature possessed two eyes, a nose, and mouth, yet remained largely featureless. Its body was tight and smooth. Even the eyes were white and pupil-less. In fear, I prayed silently to the God I never knew or wanted.

"Sorren," the thing hissed at me. It continued its forward progress. I could not react.

The thing reached to me and I was unable to turn away, unable to resist its contact. To come close to that thing was more nightmare than life.

"I know the thing you seek," said the creature.

"Who are you?" I inquired, ignoring its statement.

"Does that matter? I do not think it does. Should you not question what it is I can do for you, young Sorren?"

"Tell me what you are!" I shouted in trembling demand.

"The Devil? Is that what you would like me to say? How titillating that would be. To meet their Christian Devil here in this under dwelling."

"Is that what you are?" I asked.

"The Devil! Satan! Lucifer! Mephistopheles, I prefer, but any name you might call me would be simplicity in the face of the incomprehensible. Yet, if that aids you, well then, feel free."

He took my hand marked by that other demon creature.

"Do you doubt that I am?" he asked. I did not. His stark whiteness sent a chill through me which rivaled his touch, but he was right. I couldn't resist.

"I want to offer you something,"

"As you offered Dr. Faustus?" I asked.

"Oh, no, no. I was able to give Dr. Faustus something he desperately wanted. He was willing to pay handsomely for that which he acquired. That, however, is dealings between he and I. Confidential," he said. "This thing I have in mind for you, insight really, does not require the commitment made by our mutual friend. In fact, once you exercise this knowledge, you will owe me absolutely nothing."

"What is this insight?" I asked of him.

"Imagine, Sorren, being able to have all the things of another you desire."

"Wealth does not mean a thing to me."

"Not everything can be bought, Sorren. Father taught us that," he said. This struck deep inside of me. Morinth's last correspondence told Father's dwindling tale. The once bold and violent one was now the deranged lunatic. He owned much of his world before being locked away in a sanitarium for his own safety.

"What is it then you offer me?"

"Freedom from your physical prison! From that face! I offer you the ability to become anyone, to take any body."

"To possess them?" I asked.

"Like, yet not the same. Possession implies struggle. You would have no struggle within them. Your consciousness, your spirit, your *essence* would supplant theirs. They will be gone."

I was fascinated. I intuitively understood what he was willing to teach me. He forced images into my head. He showed me free of my body traveling into the body of another. It was mortifying. It was irresistible.

"How could I do such a thing?"

"You are so very close already. The process for your formula, the one stolen from our dear friend, Mr. Cruikshank, is very near, indeed. Those principles applied to a very special ingredient will yield something remarkable. It will allow you to separate from your physical being, to travel outside of your body. This you have done before."

Though it was painful, my eyes met his as he finished this statement. His eerie, intimate knowledge of my life struck me, but again, I was too curious to not continue.

"You will be able to enter anyone willing to exchange with you, and many whether they want to change or not," he said with a ghastly mimic of a smile.

"What of their essence? It would be murder."

"No, they will live on. The free essence will reflexively enter the empty shell you leave behind."

"And how is it that I would accept this knowledge from you?"

"By using it. By leaving this shell you occupy and entering this world anew as another."

"Yet this is me, my identity. This is who and what I am."

"No, no. You do not believe such a thing. You despise yourself and want the lives of countless others. Envy gratified. That is what I am giving you. The ultimate satisfaction of envy! You need only take the step and you could live forever, taking nearly anything on this earth you desire."

Inside of me there was a wave of crushing guilt as if I would be committing the gravest of sin. I would be.

"Yes. I will accept your offer," I stated flatly. I wanted it with the entirety of my heart.

Without spoken word he placed another series of images in my mind. I saw the elixir being poured for a stranger. I felt a chilling sensation and grave feeling of separation from myself and the physical world around me. I saw visions of my unanimated but living body. I saw a mossy plantation overgrown in some sweltering jungle. Suddenly I knew that it was western Africa. I saw an old onyx-skinned man, hunched and dressed in a native garb. Strange white-streaked markings covered his face while countless piercings lanced his body. I saw a clear path to him.

I fell to the stone floor, consumed with great satisfaction. As I drifted into a restful sleep, I looked at the moon hanging outside the hole Faustus made in the wall. All of the images replayed within my dreams. I knew that a magical time was upon me.

I awoke to birds singing, their songs carried through the hole. Sunlight poured in, capturing my aching body in its radiance. I then heard fumbling in the laboratory. My head throbbed as I stood onto my feet. I peered into the main portion of the lab. I saw Wagner there, oblivious, mixing chemicals. He did not yet know his mentor was now a god.

This I found curious. I was the one privy to the doctor's meeting with that White Demon. I was the only witness to Faustus' transformation. Poor, pathetic old Wagner. He chose to stagnate under Faustus' tutelage and was still denied the unholy spectacle.

It would be only a matter of time before he saw the damage to the wall and begin asking questions and drawing his conclusions. I was uncertain as to what to tell him. I knew I would tell him nothing of Faustus' transformation, the White Devil, nor a thing of the knowledge imparted upon me. I decided to hide from him for a spell, just long enough to collect my own thoughts.

When Dr. Faustus failed to return that day and the next, Wagner notified the constable. An investigator made way to the manor to question the house servants and the both of us. Neither he nor Wagner assumed an explanation for the broken west wall. Through sharp looks I understood Wagner's suspicion that I held guilty knowledge of the Doctor's whereabouts; perhaps that I even caused his absence. As I have set forth to you, I did not.

7

With the leased blessing of the investigating constable I made sabbatical to the Dark Continent. I found my way to the old man of my dreams. His hut was simply built, a conglomerate of misshapen sticks and dried mud. Closer examination revealed splintered bones within its bonds. There was no barrier to entry. Access was available through the log-cased void at its front.

I rapped on the frame. I peered around the casing and could see him sitting at a plain table. He stared at me as he sipped from a steaming cup.

"The ugly white wanderer arrives," he said in perfect English delivery, "as I dreamed you would. You come to know the Vella Root."

I nodded in ascent.

He waved an open palm to a chair across his table. I sat as he poured me tea from the kettle. I sipped through its bitter taste and listened.

The root had origin in both fact and fable. The term itself is an inaccurate description since the active alkaloids are located in its outward mass. It was discovered by a west African tribesman generations before. The tribesman found it spreading forth over the decaying corpse of a male lion and the surrounding blood-stained earth.

The root was white and mossy, looking a great deal like the head of cauliflower. Though it was soft and crumbled to gentle touch, it appeared as if made from hard white stone.

The tribesman, young with great ambition, carried a satchel of the vegetation to the village's eldest medicine man. As this story goes, the old man was familiar with a legend of the root. He told the young tribesman of its magical properties. He fashioned a tea from the root and other agents for the two men to drink while sharing the legend of the origin of the root.

In that day the village elder died and the young tribesman was filled with great wisdom and understanding of tribal history. He became a beacon for others in the tribe to go to for guidance and support, a lawgiver and judge. After his rise to prominence, he gathered a dozen of the strongest and most trusted of the tribe and told each of them the legend of the Vella Root.

This is what I know of this legend within a legend. Enu was a small and weak young man. He was deficient as both hunter and warrior. Despite the runt's many efforts, there was no improvement in these vitals. Many teased him that he should stay home and gather fruits and vegetables with the women and children of the tribe. He cursed himself, his persecutors, and the gods that supposedly looked over the good of his indigenous peoples. He could not accept his limitations.

Enu's hatred blackened his heart so that he drew the attention of Ka, an evil jungle demon promoting animal savagery amongst men. Tribal folklore contained many tales of Ka and exploits but none so personal as this legend. The demon came to Enu in a waking vision and offered great strength and ability. Enu would only have to bring to Ka the strongest and bravest of his tribe's warriors.

Immediately, Enu knew the bravest and strongest of the tribe to be Bol. There was no disagreement on this within the tribe. Bol was loved, feared, and respected by all members of the tribe. Dirty children fashioned small dolls from cloth, each of them playing "Bol" in rare times of leisure.

Knowing that he could not overpower Bol, Enu conceived of a plan to lead him into the jungle. The plan played on the heart of Bol, much to the pleasure of Ka. Enu told Bol late in the night that he heard the cries of an infant from within a large crevice. He detailed his lie by describing to Bol the many creatures of the night, which surrounded the hole in the jungle floor. The mighty hunter Bol knew well the crevice and darted into the night with Enu first at his side, and then lagging behind.

Bol ran to the crevice, waving a torch into the air to frighten off any animals. He placed the light over the void and leaned out to make visual contact with the child. There Enu pushed Bol with all of his might, sending him falling into the hole. Though the distance was not great, it was far enough to break his thick bones and render the giant of a man unconscious.

Ka appeared to Enu, materializing from the nothingness night. He asked Enu if Bol was of the kind and quality he desired to become. Enu affirmed and Ka told him it could be. The demon commanded Enu to cut himself in a mortal fashion. The envious one did just that, slashing his throat with a sharpened rock. As Enu's body bled out, Ka plunged into the body of Enu, gripped his soul, and the two entered the body of the unconscious Bol.

After some internal, invisible struggle Ka and Enu evicted Bol's soul from the body.

When he awoke Enu was in the body of Bol, watching as Ka drifted from the body out through the opening in the earth. He marveled as he flexed the massive arms and fingers of Bol. Above him he heard the last breaths of life gurgling from his remains. A smile emerged on his new stone face as he wondered if Ka also carried Bol to his vacant body. Enu hoped it that way. He then went to stand.

Pain seared Enu to the cold dirt beneath him. The source was no mystery. He looked down to the jagged and bloodied bone piercing the black skin of his leg. Enu shouted out in agony. The voice was not his own, yet the pain was all his. He looked up to see Ka there floating in the night sky, pointing and laughing at him.

In rage, Enu sprung upward out of the pool of blood that collected underneath him. His anger provided the means to climb half way up and out of the crevice. He balanced his weight on the ground, turning his face to see the radiant early morning sun burning down on him. He then went unconscious, a state from which he would never return. He died there, partly in and partly out of the earth.

Birthed from this union of malevolent spirit and hateful flesh were the spores of the root. As Bol's body decayed within the natural order, it omitted gases of poison, discouraging any animal from its meat. The body then sprouted white rocky patches. For years, the substance spread only a few yards from its origin.

Over the next generations, it was discovered and lost many times. The young tribesman and his twelve followers vowed to forever protect the root, ensuring that it fell into no hands that would use the power of the substance. The old man claimed he was but one of many successors.

When he finished the story we sat in silence. I was eager to find the root, but waited for him. In the following moments he stood and led me from the hut. We walked for hours.

He brought me to a patch and gave me a hefty satchel to fill with the peculiar white substance. He placed a hand on my hand that held the satchel.

"To do what you intend you will need less than a pinch," he said whirling his free hand. "It can grow on anything, in any place, at any time."

I filled the bag and my pockets. I hurried the best I could back through the jungle trail to wait for the covered wagon that would bring me to the mighty ship. On it I would return to Germany, excited and eager to begin the work of extracting the active alkaloid from the plant. But when I returned, I returned to Wagner.

8

During the months from the manor, labor piled and awaited my return. Of course there were more questions. Money could perhaps delay the inquest of Faustus' disappearance, but could not foreclose on it. Results of experiments needed transcription and analysis, while a number of chemical compounds required rendering. Wagner was desperately trying to duplicate the experiments of Faustus. He needed to know what happened to the man.

I worked seemingly endless days with Wagner and nights perfecting my isolation and extraction of the alkaloid from the Vella Root. Advancement in this endeavor assured a sample would be prepared for the bold *in situ* experiment. I took to cultivating the root as well and the old man's words rang true. I grew it on a pot of plain soil in my room and on a dead rat carcass I found in the yard.

Wagner expanded my circle of responsibilities out of his necessity and my competency. Though he hired on more help, he kept me to the secret details and the mundane recreations of the experiments. I soon bored with his copycat pursuit and was ever more the ready to try my perfected formula.

The man was rude and crude to me. He no longer masked suspicion. He scoured me for some insight into what had happened to Faustus in the laboratory that night. I acted as if equally in the dark on the matter.

Wagner was handsome with a champion physique. Many people in the village adored him though I never did. It was in part due to these qualities that he became my first subject. His maltreatment of me made certain his fate.

Brewing through the night and to the rise of morning I completed what would be a final version of the elixir. Cruikshank's process applied to the Vella Root was before me in a large glass tube. The liquid was a milky gray, somewhere in thickness between blood and water, and released a pungent odor. My stomach turned about at the thought of ingesting a thing of such sight and smell.

It was now time for the true terror to begin. I feared I could not persuade him to drink the elixir. There, too, lied the trouble of the aftermath. If the drink served its purpose and I held the power to exchange the essence of my being with that of Wagner, then what would I do next? In this equation I would still have Wagner's essence. He would be in my body, yet free to incite all sorts of havoc and commotion. Reason dictated that I must eliminate the man before any unwanted attentions could be drawn to my actions.

Murder was the only option. This was logical, but I doubted whether I could affect such a thing. I speak not of guilt or the sanctity of human life. I speak to my own inexperience with exacting such violence. Until that date I knew only the role of victim.

The plague of doubt lasted days more. I thought day and night, practicing the motions of stabbing knives and choking with barbed lengths of rope. I settled on a short, sharp blade, concealing it within the yellowed notes Doctor Faustus long ago disregarded.

I sat at the desk in my bedroom. Before me was a brightly burning lantern, a lengthy parchment, and a new fountain pen purchased for the purpose of the letter I wrote:

> *My Dear Wagner,*
>
> *Accept this apology for my abrupt absence. Our brave goal I achieved in the night! In my haste, I leapt through without you. Please forgive me. As a token of my sincerity I ask that you and our ugly little laboratory boy drink equally from the flask included with this delivery. The beverage is one of the many great discoveries. I will share the others with you quite soon.*
>
> *F*

Satisfied with my forgery, I rolled the parchment, sealed it with a generic imprint on wax, and then tied an eccentric bow. I affixed it to the bottle of smoked glass. As Wagner slept, I traveled to a neighboring village. I paid handsomely for a courier who promised not to disclose the proximity of delivery, or any description of the ugly one who placed it into his possession.

The following day the courier arrived and I answered the door to him. Per our agreement he made no recognition of me, asking if Wagner was present in the home. I called to Wagner who came and accepted the delivery.

An hour or so later Wagner was titillated. He danced around and about the house. He sang, quite horribly, songs of love and joy and tragedy and sorrow. After some time he came to me in the lab.

"I received correspondence from Doctor Faustus. He asks that you join me in sampling a special brew, insisting upon it really. Please join me at the dining table."

With that he walked away. I erred in assuming our shared drink would take place in the lab. He and I both ate and frequently slept there. I prayed that this was my only miscalculation. In contingency I grabbed the lock and chain I set aside for my crime and left the concealed blade undisturbed on the weathered notes.

On my way to the dining room, I made sure to pass through the kitchen. I found a carving knife of shining silver. Thinking it sufficient, I slid the object into the belt at my side and let my shirt hang down over it. I entered the dining room.

Sitting at the table was Wagner reading from the familiar forgery. When he saw I entered the room, he quickly rolled and concealed the instrument to his side. I saw also the bottle delivered with the parchment. It was unopened. Two wine glasses were laid out across from one another.

His attentions knew only the mysterious beverage. I quietly ran the chain through the spindles of the formidable chair and around my waist. I closed the lock, leaving nary slack for my escape. He paid such gross movement no mind and would suffer for that.

"He has instructed that we each share equally in this bottle," he said.

"Thank you," I responded.

Wagner poured the drink into each of our glasses. Immediately the air filled with that strong pungent odor of the perfected elixir. My stomach turned in response to the foul stench and the anticipation of my new beginning.

"To our great mentor Doctor Johannes Faustus. May he return to us here post haste!" he shouted.

"To Faustus!" I replied in kind.

A testament to his faith in our mentor, Wagner swallowed the elixir with not a hint of disgust. His uncompromising devotion to Faustus triumphed over the wretched consistency and taste of the drink. I was lacking in such grace.

Rejected violently by my digestive tract, I vomited that of the elixir I swallowed back into my mouth. A scornful contempt filled his blank face. It was that look, so like the look of Father, that empowered me to swallow that which had returned to my mouth.

We drank down the contents of the glasses. And then the feeling I would pursue the remainder of this tale became known to me. My vision and other senses severed. I felt no pain in my legs. I felt nothing of my physical body though I looked to Wagner through the dull eyes of my youth. I did so through choice and habit rather than necessity.

I attempted to drift away from my mortal shell. A great generalized pressure engulfed me, as if swallowed by the surrounding air, and then the pressure broke. With ease I was quickly distinct from my body. The physical and the metaphysical diverged at my will. I was moving closer to what I could see of Wagner without stepping a foot on the floor or atop the table. I was drifting unbound by gravity and reason.

I was not in this physical world as you know it. It was a separate state or realm. I still saw the makings of the room, Wagner, and the furnishings. Everything was lacking luster and color. The objects and Wagner were faint replicas of their former. I heard no sound, other than a pummeling wind of ice blowing neither from nor to any discernible direction.

The cold was chilling, murderous. I sought immediate haven despite the pure undiscovered space. In me, my spirit, my essence, my soul, I felt a frantic terror as if falling from some great elevation. There was an overwhelming sense of sin. I was no more supposed to be on this plane than Eve was to devour the forbidden fruit.

As I neared Wagner within inches, I mustered together courage and willed myself into his being. I felt the same pressured resistance for less than a second. I was passing into his living tissues. The coldness began to subside to the beat of his pulsating heart. I filled his cavity, arms and legs, then fingers and toes.

As the bonds between the physical and ethereal connected I became privy to all that was Wagner. First, the connection was too frantic to gain any single bit of information. Senseless colors and sounds swirled about. After a moment, in a deluge, I saw all the vivid images of his life and felt the emotions of his memories.

I saw his father help him climb the twisting limbs of an aged apple tree. I felt the pain of the death of his first dog, an old cocker spaniel, Nickels. I saw his first kiss of a schoolgirl and the empty feelings inside him. I saw the discovery of his first science text. I saw images of a cousin whom Wagner loved in a way criminal to the times. I felt his pangs of lust for Faustus. I felt his contempt and jealousy of me. All of these things and more came in a bold flash.

In each I felt his glee and his sadness. His flat affect gave no indication of the emotional being Wagner was within. I desperately wanted to revel in the new world of sensation and emotion. I wanted to swim in the sea of his experiences and feelings, but pressing matters stood at hand. There existed one complication in the Forbidden Knowledge shared with me by that hellish

Albino: the sacrifice of self.

He was easy prey. I was now tenfold the might of my old physical body. The chain holding Wagner was strong and tight. The iron belt negated his evasion of the plunging blade.

The confusion and terror drifted off from his face, *my horrid face,* to be replaced by a mask of blank death. His fold and fall toward the dining room floor induced an intoxicating joy. I at last ended the defective boy. For extra measure, I stomped the face of that dead thing quite hard with Wagner's polished boot. The chair toppled over. I did it again and again.

In that moment I heard the rattling gates of heaven as they closed to me forever. The decadent, worldly decision was eternal. I was an enemy of God and an outlaw of hell. The thing I became stood arrogantly outside the natural order. I ran his hands, now my hands, over the perfect contour of the face, then over the chest, arms, and onto buttocks and genitals. Pain and pleasure came to me from my petting and pinching. Each sensation was my own.

I hurried to a mirror of silver and gold hanging on the parlor wall. All of those handsome features bestowed upon Wagner in some accident of birth were now mine. I smiled and frowned, scowled and laughed, and ended with a stern gaze into my new image. The boy Sorren refused all reflective surfaces; he could not bear a single glimpse of himself. Now I was tall and handsome. My new body would turn heads in every room into which I walked.

Drunk on the remaining elixir in Wagner's blood and all my new potential, I sang a song of playing German children from Wagner's memory. *Er kann nicht mehr kräh'n, kokodi, kokoda.* I made my return to the dining room.

I unlocked its cuffed waist. With Wagner's impressive fitness at my command, I hoisted the frail dead figure onto my shoulder and carried it down to the darkened laboratory. With a lazy toss, I threw the body into a large tin vat used for the mixing of chemical formulas and the collection of blood from animals. For the tub I had my own purpose.

On a table near the bath were an assortment of caustic reagents, acid and other corrosive juices. These would devour the flesh of my old defective form.

I stayed there divided in the home of Faustus, torn in my longing for his return and equally terrified of his judgment. The knowledge the White Beast pledged to me shriveled to the abilities of Faustus. His radical powers would penetrate the façade. My new brilliance was a mere sleeved card. At first sight Faustus would know of my overtaking of Wagner in both body and mind. Perhaps he already knew.

The house servants, dismissed by Wagner, left me conveniently alone for my messy doings. There was much work to be done. I went to the business of drinking more of the elixir, remaining in Wagner's shell, but greatly enjoying the disassociation.

Moments later I stood over the tin vat holding my old deformed figure. What a hatred I held for that thing laying there bent and lifeless before me. The moment was to be savored. I poured the strongest of acid over its flesh and watched it bubble with its corrosive magic over my old gray hide.

There was a break in the sizzle of chemical teeth devouring skin. From the ground floor above drifted the distinct knock of a heavy fist on wood. Ignored for several moments, the noise persisted. I finally climbed the stairs to greet the insistent visitor. In the rear of my trousers I slid the used blade.

I opened the door to Martin Luther. Weary and tired, perhaps, but no less the man. He was a disciple of a magical man in the clouds, thinking to be dismissed. Faustus, Wagner, and I considered him a foolhardy fanatic, a religious zealot with an idiot view of the world and no appreciation for the true power of science.

"Greetings Mr. Wagner," he said coldly. There had been no love loss between Faustus and Luther, Wagner being guilty by his mere association. "Sorry to intrude over your dinner hour, yet I am in receipt of devilish accounts of an event behind this house now several months passed. May I enter?"

I nearly declined but was curious as to what had been reported and also knew the man to be quite persistent. He entered the room following my sweeping hand motion and smile.

"Ms. Garrison, a wash woman and devout Christian, was hanging linens to dry and claims she saw the Christ transfigured above the brook running south behind this home."

I nearly bellowed laughter into his ignorant face. Faustus and Wagner rejected nearly all aspects of religion as wishful mythology long before this view was fashionable. So had I.

"She did?" I asked.

"Yes. I myself have known Ms. Garrison and much of her family for years and know them to be good and fearful believers. Others validate her observations though conclude differently as to what it was."

The others had been persons of color under the employ of Faustus' most immediate neighbor. Though Luther was progressive he did not immediately offer up their affirmations of the sight.

"Do you know something of this?" he asked, scanning me for some reaction.

I denied any knowledge.

"May I speak to Doctor Faustus?"

"He is away for a spell, on a sabbatical, not to be back for some time."

His eyes narrowed in suspicion. I craved the elixir and faulted myself for leaving it in the laboratory.

"On behalf of the God-fearing residents of Heidelberg, I ask that I be permitted to inspect the workings of Dr. Faustus' laboratory," he said.

"That is out of the question, sir. I will not permit such a thing without consultation with my employer," I answered.

"So be it, for now. I have considerable influence and will not hesitate to seek assistance of Constable Hess in this matter. He will no doubt obtain court warrants for a look and I shall have it as ordered."

He turned from me into the night.

"Wait!" I yelled as if my declination steamed in error or confusion. He stopped and turned to me.

"Will you come in with me to discuss this further, perhaps over a drink of fine Spanish rum? It is here somewhere."

"I do not drink alcohol, Mr. Wagner."

"Have some water then. I have water cooled from the Shotyk Spring. It is most satisfying."

He turned and walked back into the house. I closed the door on us.

"You see," I began, "Doctor Faustus and I investigate the most noxious of chemicals which may be responsible for a number of grave illnesses. To allow you into the laboratory and subject you to such exposure would be ever so irresponsible. It would endanger both your health and mine."

"Sounds like the devil's work indeed! Sin and vice cause all disease and death. Sheer witchery. Every thinking German knows these things."

I nodded, "Nevertheless, these substances are quite dangerous and I cannot subject you to such a risk. I will share this same explanation with Constable Hess if you return this night. Perhaps you could come later so there is time for the air to rid itself of the poisons?"

"When then?"

"Tomorrow. Midday if you wish Mr. Luther," I said with a pleasant smile.

"Tomorrow then," he said standing and walking out of the home. He slammed the door as he left. I did not expect him to comply with the delay. Escape was imperative.

I hurried to my room and began to fold my clothing into a leather bag. Halfway through I realized I was in *my* room and I packed the clothing of my old form. I laughed nervously to myself as I emptied the bag on the bed.

I collected what I had brewed of the elixir, a number of bottles, a bag of the root collected in Africa, as well as what I had grown upon my return. I went to Wagner's room and packed much of his clothing. I then stormed the house for a considerable collection of money and jewels.

Hastily ready for travel, I arranged for a coach to bring me to a village two days travel from Heidelberg. Along the way I made several stops. I walked into the woods and laid out large patches of the Vella Root. I prayed for its promulgation.

The journey concluded and I found a modest room at an inn. I paid in advance for many weeks and the keeper asked no questions.

As I walked about that village, I felt a squelching thirst for the elixir and satisfied it as much. Under the influence of the beverage was the only time I could forget the horrid image of my body decomposing in the bath of acid. I felt as if every passerby could read the ill deeds from my face. The elixir was my sacrament against the sins of my doing.

I gave little thought as to where I should go from that juncture. I held the resource to travel anywhere in the world I wished to go. I decided just that. I would become a wanderer of the globe for a spell, being certain to have with me my special drink.

Into these days came an unexpected visit from a young courier. The boy claimed the stead of the most famous London barrister Harrison Beaumont. The delivery child moved in a soldier's cadence as he passed through the doorway. Within the boy's worn leather satchel was correspondence from Beaumont, a number of legal documents meeting all the formalities of the time, and a sealed envelope with the brazen sear of "Sorren" on its face. A chill metastasized over my spine. I dismissed the errand boy with a coin and broke the elaborate seal closing the envelope.

My Dearest Sorren,

Congratulations! I understand you, too, have found a destiny on this earth. As you read this I travel into the deepest recesses of space and time. I have bore witness to both the birth of this Universe and the end of our earth and yours. Find sanctuary in the fractured of mind. Covet the projected one. We shall never meet again.

Forever Yours,

Johannes Faustus

P.S. Enjoy my earthly treasures for I need not a one. J.F.

The parchment was scribed with neither ink nor blood. As was the envelope, the text of his letter was seared into the bond. I contemplated his travels. He had found the heavens. I considered his ominous riddle warnings. I held the letter in a fist as I searched the remaining documents.

The entirety of Faustus' assets were transferred to Wagner. He knew what I had done. The library alone was priceless. I was wealthy beyond the dreams of Avarice, but had no intention of returning to the home bequeathed to me. Wagner's body was a vessel, not a landing place. I had to run.

With the aid of the innkeeper, I found a man specializing in travel accommodations. I told him I sought the sights of the world. I wanted lavish places. He arranged passage on a Spanish cruiser. Just as I arrived, I left the inn in the storm of night, each and all of my worldly possessions gripped within my two hands.

9

The creaking wood swayed atop the choppy black seawater. My escape from my transference and crime left me weary. The agent booked me passage on a ship traveling from Scandinavia. The vessel was destined for a secluded vacation village on the Ivory Coast.

The grand boat catered to the elite who filled the bunks below the deck. This journey was for Spanish aristocrats to tour the Dark Continent, viewing the wildlife and rumored savagery of its native people. The passengers would land in an upscale tourist village serving their decadent appetites.

I roomed in a spacious cabin. I grew accustomed to first class treatment and held no intention of slumming to Africa. I kept to myself and was eager to touch my feet upon terra firma as the ship docked in the Bay of Biscay, eastern France. This would not come to be.

In the early morning hours I heard a gunshot, then another. Before long there was a steady stream of bangs and booms. The air took on the smell of torched powder. I clutched a bottle of the elixir and began to drink from it. Then I heard the shouting. English. As far as I knew I was one of a handful of English speaking passengers on the vessel.

The ravings and shots grew closer and the door to my cabin burst open. There stood a burly, bearded man. Rugged and battle-worn, he towered over me. I was frightened by the very sight of him.

"Please! No! My good man, please, I am an Englishman!" I shouted raising my hands into the air, one of them still clutching the bottle at its neck.

The man lunged at the bottle of the elixir I held. He smelled the open neck and wrinkled his nose. He gave me a dominant, confirmatory glance and slugged deeply from the bottle seemingly oblivious to its taste and odor. His eyes took on that distant intoxication.

As more blasts sounded, I heard the screams of the other passengers. Women shrieked as their husbands were pulled from their cabins to be beaten, stabbed, and shot. I knew that this man's approval of my choice of beverage would be my only way.

"I can get you more," rushed out of my mouth. His intrigue was apparent. He nodded and motioned for me to sit down on the bed. I followed the directive of this silent odd man.

Another appeared at the door. He was thin, hacking and coughing. Covered in blood he yelled at my captor as he pointed his fingers in various directions. He then looked towards me and ordered the silent buffoon, "Kill him! Kill all of them!" before walking back out into the corridor.

The silent pirate drank more of the elixir and his mental incapacity became apparent to me. He reached for his long blade. His actions were those of a vicious bully child rather than a man. The man-child, however, was about to follow his orders.

"Please spare me, sir!" I requested in vain.

I concentrated deeply. Then it happened. I felt the cold air, the sensation of falling. Everything went dull. I was free from Wagner's body and overwhelmed with terror. I lunged into the idiot. To the best of my faculties, I defocused the onslaught of the silent man's life and emotions. I ignored the sadness and the neglect and all of the orphanages and charities that passed him about as a boy. I still found bliss in the rip of the man's life, good or bad, but desperately focused on my survival.

Through his eyes I saw Wagner, inanimate, come to life as the pirate. His essence filled the void I left. I could see his plunge into Wagner's memories.

For a moment there was a wretched squall. This was the sound of the mute attempting command of Wagner's vocal cords. I plunged the long blade into his chest. Blood burst from the wound, covering the plank floor. I grabbed the wooden crate storing bottles of the elixir and substantial amounts of raw Vella Root.

I hurried from the room. The jewelry and money remaining on Wagner's corpse were now in my pockets. The thin little pirate returned and was happy to see his orders followed. He inspected the crate and looked at me disapprovingly, but I grunted him off handing him the riches.

When I arrived on the top deck I witnessed the remnant carnage laid about. Limbs, torsos, heads, and blood were everywhere. A modest but progressive fire was burning across the old Spanish vessel. The captain's head was perched atop a flagpole.

A series of large flat planks connected the attacking ship to the target vessel. Fleeting images from the mind of the idiot showed his quarters. I could hide the elixir safely for later consumption.

I stored my intoxicating booty and returned to the plundered vessel. There I saw the most horrid of sights. I watched as the pirate underlings laid waste to the remaining female and the few children passengers. This was the conclusion to all the brutal rape and evisceration. I could neither watch nor look away.

The thin pirate led the mayhem. He ordered the marauders back to their vessel. I watched as they carried armfuls of stolen goods. I assisted and returned to my new ship. I attempted to make conversation, to learn something in the chaos, but this new shell was a mute, his memories so ever simple. His maladies of mind and mouth hindered me.

After loading our treasures we were served a foul gray gruel in clay pots. I ate to draw no attention to myself.

"Now we eat!" said a clean man. Following him from behind were shipmates carrying much of the fine foods pilfered from the travel ship. Fowl and cured meats were placed on the tables and devoured as quickly.

This kempt man was no sea mongrel. He walked with a defined motion, a statured elegance. His hair was curled and red. He was an Englishman named Drake, someone whose name preceded him. The man was another duality of the world. English hero first class here, yet moments ago a monster of the sea.

"Today was the work of fine men. We have done well and each one of us will be rewarded for these efforts," he said pacing about amongst the men. Raising a wooden mug, he shouted, "For our Queen!"

"Our Queen!" shouted out the ragtag collection of former military men, lifetime sea barons, and hapless criminals. I found my own glass rise up in systemic reflex, though no words would come from my mouth.

Drake was not a pirate by conventional definition. He operated his crew under letters from the Queen; a license to plunder and kill. He made a career out of targeting Spanish cargo. The Spanish efforts were thwarted for Britannia, while Drake became wildly rich off the captured booty.

He was neither particularly handsome nor well spoken but he was commanding in his presence, respected by all under his orders. Drake ate and commiserated with his loyal men. While my simpleton-borrowed brain sought his approval, I dreamed of an opportunity to overtake him, to become him.

Being mute made it easy to travel to and fro throughout the boat. No questions were asked of me nor were any answers expected. They assumed me unintelligent because I could not speak. I was assigned the most basic of duties. These simple tasks, though utterly repulsive, afforded me a great deal of time to plan and drink the elixir at my leisure.

I was successful in a controlled search of the oaf's memory. Within his simple thought structure I honed my fledgling abilities. This mind offered me all it had. I relived his first sexual encounter with an aged Spanish whore. From there he had been lost in a hand of poque to the skinny man. His memory and emotion were neutered compared to those of Wagner, but vivid and new all the same.

I binged on the memories and fantasies of this idiot. He did not know how old he was or where he was from. He had seen much of the world. The thin man provided him a companionship unknown in his rejected youth. All the meaningless slaughters at his own hand were just that to him. This man-child monster was a murderer without bloodlust, a thief without greed.

And this is how it went for thirty-five years. Though I did not remain the oaf, I plundered and coveted my way through the decades. In the old seaside taverns and whorehouses I always found those willing to drink from my tainted chalice. In each place I spread my Vella Root in the nooks away from plain view.

I enjoyed the flood of their lives pouring into me more than I detested that cold nether region between us. I became adept at absorbing the deluge of emotion, body, and mind. The killings became easier and easier, as did building my confidence in leading men to drink my elixir.

I went from ship to ship, body to body, long leaving Drake for bolder, crueler legions of pirates. I carried nothing from life to life other than a satchel of the Vella Root and whatever bottled elixir I could carry. I partook in atrocities large and small. I found that guilt could almost always be quelled by my consumption of the elixir or a new shell.

I pondered much about my life near the end of these years. *Was I even alive?* I began to think of myself no longer as a man, but as a demon, some devilish instrument which did nothing but take and destroy.

There was also the issue of my own will. *Was I in control of myself?* I did not think so. I consciously tried to limit my use of the elixir and found I could not. I also found myself stealing lives on a whim.

Seaside taverns filled with tales of the evil ghost pirate named "Sorn." This folklore, still in its infancy, spoke of a satanic aberration pirate drifting throughout the coastal world, possessing the weak and mild mannered. Legend told that the ghost would possess their bodies and minds, leading them to leave their lives behind and turn out to the sea. There was even a children's rhyme that went something like this:

Turn your back to the sea
and pray the Sorn come not for thee
it's the thief of body and mind
the things you love left behind

This fable was my doing. I was in the body of one-eyed Marcus of Italy. One cold bitter night I found camaraderie in a port bar. Drunk on strong rum, I carelessly shared the elixir with a handsome English teacher. Before a small crowd that gathered around, I boasted I might overtake the teacher and give him my body in exchange. He and those gathered egged me on.

"You will make a fine pirate!" I said to the teacher before the switch.

The naked eye detects nothing of this process. There are no faint images of the spirit. What they saw was the absence inside our bodies. The basic and most primary functions require nothing from the essence for some time. The body is able to live for minutes without occupation by the essence. Core functions such as breathing, metabolism, and blood distribution by the beating heart continue on while the body stands vacant.

Humans, though, have some sense of this happening. Some more than others. Newton would see something. The Taxman even more so. It is not detected by the eye alone or the ear alone or the hands alone, but of some other sense or some synergistic combination of the senses. They believed. As those in the crowd realized something inexplicable occurred, they separated and moved away from the both of us. Most left the tavern all together.

As for my friend the teacher, now in my old rags, I simply looked at the horror in his face and laughed cruelly. I basked in the glory of the rush of his emotions and experiences as he realized I did that which I warned him I could do. He was overwhelmed by the horror of emotion and memory I bequeathed to him.

His final insult came when he rested his eyes on his old body. I did a little jig to torment further. He stepped forward as Marcus into a great stumble, his perception of depth skewed by the missing eye. This was all that had been needed.

He began to rant and rave. The disturbance brought a passing constable who removed him from the tavern. I followed them out of the bar.

10

In the jungle of the teacher's mind I found an obsession. Many men hold such desire. Sometimes sexual, other times for great fortune, but always to escape in some fashion from monotony. Through memory I saw his most valued possession. It was something he spent all of his wealth upon. It was something magical and mystical to him.

His sense of adventure excited me. While I overtook him for his look and his education, I found beneath a much more appealing figure. In this mild mannered man I discovered a fledgling treasure hunter, a seeker of long and forgotten relics. His interest was nobly academic though deeply heretical as well.

His cherished object was a map and accompanying journal entries purchased from an embezzling courier. The eager thief stole the instruments in transit to a memorable man of the sea. The teacher's obsession drove him into the darkness, consorting with thieves and murderers to obtain progress in his plight. A shaking virgin fear filled him as he entered the dark dens to barter for the stolen goods, his guilt subdued by acquisition. This is where he developed a taste for the rowdy sailor bars and the loose women within them.

Before the intervention of theft, the documents were destined for the hands of the great explorer Henry Hudson. If the teacher deciphered the instrument properly, Hudson was in search of a supernatural artifact of unknown origin. Though his decoding left him with a number of questions, this thing promised its holder great power over the elements of the world. To the best of the teacher's deciphering, the thing could be described only as "the box." It was my hopes that the power could be used to aid my maddening addiction to the elixir. Maybe I just needed something to run toward.

My own rendezvous with the mystical made me keenly able to

appreciate such things. I needed no persuasion. My faith was absolute in such matters. I agreed with the position of the teacher. His own pursuits were fruitless to the date of his unfortunate meeting with me in the tavern, yet he stood on the precipice. He knew the approximate location of the artifact, but would need an ice cutting crew and a large ship to reach it.

In frustration he considered an allegiance with Hudson, the two sharing in the spoils. He considered the man to be a competitor for much of the endeavor, but Hudson's resource and skill proved too much to pass upon. With this I agreed also.

Over the next many months I traced the progress of Hudson and his vessel. Binges on the elixir delayed and confused me for my purpose many a night. I found myself unable to rise from bed without a good swallow of the drink. The body of the teacher proved remarkably tolerant of my abuses. For that I was thankful.

I finally caught up with Hudson in some now forgotten Irish port city. He and his crew arrived stateside for a good bit of rest and a restocking of supplies. Hudson himself roomed at an inn where I, too, enrolled.

I learned from some of his crew at a tavern that the stop was neither rest nor replenishment. Hudson ran his resources dry in pursuit of a treasure he would not describe to even his closest mates. Most of those remaining on the ship thought him mad. Those who did not shared in the belief that the venture hobbled on failing legs.

Many of his crew abandoned or threatened to abandon him due to the depletion of food supplies and a serious cholera outbreak on the vessel. The men resented throwing their dead sea mates into the icy waters at such a maddening pace. No merchant would extend Hudson goods on credit and most of the crew were unwilling to continue the journey without guarantee of fair payment.

There laid my opportunity. As always, I carried with me an ample supply of cash and could collect a great deal more without fail. I wore timeless jewelry of rock and gold on my fingers and around my throat alone that could pay for the venture.

Arriving at Hudson's inn I rented a room and waited in a common parlor. I sipped on the elixir for all of a day. Hudson never appeared. After a small gratuity a bag man brought me to his room.

"Yes?" he asked after opening his door, clearly puzzled by his tricked out visitor. The brave world traveler was not as I had envisioned. He was gaunt and his skin was a waxy yellow coat. The tremor of his hands could not be concealed despite his white-knuckle attempt to do just that.

"My name is Nigel Sands and I am very much interested in discussing an important business venture with you."

He took interest in my words, weakly motioning for me to enter his room. I did so. We both sat on woven bamboo chairs. He waved with a shaky hand to the pot of hot tea and cup that sat on a like bamboo table.

"Let me say first, Mr. Hudson, I am a great admirer of your many exploits," I said. He smiled. "In my travels I have come across a bit of chattel that I believe you to be the true owner."

His eyes widened, "My map?"

"Yes, a map and some notes. I paid a handsome sum for the instruments before discovering that they were your belongings and would be happy to provide them to you for the price which I paid for them."

His eyes fell to the floor. There was a silence in the room. I found no discomfort in his disappointment as I anticipated it and had known its resolve.

"And I understand the straits in which you have found yourself. I am a professor of histories and have good understanding of the thing that you seek. I have also been fortunate to collect great wealth in these last years. Let me suggest a venture between us."

"A venture?"

"Yes. You provide your ship, crew, and experience and I provide the map and finances for our mission. At its resolve, we will share equally in the knowledge and ownership of this thing."

"What do you know of it?" he asked me curiously. Though I had come to him for greater insight, he was now asking me.

"I know only what is contained within the four corners of the writings that accompanied the map. I know you seek a thing of a supernatural nature, a thing of great power. It is simply the box."

"Yes, the box. That much is true. But there is more. It is a living thing," he said with a small showing of fear, "and that is all the more that I know."

Another silence came over the room. This thing developed a new meaning to me. I thought of the White Beast and that creature from my misaligned youth. It had to be that same creature.

"What of it then?" I asked bluntly.

"Yes. Let us do this!" he said with a smile championing over the illness and depression that filled him.

Another additional condition to my kindness was that I join the crew as his first mate. He desperately and graciously accepted.

Having reached an agreement in principal we were partners. In mere days I stocked his mammoth ship with quality supplies: foods, medicines, and liquors. The provisions and guaranteed wages enticed many of his crew members back on board and brought on a number of recruits.

I spent the days leading up to our voyage with Hudson. I found his tales as fascinating as any I heard. I thoroughly enjoyed the company and insights he offered to me.

It was shortly after we set sail that I acquired a greater sense of what led him to the depths I found him. Hudson was ill in both body and mind. I was not the only one to notice the captain's shortcomings.

The further we journeyed the greater the map parted from geophysical reality. This was clear to everyone, save Hudson. The map was a fabrication of greedy imagination. The back pay and new supplies had quelled his crew for only a short time. Soon whispers of plans to abandon the ship at the next port echoed.

The venture would yield not the blasphemous beast of my youth. Everything changed in that moment. There was no grand adventure. I merely lent myself to the ambitions of a foolhardy teacher and the dementia of a once great and brave man whom time had put to pot. I felt venomous. I was back to just plain old me, without purpose or reason to go on. I grew more and more vengeful with the ebb and flow of the ship.

It was then I began to whisper back to the members of the crew. As the chief financier of the journey my words carried with them great weight. I spoke of my concerns regarding Henry Hudson, particularly his fitness to lead the vessel.

"We should fear for our basic safety," I told each of them.

Some of the men were eager to jostle him from the boat, still resentful for the conditions prior to my bailout. Others held sentiment and admiration that required the time and pressure of desperation to let it melt away. Eventually, nearly every man on the ship agreed that Hudson was to be removed from his post most hastily. Misled by a madman, I would have my mutiny.

My co-conspirators and I drank rum and whiskey before we approached his quarters. Hudson was defenseless.

Into the black night waters he went, letting out a great scream as his nude, old body connected with the icy ocean froth. The men, my men, cheered before they looked to me for direction. There came my bastard epiphany. I had not a scintilla of where it would all go next.

"We ride into the night," I shouted, "to our great destiny!" The roar of the men filled the emptiness of my words. I had no plan for them.

I calculated my escape from the pack of animals I birthed. I needed a stronger body and a new face. I looked at the crew and made my target. He was a young and fit man named Andrew Kates. I promised him some of the elixir and he followed me into the bowels of the ship. We traded shells there before I stabbed him in the heart.

After hiding the body, I waited for the crowd on deck to dissipate. I lowered the dinghy into the waters, thankful of the lights visible off the starboard side.

In the small rowboat I paddled away from the ship to the nearest port. I carried only the clothes on my back, the Vella Root, and a bottle of the elixir. This new body I had taken was young and powerful. I was quite pleased. I pumped the oars like a machine, traveling rapidly over the black waters.

I made my way first to shore and then back to Germany. I would remain Kates for a spell.

11

I wandered Germany. I laid out more of the Vella Root. I brewed the elixir a bottle or two ahead of my needs. I spoke to priests, scholars, and elders. I searched for some comfort of my condition, but tired when it did not come. I returned to England.

One day in London I hailed a carriage, but offered it to a pregnant woman and her betrothed. She smiled in gratitude as the two climbed up and into the coach. It was then the thought came; I did not know the inside of womanhood.

Gwen was her name. She was the youngest daughter of a wealthy English spice trader. She strolled along the shore of a placid pond. She was barefoot and beautiful. I stood behind a spreading chestnut tree to watch.

She flipped her blonde ringlets between tossing brightly colored flower heads on the surface of the water. The petals floated atop, spinning gently with the mild breeze. Gwen took practice at the petals with stones gathered from the shore. She sunk a great number of the flowers.

A carnal desire emerged. Her hair radiant; eyelashes that were thick, long, and dark. Gwen's eyes were a deep, crisp green. She was an unavoidable blend of innocence and seductive charm.

"Hello my dear," I said.

"Hello my lord," she responded through a blush, half afraid and the other half curious of the handsome man behind the tree. She cupped a rock in her tiny hand.

"May I?" I asked.

Her face broke into a smile of beautiful white teeth. I reached into her hand and took the rock. I threw it at a floating flower top and sunk it. She clapped her hands in glee and began collecting more of the flowers. I revealed a flask from my overcoat and sipped from it. The flask was painted with swirling dragons around it. I purchased it for a handsome sum at an English market. Her eye caught its seductive luster.

"That is quite beautiful!" she said reaching out for my flask. I placed it into her hands for examination.

"Drink from it," I said softly. I saw the mischievous devil through her window eyes as she raised them to me.

"It smells awful!" she said as she wrinkled her nose.

"Yes, but it tastes so sweet."

The beautiful Gwen took a brave swallow of the magical fluid. I saw the ecstasy. I felt her divide before me. I lunged at her with my essence. I filled her from within, extending myself into her small fingers and toes.

Kates' body animated as her essence entered. She shrieked in terror. I attempted to subdue her, but found I was now the far weaker creature. This I failed to include in my shallow, lustful considerations.

She struck me hard with a closed fist. She kicked me to the ground demanding explanation. The delicate skin covering me split and tore upon impact. The blows weakened me to concession. She climbed on top of me, shaking her former body with great violence. That was when I felt it.

Her breathing accelerated and deepened. Along her thigh, her organ swelled erect plucking a memory from a forbidden place. It was a terror from a year earlier at the hands of a drunken friend of her father. After a night of hard drinking and storytelling the man, Reginald, slipped into her bedroom and climbed upon her. She awoke to his liquor-soaked breath and him inside of her.

The next day she told her father. He dismissed the tale outright, blaming her for a lurid imagination, sparing her the whip if she promised to recant. She did so after some badgering, but now she would have her twisted revenge on the kind.

She tore the delicate cloth of my gown from me. Gwen forced my legs spread. She thrust inside of me from a vantage of power and rage. There was no sense of pleasure. I remember only alien sickness and fright.

The male figure finally rested atop of me and the moment was mine to seize. I tried to push out of her, but could not. I thought of the shiny blade in the jacket she now wore. I pulled it from within the coat and thrust it deep into her pulsating throat. The warm blood spilled over my bosom. And there I lay until it was over.

I pushed the bled-out body off of me. It rolled to a standstill, looking blankly into the heavens. I stood and leapt into the pond water and rid myself of the awful contamination both inside and out. The scrubbing removed the blood and other fluids though no amount of washing could cleanse the filth of experience.

I ran from the place naked. My heart and lungs raced. My feet were cut with the sticks and stones riddling my path. My eyes and ears were open to the sound of human beings. I needed to escape from the fleshy prison of emotions; anyone would suffice. I urinated down my leg as I ran, unable to control such a release. It was then I saw the filthy vagrant.

His hands, face, and clothing were covered with pitch black soot of inexplicable origin. He hid away behind the burnt out shell of a large barn. It was there that he roasted some unrecognizable small mammal over an open flame.

His eyes, wide and white under the soot, scanned me in disbelief. His posture tightened, crouched down like some predator animal poised to advance upon its game. He grinned a row of rotting teeth. I teased my hair and offered him the extended flask.

The prospect of liquor seemed to excite him more than the seductive youth of my form. He greedily grabbed the flask and drank from it. He wiped his mouth with his grubby sleeve to no effect and returned his attentions to me. I infested him and watched as he defaulted into the female figure. I strangled the now female vagrant to the ground.

As I hid the body amongst refuse and piles of cut brush, I heard the not so distant rumblings of crowded hate. I smelled the burning of torches before they began to bob up and down under the setting sun. The mass moving toward me became quite clear, a mob screaming, shouting, and waving the torches.

I raced through the mind of the vagrant. I found no clear narrative within the diseased brain. I saw from his crazed perspective the most brutal of murders. A boy, a child not more than six, wandered from his mother as she rubbed linens over a washboard in a small stream. The vagrant waited only feet away, calling to some dark god to bring the child to him.

The vagrant, deep in mania, saw something more than a child drifting from his mother. He discovered hell's spawn loose on the earth, ready to desecrate and devour the innocence of the world. In irrational fear for his own life, he lifted the child and smothered him with a forceful hand. In both this practice and mythology he had been trained.

I ran from that place, but they overcame me. I was kicked, punched, burned, and whipped as they bound my legs and arms. They spat saliva and curses over me. My death was again so near.

12

"Cease!" shouted some booming voice of reason. The speaker, an older man, spoke slowly and softly, but with great command. The mob showed him a great reverence and immediately stopped their torment. I looked through battered eyes to the groomed man in a long, rich coat. His eyes were a kind blue. The vigilantes parted as he approached. He offered me his hand. I reached out and took it, relying on it greatly to pull my beaten body upward.

"Come now, Mackrey," the man said as he directed two of the crowd to loosen the ropes on my legs. He handed each of my persecutors coins as they freed me. My mind told me the man's name was God. This was who the vagrant, Mackrey, knew him to be.

I walked on pained limbs behind him for miles until we reached the apex of a large rolling green hill. There stood the castle of rock and forged metals.

A flooding of Mackrey's memories came forth; haunting images of medical experiments being performed on elderly men and women, the mentally retarded and insane, but mostly on children. There had been experimental brain surgeries performed on… me. I touched my head and ran my fingers along it. These were remnants of ghastly poking and prodding inside of my borrowed skull on its man-child mind. Mackrey once loved children. Now he feared and hated them.

When we entered, I sluggishly walked to quarters I knew as my own on the ground floor. The simple unmade cot glistened. I fell into the bed and closed my eyes.

"Rest now my son," he said from the open entryway.

Days passed. In time the man called God pulled me from bed. Confusion overwhelmed me as I simultaneously knew a mere man cared for me in the castle, yet also thought him to be a deity. This was the paradox that caused me such dismay. My mind and my host's were both combined and separate.

"Oh, Mackrey. My lost sheep. Why do you stray from me?"

I was filled with terror and doubt.

"I have brought you back again, for you know that we have much work to do."

He brought me up winding stairs toward a musty tower. He stopped and turned on the stairs, "What is this?" he asked holding out the flask and a small satchel of the Vella Root. I did not answer. "Dispose of them," he said returning them to my possession.

We reached the turret. A wooden chair was centered in the upper most room. A helmet laid on the chair with a chain attached leading up to a metallic pole passing through the roof and into the sky.

More memories: a bolt of lightning, sizzling flesh, the smoking body of an orphan child. All of the senseless experiments and the monies paid to obtain subjects for the madness. I felt his terror, but impotent to defy his maker and personal savior. God checked the chair and its connections.

"Bring one to me!" he said vigorously. Without the benefit of thought or reason, I plodded back down the stairs and entered a dark room filled with whimpering children. I left and then returned with a torch to illuminate the room. Four children held in a cage looked up at me. I drank from the elixir at the sight of them. I opened the cage and pulled out one of the children by his arm. In a flash of defiance I did not lock the cage.

"Run," I whispered.

I picked up the sobbing child. We ascended back to God and his infernal chair. He was tinkering still with the chair. I stood there holding the child tightly.

"What ever are you waiting for?" God asked without turning to us.

I honored this call for violence. I forced a firm palm over the nose and mouth of the child. The little boy's purpose could now be realized.

The dead boy was chained to the chair and the skullcap placed on his head. I smelled lamp oil in the air. Then we waited for the rolling gray thunderclouds to approach from the east. First the rains came down in trickles, and then in a downpour. In the distance, the crackling boom of thunder edged closer with preceding bolts of lightening. My eyes returned to the man called God as he drilled into the forehead of the dead child. My defiance was re-inspired. I pulled God up into the air by his regal neck and broke it in a motion of violent physics. God was dead.

The lightening drew closer as I furiously tried to unbind the child from that horrific chair. The futility went unrecognized. I was pulling off the skullcap when lightning struck the elevated pole in a brilliant flash. Through the blasting electric sun came the pause of time and space.

I felt the intense heat rendering my blood red molten magma. I was burning from the inside out. Looking down I saw the same skin and limbs, noticing no damage to any outer layer tissue, but my insides seared from the bone outward. A faint gray smoke rose off of me.

I was no longer within the castle tower. There was no lightening, rain, or thunder. What I heard were desperate screams echoing from some deep recess. Menacing shadows came in and out of the surrounding darkness, each a perversion of the human form.

Beyond the burning pain within, the pitch darkness, and those monstrous figures there had been the odor. It was a combination of unpleasant smells: rotted meat, human waste, vomit, and burnt flesh.

Then it came for me. The thing was monstrous and scaled white. Recessed white eyes held captive my reflection within. The unearthly brute looked to be some bastard cousin to the White Devil of my history. The reflection was ugly and sickly with its cleft palate. It was my true reflection. The boy grew into a man, the man I would have been had I never made that first leap of faith into dear old Wagner. The creature reached out for me, but the shadowy place vanished to the light.

The world was a dull sheen. I felt the icy cold winds of nowhere and the undeniable sense of falling. I was yet again lost to that netherplace.

I know not how long I left this earth for that other plane, but my essence was ejected from the body of Mackrey into the surreal void of black menace. I fought the icy winds and looked upon the charred child in the chair and the smoldering giant Mackrey. I was there, trapped between the world of the living and the world of the damned and the dead.

I fought my way back into Mackrey's shell. It was dying, but there had been nowhere else to go. I forced open my eyes.

The faint images of the world became even fainter. The washed out colors faded to dead pale gray. The light continued to dim. I knew the essence could not exist without the flesh, but this flesh was spent. I closed my eyes in anticipation of the end.

A tiny hand pushed my face. I felt a liquid splash over my mouth and nose. The taste was undeniable. It was my elixir. I opened an eye to one of the boys I had freed from the cage.

"You drink," was all I could muster.

He put the bottle to his lips. I nodded and he took a small drink. I bolted from Mackrey's scorched frame into that of the child. I would live.

13

I was a child again. The onslaught of his wretched memories came in bursts. There had been a drunken whore of a mother, a sale to a twisted man for unspeakable buggeries, and then an escape into an orphanage for a time. It was there the child came into God's possession.

It was an uncomfortable mixture of the boy's innocence and darkness the world brought him. I did have the sense to gather the bag of the Vella Root and what remained in the flask. I ran from the castle and came upon another of the children from the cage.

The boy was older, but not by much. He was my new shell's closest companion in the cage, but lacked the bravery of the boy who unknowingly sacrificed himself to save me. In allegiance he waited while the other two children disappeared into the countryside.

The waiting boy's name was Godwin. He said little of how he arrived in the same cage, but I could imagine it was in a like shameful path.

We made distance between the abominable castle and ourselves. Along the way I told him what I had seen in the tower, namely the mad Doctor's attempt at the resurrection of the dead.

Godwin seemed less troubled by this than I. He wondered if any success had been achieved and asked questions to which I had no answer. The horror seeded his imagination. We talked through most of the night before drifting off to fitful sleep. We walked hungry for days and I had exhausted what little of the elixir remained in the flask.

With the sense of children, we missed the neighboring village and travelled deep into the wood. We entered a third day without food and I entered a second day without the elixir. Though a dose remained in the flask I did not dare drink it. I needed to ensure an escape from the shell of the tormented little boy.

My little hands began to tremor and sweat poured from me. Godwin walked many yards ahead of me driven by a voracious hunger. My withdrawal did have this advantage. He called back to me every few hours, but gave up on this as we plodded forward.

Then drifting in the air came the smell of baking bread. He walked faster and I stopped to vomit. Collecting myself, I followed him to the smoke trickling out and over the trees.

We arrived. It was a small stone cottage. From our vantage we could see the fresh loaf cooling in an open window. There was not a soul in sight.

"Stop," I mustered.

Godwin was beyond reason. Like a rabid beast he propelled toward the bread. I set the flask and my satchel behind a towering oak. I gingerly followed and saw the master of the house. The man reached the hungry boy just as he pulled the bread from the sill. With a mighty blow, Godwin fell to the ground without a bite. The man saw me and gave chase. Within steps I was at his mercy.

He threw me to the ground and gave me a kick. Of course he reminded me of Father, but he was just a simple man protecting his dinner. The man held the both of us at bay with a long rod.

"I hate nothing more than thieves," he told us.

Authorities came and marched us from the place. The policeman brought us straight to a ramshackle of a hole. A handpainted sign, worn and dangling, indicated the place to be a "Home for Wayward Boys."

After a good bit of washing and spanking we were fed a brown paste of a stew. I had something of an appetite and ate. It was quite tasty. Godwin ate much more, finishing what remained of my plate. We met the other boys, lean and angry, and were put to cots in a room with the bunch of them. It went on like this.

Day in and out we slaved for Ms. Lanson. Scrubbing and washing, cutting and trimming. She was a hard woman, but in some way must have cared. Godwin blossomed and a month later he was gone. I only saw the smiling man and woman for a moment. I was alone again.

About a week later Ms. Lanson put me to pulling weeds. I was recovered from the withdrawal, the child's shell having digested little. This did nothing to inhibit my psychological cravings. These desires traveled along with me from stolen body to body. I thought each day about the flask and the Vella Root outside the house where Godwin and I were captured. It was not far.

Escape was no great feat. It was the fear of being alone again that kept the boys at bay. The steady meals and warm rooms were a greater comfort to those who had not always known such privilege. I fought the weary waves the hard work brought and outlasted the other boys. I crept through a pried window and climbed down a defunct piping.

I arrived there in the dusk. Smoke billowed from the cottage and a dwindling lamp lit its innards. Nevertheless I braved across the lawn and found my flask and satchel unscathed. I shook the bottle and surely as I remembered there was a small amount of the elixir inside.

Producing more would not be difficult, but I needed basic reagents and some glassworks. I had no money and childhood was no way to move through the world. Without money or strength, power or influence, there was little I could do. I saved the dose and walked into the night.

14

I came upon a moor illuminated by a dim moon. Beyond it laid an apple orchard. There I saw a magical presence. Lights flickered and danced in the sky. I traced the object back and forth before catching the reflection off of a long string. It traveled to the hands of a boy no more than ten. The dancing lights were two oil lanterns attached to a kite fashioned from retired linens.

"Isaac!" shouted a voice of age-old motherly concern.

With the beckoning the boy retrieved his kite from the night sky and ran towards a well lit home. He embraced the kite, holding forth the lantern to guide his way. I followed slowly behind him.

The place was isolated and perfect to wait for opportunity. I gave myself the night, watching the house from the robust trees. I ate the juicy, red apples scattered about the ground. As the sun replaced the moon I saw the boy and his family begin the new day. Despite the night to reflect, I did not know what next to do.

I waited some more. In the full moon light I saw a hulk of a man emerge from behind the house leading a sickly goat to a fenced pasture. He was mumbling to himself. He swatted in the air as he ranted to unseen torments.

He became more agitated. I became bolder in my approach. I recognized him to be a lunatic. *Find sanctuary in the fractured of mind.* I pondered over the words of Faustus and knew then their meaning. The crazed man's essence was "looser" than that of a sane man. It seemed a practical chance and my only option with such diminished holdings of the elixir. As a grown man, even a mad one, traveling and collecting reagents could only become easier.

I darted at the disturbed man. As I ran I drank the remnants in the flask and threw my satchel of the root forward. The familiar feeling came.

Then followed a fiery agony. Something from the night behind gashed my back. I felt the blood, warm and spreading, absorb into my shirt. The crazed man saw this and hustled to my aide. This brought him close enough.

I assaulted the lunatic with all my astral might. Though I felt the impact inside him, he remained steadfast within the body that would be mine. Again I tried with even more force, propelled by a unity of desperation and fear of the ravenous beast. With this blow, I unlocked his essence from its physical doppelganger.

My perspective changed. I watched the wolf, mangy and crazed, tear the little boy I had just been to pieces. I pocketed the satchel before it lunged at my new limbs with demonic veracity. The beast locked its iron jaw upon my forearm, causing a copious flow of warm madman blood. I set out to scream in reaction, but from my mouth came only maniacal laughter.

The wolf ensnared my other arm and tore from it. This lunatic form possessed great strength. I kicked the beast with heavy boots and dropped my weight down upon it. The thing yelped out and squirmed away. It hung its head in defeat as it made way back into the orchard.

I removed my outermost shirt and wrapped it around my bleeding arms, clutching it in front of me. I continued to laugh and mumble throughout the ordeal, only stopping when the world faded to black.

I awoke in a bed. I examined my arms that were tightly wrapped in a white bandage. I smelled the putrid chemical that stained both my skin and the bandage. The injured limbs swelled and could not be moved. I felt a feverish heat throughout me. My visions seemed to pulsate with my heart. I craved the elixir as I giggled and mumbled to myself.

I heard rumblings from outside the room. The door opened and in walked the boy who propelled lanterns into the sky with his kite.

"Hello Uncle James," the boy said.

"Isaac," I said as the troubled mind furnished me with the child's name.

I went to stand, but found that I could not. My heavy head weighted me back down to the bed. With some effort to keep the words straight I said, "Would the boy do Uncle a great favor?"

"Yes, anything Uncle. What is it?"

"A burlap satchel was-"

"Yes, Uncle," he said holding out the Vella Root.

"Good boy."

The boy tended to my wounds and wiped my forehead with a watered rag.

"Could you get your uncle some things?"

With that I recited the catalysts and suggested where he might find them. He possessed a grave intelligence and aptitude. My request for the glassware was accepted with equal competence. The boy hurried from the room excited by the prospect of applied science. The crippled arms and brain with its inane mumblings would not deter me.

The boy returned after many hours to my appreciation and his grandmother's anger. After much nagging and castigation, the boy joined me and built a makeshift laboratory in the room. At my direction Isaac isolated the active ingredients of the Vella Root and hydrolyzed the yield.

At the conclusion of all the time and effort, there it was. We yielded several pints. Isaac held a bottle to my mouth and I drank a hardy swallow. The detached euphoria came over me. I easily separated my essence from crazed Uncle James. The child's eyes widened. It was an unmistakable observation. I settled back in to the witless.

"What did you see?"

"A ghost," he answered. "May I?"

"This is not for any boy to know," I told him.

The child was special. He saw the invisible, the impossible. The notion to know his perspective was fleeting and I thought better of it. He thanked me for allowing him to aid in the "experiment" and went on his way to the apple orchard.

In a few days I was elated to find my arms improved. I fought the mind demons off to wash and shave my face. I finished bottling the formula and headed to the nearby village with a pint. I needed to find a new identity as the mumbling and laughing grew unbearable. I never saw the child again.

I found a sturdy young carpenter in the village, Jon Earl. He bore rough features. He enjoyed drinking rye and smoking imported Jamestown tobacco. He dreamed a future beyond the confines of Colsterworth. He enjoyed the smoke so much that he booked passage to the fledgling American colony. The man hoped to reap profits from the dealings in the pleasant weed. It was not much to convince him to taste the elixir.

His dreams became mine. I did not kill him. I watched Uncle James' crazy mind overtake the carpenter as he went away mumbling and laughing. In stealth, I crept back to the Newton home and retrieved the unspent Vella Root and bottled elixir.

I was sound, healthy, and well stocked in elixir. I smelled dampened tobacco in my dreams, imagining walks through perpetual rows of the tasty leaf. I awoke to begin the carpenter's long lusted journey.

15

The population of the New World swelled. Its borders filled with every color and creed, though men looking as Jon Earl did reigned. I arrived with the monies Earl saved and purchased a small farm. On it I threw down some of the Vella Root, but otherwise placed the elixir and the tools I used to make it away. In this period of clarity, I abstained.

Working hard, I made great fortune in the sales of my premium tobacco. The money was parlayed to acquire vast amounts of land. I leased homes and farmland to fellow colonists, avoiding the greedy cruelties in which Father engaged.

I found a conception of God and the church, the Roman Catholic sect, and began a devotion to the tenets of the religion. My dollars raised a great cathedral of cut stone. I prayed for my sins to be forgiven. I developed hope within my voided heart they could be.

In my religious fervor I found Mary. She worked hard on a rival plantation, but attended the church I paid to build. We courted for a year and then married.

She shied from sexual relations, believing it to be sinful in all contexts other than procreation. In the dark of night, perhaps once of every other month, we made the attempt, but no child would ever be conceived. She entertained no pleasure beyond her strict reading of the Bible and prudence. I enjoyed her companionship and instruction in the Catholic faith. She was good in the plainest sense.

I toyed with the idea of revealing the dark science to her, making her my companion for the ages. I concluded her religiosity would preclude it. I enjoyed my moments with her. Over the many years with Mary and my fledgling faith, I drank nary a drop of the elixir. These were the happiest times of my over long life.

Mary and I built upon my vast fortune. We hired a competent man, Leland Hardy, to oversee operations. He served as an agent and confidant, but most importantly a friend. His ability freed me from the daily works of the plantation, permitting me to focus upon new business in America and abroad.

We set out in the late of November for several meetings in Massachusetts to negotiate merchant contracts. Dealings with the northerners proved too lucrative to send agents. Mary also enjoyed the turning of colors and wanted to see a true snowfall.

It was a nasty lead-in to winter. She first contracted a bold flu that progressed to pneumonia. Her wheezing coughs gave way to bloody projectiles. Thick sputum choked her to death. I went from my bed to hers and held her until the morning sun shone through the glass of our rented rooms. I remained sober long enough to bring her body back to our farm.

The pain ran deep in me. I found some subdued version of love and lived it for over thirty years. All my old works were waiting where I left them. The Vella Root was growing over a back portion of the property I had sewn after purchasing the lot. Within days I fell headlong into a dangerous binge with the elixir.

I hid away for days at a run, drinking the elixir and dodging responsibility. My friend Leland made the mistake of intervention. He thought he could show me that life was worth facing and this was Christ's plan. I had plans of my own.

"I am dying," I said.

"No," he said.

"Yes, very much so. I have no heir to speak of. With Mary gone you are the closest thing to family I have."

We sat in labored silence.

"I am making arrangements to transfer the plantation and company to you," I continued.

"You cannot!"

"I am and I must. Do you accept these things?"

"Yes, of course," he answered.

"It is settled then."

Within the week I brought the lawyers and notaries in for the transfer. I signed all the documents and Leland did as well. I dismissed them so Leland and I could speak.

I asked Leland to join me in a last drink. He was certainly no teetotaler and obliged. When he wrinkled his nose to the putrid-smelling elixir I assured him it was exotic and fine. Drunk on the elixir and his new wealth, I easily overtook him. With tears in my eyes I overpowered the frail old frame of Earl and smothered him with a pillow.

I was again young and wealthy. The year was about seventeen-fifty and a fledgling America rumbled to break the chains of its British master. A bloody war was fought. There was much suffering, treachery, and destruction but I remained unscathed. I financed a considerable portion of the war on both sides but paid little attention or effort to it. With the hedging of my bets I lifted a finger in neither direction.

I remained within Leland until his body was weakened prematurely by my excessive ingestion of the elixir. With his eyes I saw the independent United States of America arise. During the years I held discourse with a number of the notable. I met General George Washington and his compatriots. Neither they nor I played any considerable role in each other's affairs. I was never part of any of it. I was always alone, something unavoidable.

I shouted out to the White Devil in the darkness of night. I demanded meaning and purpose for what I was. I wanted it undone, but feared death beyond human comprehension. I prayed to forget. My cries were dismissed as drunkenness or lunacy.

Catholicism and its God failed me. The mirage of a life faded with the death of Mary. I sought solace from other world religions. I traveled to India, China, Africa, Australia, and throughout the remainder of Europe and Asia drunk on my elixir. I consorted with mystics, witches, shamans, priests, bishops and laymen. I found no further record or memory of any entity such as myself.

I traveled for decades, body to body, until exhaustion and desperation mandated one conclusion. No answers existed for me. I was in an infinite cyclic hell. I was unique, a novelty. I existed within no context. I was a plague. I was wicked. I was death.

16

These were the years I wandered the western world, destitute and crazed, binging on the elixir and so many personas. I ravaged three or four lives in a day at times. I lived only for the euphoria and the onslaught deluge of identity. There came all of the pain, all of the pleasure, all of the bliss and torment. Much of the time I was riddled with confusion and chaos. I remember so little. Inevitably, I would end a binge in some hospital bed or at the doorstep of some charity.

My addiction to the elixir was physical and mental. In each body I occupied, the mind obsessed over all aspects of taste, texture, and in the end its putrid smell. After one ingestion each body became addicted. Those bodies that knew only that first drink would experience a slight sweat and a subtle tremor. This was a mild depravation. The greater the body's exposure, the more intense this withdrawal would be. On the outer realm of denying the drink was vomiting, fever, dementia, paralysis, and maybe death.

No two bodies were alike. Some could withstand several bouts with the elixir while others would deteriorate almost immediately. First affected in every body were the teeth and soft tissues of the oral cavity. Teeth would yellow, darken, and then rot. The tongue and gums burned and bled. Eyesight and hearing faded, then balance and dexterity fell away. The heart would beat inconsistently, sometimes stopping entirely. Each breath was consumed fire.

The brain went last. Beyond the disorienting confusion of withdrawal, language would be forgotten. Memories, both mine and those of my host, would blur and bleed to meaningless disconnected imagery. Everyday objects would become baffling mysteries. Only incoherent insanity could follow.

Adrift in combined discomfort and madness, I rarely stayed in a host for any real duration. I was incapable of controlling my ingestion of the elixir. My obsessive consumption proved insatiable in any form I entered. Everywhere I went, there I was.

I wanted a cure. I read of measures being taken with men driven insane from alcohol consumption. A Scottish physician claimed successes with a sugar-based mixture. Ten "wayward, hopeless drunkards" abstained for one year. Credited was a daily consumption of the sugar drink, diet changes, and exercise. To my regret, the physician was murdered. I learned his papers were bequeathed to a former student I could not find.

The libraries ran dry. I needed to take action. I traveled desperate and lonely to Scotland. I drifted between small reading houses. I discovered three bound-written pages from a pseudo-scientific journal titled "Modern Alchemy." Copious notes appeared on its pages. Other notes were written on loose sheets of paper folded inside. The article discussed the experimentation of a permanent personality change through administration of some mishmash of acids and isotopes. The loose sheet of paper was letterhead. At the top it was engraved "L. Stevenson" with an address in a nearby village.

The notes provided narrative. They outlined the bold experiments. They told of a man searching for an elixir to ascend him to the apex of human potential. My eyes swelled with tears at the prospect of finding another such as me.

I shortly thereafter found his quaint home. His full name was Robert Louis Stevenson. Of historical fame to you, he was but then only regionally known. There was no *Treasure Island*. Yet, there was a Doctor Jekyll.

After some polite refusals, Stevenson finally let me into his abode. He offered a drink of rye. I offered a taste of the elixir. He was keen on it. When we first drank I thought of stealing away with him. I dismissed the temptation. I dared not risk the chaos. I was on to something.

I opened my satchel to the pages. His eyes brightened to the notes. He reached out for them, but I refused. I placed them away from his grasp.

"Is this man real?" I asked.

With slight hesitation, he answered back in the affirmative. With more sips of the elixir he verified the man and elaborated.

"Yes, oh yes, indeed, He is real. He is as real as you or I. He is extremely unpredictable. Dangerous," he said, "as is his wicked drink." A shuddering terror ripped through him. There was substance to this man Stevenson wrote about. The thought of one with such an elixir sent a sharp exhilaration through my body. Perhaps together he and I could find a cure for my compulsions.

I made passage back to England. In one week I arrived at the humble wood-sided home of Doctor Harold Jenkins. Stevenson changed his name to protect the unholy. The whitewashed domicile rested on the hillside of an old

Dutch community in western England. Opening the door to my respectful knocks was a gray-haired manservant. He let me inside the home after much badgering and a handful of rare silver coins. I declined his offer of brandy. I did welcome a small glass of well water, a sufficient base to which I could add my elixir.

I wanted to be alert, but needed to exercise prudence. Without at least a few drops of the elixir my brain was quite sluggish. More than that and I would lose myself again. As I sipped away at the water-elixir, an unearthly growl seethed from the cracks of the floor beneath my feet.

I saw the knowing fright in the butler's eyes. He was fearful of that which was underneath us. Crashing through his feeble attempt to stop me, I opened each of the doors on the level. I finally found the one leading to the basement. I opened the door and ran down the stairs.

What I first saw was ordinary enough. It was a man. He was dark, harried, and slightly overweight. He was tall with a gross bend in his spine sending him looking downward. What was extraordinary was the massive wooden table he held over his head. The piece clearly weighed hundreds of pounds. In animal fury, he launched the table toward the flush stone wall where it splintered apart. He displayed the strength Faustus had when my nightmare life began. Then in a violent flash he turned toward me.

"Who?" he asked through a gnarling fire in his eyes. The voice was demonically human. Before I could answer, he lunged at me with lightening speed across the room. He grabbed me by my throat and lifted me. He peered into my eyes, rotating me so he could look into each. He sniffed at my body. He then hurled me across the room into blackness.

I awoke to intense aches about me. I rested in a cushy bed. I was warm and extremely thirsty. I rubbed my scalp, feeling a large nodule and dried blood. I was not alone in the room.

I opened my eyes to the two dim figures seated alongside the bed. As my head cleared, I recognized the first man as the elderly butler who received me. The other figure I did not first recognize. I then recalled my purpose for entering the home. I explored the blunted memories of the basement. The seated man was the same who hurled me across the cellar. He held a completely different affect. He sat there in a tweed hound's tooth jacket, his face and hands delicate and reserved. The subtle movements were effeminate and dainty. I tried to speak but could not.

"I'm afraid you struck your throat when you… fell… in the basement. It is swollen, but I have examined you and it will be fine in a day or so. I am Doctor Harold Jenkins," he said. He gently placed his hand on my linen covered knee. How different he was from the being that grappled me in the basement. "I must apologize. You startled me when I was… in a delicate state."

I knew his "delicate state." It was that which Stevenson warned. He drank his elixir and transformed into that wild brute that attacked me. The contrast between the man now and in the basement could not have been greater.

A rush of panic overtook me. Tremors, then nausea. My mouth salivated as an agitated rage overtook me. This was the phenomena of craving. Plunging madness could follow.

"Would you like this?" asked Dr. Jenkins. He literally read my mind. He held up my silver flask.

I reached forward and he mercifully placed the opened flask into my hands. I slugged deeply from the bottle as each nerve sent a burning scream for its absorption. Within seconds, the pain and discomfort dissolved. I was complete again. My eyes met with those of the doctor and he understood instinctively.

"Two days without my special beverage and I am unable to walk," he said with a defeated smile. I was in the presence of another like me. I closed my eyes and returned to dreamless sleep.

Hours later I awoke. In courtesy my flask rested on the adjacent nightstand. A wonderful aroma of grilled beef filled the air. I was famished. I sipped my elixir and stood from the bed. I spoke softly to myself. My throat housed an uncomfortable pressure, likely the pain masked by the elixir. I followed the scent into the dining room where Dr. Jenkins sat, looking up at me in warm surprise.

"My new friend! How wonderful to see you up and about," he said with a genuine smile. He motioned to a set place at the table. There was only room for the two of us. He lived with no other person.

"Yes, I am a bachelor," he said, "and quite happy that way. It leaves me open to the things I wish to do rather than hold me to obligation or routine."

He poured us glasses of blood red wine, assuring with his eyes that he had read my mind. My thoughts were his for the taking. He placed the confirmation inside of my thoughts.

"I, like you, am a prisoner to my own discoveries. I, like you, am dependent upon them. I searched for decades to find some combination of chemicals that would allow me to reach maximum mental and physical potential. Now I spend each day regretting the dreadful door I have opened as I, like you, am forever damned for it."

"I have seen that," I responded.

"Like you, I cannot seem to stop," he offered with a directness that placed a chill in my heart center.

I very much liked Jenkins, respecting his presence and intelligence, but disliked his unnatural abilities. I felt my mind was completely open to him, that he could on a whim uncover and understand the totality of my life. He knew my secrets. He knew my pain. I believe he knew of my time with the White Beast, a secret of which I never spoke.

I wanted to leave the place. I was never so exposed. I no longer wanted his companionship, insight, or understanding. No cure was worth this. Escape was my only desire. I remained seated.

The food was served by his *majordomo* and we ate in silence. I chose to eat over speaking. He chewed his food and drank from his cup, never taking his eyes from me.

After dinner, he said, "I am in desperate need of a partner. I need someone with a strong grasp of the physical sciences and modern chemistry. I can offer you both room and board, handsome pay, and all of my knowledge to date."

I remained silent.

"Your cure may lie in my project. Synthesis," he stated. "Isolation. Injection." He sent to my mind his skin-piercing syringe. This was years before Pravaz and Wood introduced the invention. Against every urge of reason, I remained for more.

"There is a way, you see, to isolate the principles of our respected medicines. Together we can find a way to take the best of what they offer to us and leave the remainder for waste," he said. "Let me show you."

We stood from the table and walked down to the lab. I consumed enough wine and elixir that my throat loosened. I could speak without the torturous pressure. He brought me to the laboratory and showed me his rudimentary hypodermic needle.

"Whatever is that for?" I asked, having never seen such a device.

"Let me show you. May I see your flask?" I held what remained in my flask. My reserve was in the rented room miles away. I reluctantly passed it to him.

He poured the thick fluid from my flask onto a conventional metal spoon. He dropped an ominous liquid into it and placed it over a burning candle. The liquid sizzled and bubbled.

"This is only burning off the excess water and impurities," he assured me. "Lift up your sleeve and come to me."

I followed his instruction. He drew the remaining liquid from the cooled spoon up into the needle. He motioned to me, jabbing the needle into the vein in my right arm. Nothing. Nothing. Nothing. And then it happened.

A wave of pure ecstasy overtook the entirety of my being, the room, and the world around me. My stomach tightened and my knees buckled under the weight of my modest frame. A rush of emotions flowed throughout me, those from the lives I thieved. I felt all the happiness, the sadness, the fear, the joy, and love of dozens of lives all in an instant. I found sense in my place in the world. I had purpose. I had a destiny!

He offered me a chair and I accepted it. I sat and watched him smile down at me. He then poured fluid from a bottle native to the lab into a spoon. He placed it over the flame. Jenkins injected himself with his own concoction. He became that beast. He predatorily hunched forward, growling and animal-like.

Jenkins approached me and began to feel my face and my body. He smelled my neck. "Woman," he growled as he headed to the staircase leading out of his basement laboratory. I followed.

He galloped under the moon across the village cobblestone street. He was savage. To keep pace I ran at my fullest speed. Jenkins led me to a seedy, gas lit community of taverns and run down flats. Women of all ages, shapes, and sizes stood seductively before the row houses. The savage selected two of the women. He handed them coins and carried the both into a first floor flat.

I scurried to the neighboring alley, hoping to catch a sight of the room. I found an open side window from which I heard his monstrous growls. I saw the two women naked in a large master bed. Jenkins was between them. He began to bite roughly at their knees and thighs. An eerie familiarity overcame me. I was again peering in on the sexual acts of others. There I was again, the deficient, ugly, unwanted pervert child.

My heart raced and my hands trembled. I caught the smell of lamp oil in the night air. I watched only seconds more. It was long enough to witness Jenkins' malevolence. He tore flesh from the inner thigh of one woman as he held the other down with savage strength.

As I turned my eyes from that view, I was struck hard in the head to the sound of shattering glass. Though not rendered unconscious, I fell to the ground. Grubby hands ran through my pockets as a cruel laughter filled the air. I looked up to the rotted teeth of my attacker before Jenkins leapt through the open window, blood already drying around his mouth.

Dr. Jenkins pounced with a frightful might. He dug into the man's flesh with strong monster hands. He hurled my attacker against the stone wall of the neighboring building. The man's head collapsed on impact with a sickening thud. I did not bother retrieving the money he removed from my pants before I ran off after Jenkins into the night.

I tried to speak with the Jenkins beast, but the thing was incoherent, babbling a mixture of chemical formulas, historical events, and Bible passages.

Upon entry into his home he ransacked the place. I considered no intervention. I craved another shot of the elixir for myself, but feared turning my back to his savagery.

With time he slowed and drifted to unconsciousness. I descended into the basement to my flask, the spoon, and syringe. I dosed and left into the night. I would never return to that place again.

17

I ran to Paris. A filthy wretch, I rambled about the streets of the French metropolis. Decades passed. More lives were stolen and destroyed. There was no direction or purpose or meaning. It was in these dark hours of despair I found her hope-shine.

I neared a pleasant area of the West Bank. The setting was clean and peaceful. Hands jammed in my pocket, crashing from a freefall bout with the elixir, I shuffled across a brick lined street to what I thought to be a desperate mirage. My aimlessness landed in purpose. She was a vision.

The woman, Karen, moved with a confident elegance. Her eyes were blue and wide. She scratched away at a notepad with a unique blend of grace and elegance. I knew something of love again. I dared not approach her. I looked more like a hopeless derelict than an experienced traveler of the globe and the ages.

I took visual reference. I briskly walked toward my rented room. Inside the dwelling housed my neglected finer things. I bathed quickly in cold water and shaved my face. I dressed in a custom gray suit.

To my dismay, my frenzied rush was in vain. I returned to the café and she was gone. I stumbled through the little French that I knew with a friendly, attentive server. He identified her as a Dutch woman named Karen Osterhoudt. She was in Paris for several weeks on extended holiday. He assured me she spent nearly every afternoon at the very same table filling the pages of a leather bound pad. If I returned the next day I would certainly see her again. I tipped the helpful young man generously and began the business of waiting.

I knew the name. I read it in the pages of an English tabloid sheet a year prior. She braved her way against convention and scandalously divorced her nobleman husband of a short time. She found and lost love in the arms of a game hunter. She went about writing novels and traveling the world.

The following day did not offer her to me. I waited, sipping a twisted concoction of the house red wine and my elixir. I found no solace, only the heightened drunkenness I knew so many times before.

With all the earnest at my command, I awoke early the next morning to try again. I arrived at the café even earlier than the day before. I ordered tea and a raspberry pastry with no intention of consuming either. I watched the people over the second book of *Paradise Lost*.

She appeared. Karen looked unkempt and tired. Her hair was tied back and she wore no makeup. She was beautiful. She led herself to her familiar table and sat there to write. She ordered a lunch from the wait staff without looking upward.

I smoothed my soft brown vest. I continued a gaze across the table, sipping from a flask of the elixir until our eyes met. This was my cue to approach her. She watched me walking towards her in the form of a suave young physician. I commanded her attention.

"Bon jour, Mademoiselle," I said.

"An Englishman," she remarked, "Hello to you." She was comfortable and fearless. She eyed the work in my hand.

"I find myself alone. A stranger in a strange land. I wonder if I may join you for a glass if that isn't too much of an intrusion?"

"I think I would enjoy that very much," she said. Karen closed the open notepad and motioned toward the vacant seat across in fluid motion.

"Thank you. Dr. David Addison," I said.

"Karen. Karen Osterhoudt. It is a pleasure to meet you, Dr. Addison."

"Likewise. Let me order us a bottle of the house vino if I may." I motioned to the passing server. He acknowledged my order with a combination nod and bow before entering the café.

I gave her Addison's history. This young doctor was an accomplished man. He rose from the tenement slums of Old London, working two jobs to support his widowed mother. He became wealthy and esteemed. She was impressed and attracted to me.

She, in turn, told me of herself. She told me of her time on the Dark Continent as a burgeoning woman. Her father left her to wander and learn. She spoke of her eye opening return to England. She shared with me the details of her still mostly unwritten erotic tale of rapes and incest and falling in love.

I enjoyed the rapport. We spoke of the ambitious urban renewal projects of Napoleon III and its blight on the city. We so clearly came together.

I asked if she would join me the following evening for a walk through

Parc des Buttes-Chaumont and dinner. She countered my proposal with an offer to join me that very night. In that moment everything illuminated.

We dined in the evening and each night after. I loved to look at her face glowing by the dim light of the flickering candles. I felt the completing of the age-old void inside which echoed since my maligned beginnings.

Over the following days the more heretical the subject matter became. She held fascination in the macabre. We spoke of past lives, witches, angels, and demons. She shared her observations of rituals performed in the darkest jungle corners of Africa. I shared my most benign tales.

I was anxious to share with her the secret, yet she needed time. She needed to trust. When the moment was right she would cling to the gift I so wanted to give her.

She spoke of a one hundred-year-old mystic in Kenya. This was Karen's sole encounter with the supernatural. The mystic, neither man nor woman, channeled a specter capable of much mayhem. The energy thing hurled stones and broke pottery. Her fascination with such things mushroomed since.

"There is a bit of magic, science really, I learned years ago. I am sure it would interest you," I said.

I paused hoping to instill in her a greater sense of mystery. From her eyes I could see that it worked. She reached and grasped my hand.

"Well, what?" she asked.

"It is far too fantastic to explain to you here. It is really something you would have to see to believe. It is also something you will want to try."

The curiosity spilled from her emerald eyes. As I had thought, her rebellious, adventurous nature triumphed. Her curiosity led her on the path to forever with me.

I brought Karen to my rented rooms on Boulevard Haussman. The area remained unscathed by the painful improvements inside the city limits. Without direction or suggestion, she kicked off her black leather boots. She sat on the edge of the bed with a foot tucked under her. My wrongfully borrowed heart thumped in anticipation. Soon we would have the elixir and then forever we would have each other.

I rolled open the writing desk where I left a silver flask of the elixir.

"Some Yankee moonshine?" she asked throwing her hair back.

I poured the brew into two small, cheap cups. I left the bottle uncapped on the table. I held out my glass. She reached for hers and met mine in the air.

"To the end of boundaries between us," I said. This caused a puzzled, but interested look. I sipped first and then swallowed the contents of my cup. She looked at me and did likewise.

I saw the glow. Her eyes glazed in the unmistakable frantic euphoria. She looked at me with a satisfied, sexual glance. She pulled me to her and kissed me.

"This is not all," I said.

"So what is it?"

Separating from my physical self I placed my essence inside of her. I fell perfectly within. I felt the charged sexual energy remaining in her being. Each part of her body tingled and hungered for touch.

It was now I who sat on the bed looking up at the standing body of Dr. David Addison. The doctor's body stood swaying inanimate and then suddenly filled with a shrieking, flailing terror. She knocked over an unlit oil lamp onto the floor. I froze under the smell.

The arms and legs of the body swung sporadically. She tried to stand only to send her new body crashing back to the floor. She looked up through Addison's eyes. They were poison. She focused onto me inside of her form. Sheer horror flooded her face as it became ghost white. I thought the better of leaving her within the body any longer.

I left her body with great force. I reclaimed Addison. She returned to hers. I felt the shrill terror left remnant in the doctor's body.

The exchange did not stop the screaming. Hatred and fear became her. She ran from the room. I made no motion to stop her. I crumpled down on the bed and wept. For days I knew the beginnings of love and companionship. In a moment it was then lost.

The roaring mob broke me from my grief. A flaming bottle crashed through the street side window of the room. The bottle exploded fires over the stained carpet. I fought flames and my own panic to peer through the broken window. From there I saw the masses, angry, hungry for the blood of the witchcraft practicing Dr. Addison. They did not know that they sought Sorren, the demon. I took two bottles of the elixir and a stack of bills. I made my way from the room post haste.

I found escape down a shaky flight of stairs. They led to the rear alley side of the building. I ran to a stable where I purchased a strong riding horse. The well-bred creature brought me far from Paris to a small mariner town. I booked passage back to native England. It was then I first took a breath.

I landed in England and stayed nowhere or nobody for any length of time. I lost myself to a deeper obsession and compulsion. For two decades I never drew a sober breath. I began a reign of body thieving more abusive than any before.

My binge led me through the lives and bodies of a butcher, an adulterous preacher, a crooked constable, and a drifting lunatic. The derelict claimed apocalyptic visions of the distant future. In him I dreamed of a vivid battle between two men of godly strength. I saw a man and his machine take the world. I saw the earth burn to cinder. I could not take the dreams of the madman.

None of the bodies could survive the weight my consumption placed upon them. My mind, my consciousness, could not sustain such a binge. Each and every of my identities gave way in body or mind or both. I knew no stability. The feverish pace through all the lives sent me to my knees. I prayed to dark gods for some stationary point. I sought out some purpose for my life.

Sick and tired, I settled myself in the White Chapel district of London. I found a target easy enough. I became a tailor with a simple, lonely existence. I liked the man a great deal before I overtook him. He had crafted me the finest suit. Regretfully, I needed his space in the world. He was a fine craftsman. I catered to aristocrats and wealthy businessmen who paid me handsomely for the fine wares I created. It was then I learned of the murders.

18

Scotland Yard speculated the fiend to be some deranged barber or a medical doctor. He murdered prostitutes throughout the Whitehall district. Post mortem, he carved them in an ill, meticulous manner. He removed varying organs from them. He was aloof, insane. These things you know.

I imagine I have lost all your sympathies developed over my childhood. I am no hero. That is evident. It was selfish really, just needing something to go on for. His puzzle attracted me. I would make his mystery my purpose. I wanted to find this night creature. I sewed, measured, and hemmed by day. I prowled into the hours of the night, my senses heightened by the elixir.

I walked the neighborhood, practicing in a low-grade telepathy. Jenkins inspired this pursuit. A less than complete separation of my consciousness from myself permitted me the mildest of bonds between my mind and a stranger. This learned power was great, but unreliable. Many minds remained closed and the power peaked and faded only minutes after a strong boost of the elixir.

I scanned the minds of the night people for some hint of his identity. This endeavor proved fruitless even after several months. I found no new patterns. I was without a scintilla of evidence. I understood the monster less than when my quest began.

After he killed a woman named Mary, I concluded I would never find him in the body of the tired old tailor. I needed to cloak myself in order to draw him out. Yes, that was it. I needed to become the object of his twisted desire.

An eerie recollection overcame me. I remembered that day those many years ago when the very woman I thieved raped me. My moment in Karen was only disaster. I did not like being a woman. The quality of thought and the emotions were so alien to me. But, as with my other obsessions, the choice would be made by my behavior. This killer became my reason to be.

In preparation, I rented a separate flat, storing much of my money and other valuables accumulated as the tailor. I would need these things when I left the tailor for a new haven. I warned the landlord that my lovely niece would be moving into the second flat and would be there more than I. He rolled his eyes to me. Nevertheless, he readily accepted the money I offered.

Finding the woman was not difficult. I compiled descriptions of the other victims. I noted a number of similarities amongst them. Age varied, but each had a head of long brown hair and thin frame. I scoured the night and found her. My target was young, less than twenty, but lewd beyond chronological measurement. She spewed foul, sexually charged words as she drank greedily and openly on the cobblestone streets.

She caught a glimpse of the fist of bills waived under the gaslight. I could see the hunger in her eyes. For the money offered she would have followed me to oblivion. She was going to do just that. I brought her to the newly rented flat and offered her a drink. It was a fine scotch cut with a fresh batch of the elixir.

The whore accepted and drank directly from the bottle. I admit a certain dark fascination with her as she slugged down the precious liquid. Breaking from plan, I offered her an injection, more of the elixir, and she accepted this. I shot some myself, something I avoided for some time and watched her sprawl back in bed.

Her young breasts pointed skyward, rising up and down with her slow methodical breathing. She opened her eyes, pale blue, and twirled her hair slowly. She opened her legs and pulled her dress upward to reveal the white stockings. She was beautiful and would no doubt draw the attentions of the beast.

"Take me, love," she commanded. I breathed in deeply, mentally preparing for entry into her subtle feminine form. I penetrated her in a way she could have never imagined.

I stood from the bed recognizing the old horror in the face of my vacated tailor. Before even a shriek I stabbed her with a blade left along the bed. She fell to her knees clutching in vain to stop the blood from squirting out of her severed Adam's apple. A wispy, gasping cry was all she could muster before her head slumped forward.

This time was different. I had the time and privacy that evaded me on my first ventures into the female form. Her figure was pleasant and toned. Her memories were horrible and cruel. She was an object of sex since her beginnings and in no small way I freed her from that pain. It was now all mine.

My thoughts returned to the task of finding the one known as "The Ripper." In the mirror I found an object of his twisted desire. The bloody mess on the floor was no more. Two goons hired for gold disposed of the tailor's body most perfectly. Now I was in a position to draw him out.

I thought of arms. Surely a woman of my size needed a gun or dagger. Clarity seized me. A weapon was meant to harm. I did not want to kill or even injure him. Any plan should keep him safe. My intentions became evident to me. I wanted to become him. I wanted to know his tortured mind. I wanted to know his appetites. I wanted to know why.

That very night I set to the streets. I made eye contact with every gentleman passing. I expanded, but caught not the faintest sense of the savagery. This went on for several weeks. I used the elixir to drown out her screaming memories. For the madman's pleasure I concealed a loaded syringe in the thigh of my stocking.

Then we found each other. I sensed him. His mind was dark and tormented. I could hear the screams of tortured youth rattling inside his skull. He was traveling my path. I remained a healthy distance behind. I was kept in his predatory stare. His guts mirrored my own in an electric churning. I again expanded into his mind and saw only disconnected images of blood and mangled flesh. I felt the arousal in his pursuit.

I resolved to force his hand. I drank deeply from my bottle and turned into an empty side alley. There he went too. I feigned a stumbling drunkenness and fell to the ground, dropping the empty glass bottle for dramatic effect.

"My pretty picture!" the man yelled as he entered the alley behind me. The voice was smooth and steady.

"Are you looking for a date, love?" I asked. He was close enough now to smell his unpleasant sweat.

To him, time was of the essence. The beast threw me against the ragged, red brick wall. I shrieked in pain and terror. The man was rabid, lost in a world of bloody violence. I was intrigued by the sheer contempt he held for me. The hatred burned in his crazed eyes. I knew then that I could become him, and force him to the most ironic of spots. This was irresistible.

In my arrogance, I extrapolated that his crazed mind would be open to my assaults without benefit of the elixir. This proved untrue. His illness was not the illness of Uncle James. Faustus' advice did not apply. He remained fastened within himself. I leapt from the whore only to be crashed back in through his firm rejection. He struck me to the ground once back inside.

I waited until he brandished the weapon. It was an exaggerated scalpel with a long blood-rusted blade. As he pulled his arm back I plunged at him with the syringe. He was stunned. This allowed me to inject him with the totality of the needle. I separated and assaulted him with my essence. His crazed rage fought my entry. I forced him out and he was drawn into the vacated girl.

I shuddered in ecstasy as the maniac's mind became my own. I saw all the violence. I felt the mad hatred pour into me. I looked into her eyes and saw his fear. I carved her in his signature way. I secured the flask and the satchel of the Vella Root. I also took a part of her.

Compulsion demanded the kidney be brought home as a souvenir or to eat. What a mind I found. I wanted to throw the kidney down a storm drain or into a trash heap for a stray cat or dog to consume. His remnant willpower would not allow it.

Despite the carnage, my appearance remained mostly clean in a storefront's reflection. I closed my coat to the splash of blood on my shirt. Only my hands showed the blood. I placed them in my pockets. One rested while the other hand gripped the severed organ.

I then traveled to the lunatic's flat. It was only blocks from where he met his bloody end. I was eager to inspect the quarters of this infamous Jack the Ripper. His cognitive differences did not offer me a coherent look through his memory. I would have to see his lair for myself. I would not be disappointed.

It was a brownstone in a neighborhood of the row buildings. The home was inherited from a deceased brother. Its ground floor was richly furnished and impeccably clean. There was a remarkable lampshade adorning a reading lamp. It appeared reptilian. Fragmented memories told me different. Cured human flesh, white from age and chemistry, was stretched over the metal skeleton. He meticulously cut and treated the human flesh carved from some nameless streetwalker.

Under the lamp I saw a written letter addressed to a George Lusk of Scotland Yard. It read as follows:

From hell.

Mr Lusk,

Sor
I send you half the Kidne I took from one woman prasarved it for you tother piece I fried and ate it was very nise. I may send you the bloody knif that took it out if you only wate a whil longer
signed
Catch me when you can Mishter Lusk

Next to the letter was a carved wooden box. Inside I found a glass jar containing a pungent liquid. There was nothing in the jar. I understood the drive to keep the kidney. Whether to mock God, or continue the sensational tale, I cut the kidney in half and dropped it into the jar and sealed it in the small box. I folded the letter and affixed it to the top of the box with a noxious glue. I would post the package in the morning.

I examined the house. Nothing was outside the ordinary on the ground or upper floors. Home was in the basement. I walked down the creaky winding steps into another world.

The smell of death and decay permeated the air. Somehow the odor did not escape to the upper levels of the house. There were entire rotting bodies. Limbs and bones were strewn about. There was an altar without denomination or deity erected before a few baffling torture devices.

I fleetingly imagined a good deed. I could turn myself in to the authorities. I could lead them back to this lair. I would then leap from this body before it was hanged which it surely would be. Or maybe I would remain for the noose. Then, darker, stronger thoughts overwhelmed me.

I imagined life as this new creature. Perhaps I could stalk and wait and kill in his stead. It was only I who could act without consequence. There was no earthly authority over me. I could walk the slummy streets watching the whores. I would isolate one in some secret corner, and then tear her to shreds. My heart raced at the proposition. I left the home and returned to the streets. I merged wholly with the lunatic.

After some time I found a young girl. She was about sixteen years of age. She was brunette with rotted teeth. Her pretty young face was aged prematurely through alcohol and disease. I paid this no mind. It was an unholy bloodlust that I had to satisfy before I moved on from this lunatic murderer.

Sparing gory detail I had my way with that wretched tramp. She put up quite a fight, tearing at my eyes so. I walked from her corpse in a moment of lucidity. I had to leave the Ripper then or never.

I found some gold coins and paper currency. I changed into a fresh suit and took a carriage out of White Chapel. I traveled to a nearby inn where my late arrival was unquestioned. I fell into a deep sleep. I was at the mercy of the madman's nightmare. Death, torture, and brute mayhem flashed before me without any coherent narrative. While I retained myself I had also been poisoned by this decaying brain. My time was short.

I traveled by steamship to New York City without significant incident. I slept restlessly; tormented by the nightmares of a raging hell plagued by his world of death and rot. Only sadism and murder could calm his panics. I sliced through his demons night after night.

New York was a city of night. Bars rolled without cessation. Street prostitutes swung their wares up and down the brilliantly lit downtown. Drunken night people crowded the streets. Shouting and laughter filled the sky.

I found a hotel renting at a weekly rate. In a makeshift laboratory I yielded an imperfect batch of the elixir. I committed error and overexposed the elixir to adulterants. This mistake yielded an inedible rudimentary gum. I found it to be painstakingly smokeable. The sensation from smoking the gum was weakened, yet held promise. In my error lied another great discovery. Within days I perfected the form.

When I could not carry the drink or lacked the works to shoot my formula the gummy elixir could be puffed in the opium dens of Chinatown. I could roll it in tobacco and smoke on the streets. I could escape the shadows and socialize. I could dip into the minds of those around me.

The madman's persona overtook me once more. I left his mark on this New World. I did it just the once. My bloody crime furthered the agenda of a newly appointed police commissioner. The man set his sights on the many vices of turn of the century New York. He said, and many agreed, that the violent murder, and other like killings, demonstrated the logical conclusion of the New York nightlife. The commissioner was Theodore Roosevelt.

Roosevelt was a raging bull of right. Charismatic and powerful, he was destined to craft a right path through all the debauchery. The City was going to change at his whim.

Only circumstance could stop him and it did. The abrupt death of his wife proved more than he could bear. He receded from public life and duty. While he mourned, I found a new body in a man named Simon. I met him in an underbelly den shooting morphine and playing cards. He quite liked the elixir. I could not let the Ripper continue, so I killed Simon after the switch with several blows from a lead pipe. There was something new to chase again.

19

I chased him westward. It was no secret he stopped in the placid hills of South Dakota. I was eager to make his acquaintance. I would need his assent. A man such as he could not be tricked or overpowered. This made him ever the more appealing.

I rented a cottage near his ranch, but spent most of my time watching him from the brush. I left my view of him only to refill my elixir or brew a new batch.

My health was failing. After leaving New York I felt feverish. My temperature soared. My new left arm was infected. The counter side of my elbow was painfully swollen with an abscess at its tip. Throughout the rest of my body I felt a dull throbbing ache, a pained blood stream.

I watched him ride hard on a handsome black mare, chop wood with one mighty swing after another, and rise with the morning sun each day. He was desperately fighting off the sadness of his loss. I was willing to free him from his demons. I would not kill him. I would irrevocably trade.

Sweat spilled over my eyes in an itchy sting. I lost sight of Roosevelt. I sat back to rest. The burdensome pain inflamed. My vision dulled, doubled, and then tripled. I closed my eyes for a rest.

I awoke to grass that spiked my skin. It was an organic bed of nails. I next heard a booming, gentle voice. It surely was God himself there to cast judgment upon me. Any escape from the painful fever would do.

"I am going to place you in this cart and bring you to my cabin," Roosevelt said. "You're going to be all right young man." My eyes opened, but I could see nothing more than obscured outlines and a bright dot sun.

I awoke next to a white ceiling overhead. I was flat on my back in a bed sided with metal railings. A thin sheet covered my emaciated frame. The sheet was faint yellow and damp. The general pain throughout my body was greatly diminished. My fever broke. My left arm no longer ached at its elbow. The arm was gone.

My shoulder was wrapped snug with only a trace of blood soaked through. I weakly wiggled the nub. I heard muffled voices and squeaking shoes.

Next I heard the twisting of a metal doorknob and the opening of the door. I turned to see Roosevelt standing there at my bedside. He stood tough, stoic, and sympathetic.

"Hello young man," he said, gently shaking the metal bed handles. I tried to respond, but only an indecipherable scratchy sound came from me.

"Try not to speak. The ether has dried you up mostly inside," he said. "You, young man, have a serious problem. You are addicted to morphine and nearly killed yourself with this infection. If you do not treat your condition you will die."

He paused to offer me a compassionate look over. "I've taken it upon myself to seek a commitment for you to an asylum that specializes in these matters. This may not seem desirable to you now, but over time you will grow to appreciate it. The doctor told me that had I not found you and brought you here you would have surely died. In many cultures in this world you now owe your life to me. All I ask is that you get well of this."

Tears swelled in my stolen stranger's eyes. The tears were mine, half desperate for the drug and half lost in another's caring for me.

Roosevelt placed a firm hand on my leg, "You will ship out tomorrow."

I craved the elixir quite horribly. I lifted my head to look around. Roosevelt held out the satchel and flask. "I took the liberty of pouring that poison into the toilet. You will not be needing it from here," I went to spring completely out of the bed and realized I was strapped at the waist.

"Let me up!" I commanded. Roosevelt looked down upon me with a deep compassion and reserve. I wanted to kill him and burn the God forsaken place to the ground.

An old nurse entered the room holding a needle forward. The site of the instrument calmed me. She jabbed the needle into my right thigh, instantly transporting me into indifferent darkness.

I awoke to a hot summer sun beating down on my face and a gentle warm breeze. My eyes opened slightly, enough for me to see I was laid back on a gurney, traveling through large, glass double doors. Another needle was plunged into me by a faceless practitioner and I drifted again to nowhere.

I awoke strapped to a metal table by leather bounds. I was cold. Water dripped somewhere behind me, but I could not see. There was only the solitary dim light hanging directly over me.

Terror overwhelmed me. I fidgeted and fussed, but could make no progress forward in undoing the leather bindings. I closed my eyes in desperation and fell into sleep.

Hours later I heard the rubber soles of shoes hammering across a laminated tile floor. A pleasant looking young man, maybe thirty years old or so, stood before me with a clipboard.

"Hello there. My name is Dr. Silkworth and I am going to be treating you," he said politely. "You are in Baltimore. This is the Jefferson Asylum. You are very fortunate indeed. This is a special wing of the hospital where we treat people who cannot refrain from drinking alcohol or habitually using drugs."

"Let me out," I said in my kindest way, "please."

He smiled and gently placed his backhand over my brow. He asked me to hold my remaining hand outward. A tremor revealed the rage of deprivation that burned within me. I would have sold my soul for just a taste of my elixir or morphine if I had not already spent it outright.

This newest benevolent captor meant well, as had Roosevelt, but the withdrawal pains were unbearable. I became lost in tattered memories of people, places, and things. I thought of Rosetta, Cruikshank, Faustus, Karen, the Ripper, and I could control nothing. My primal desire was for the elixir.

20

Days went by with a series of attendants beside me. The straps were only removed when I was rendered unconscious from heavy doses of tranquilizers. It was then they would change my soiled linens and wash me.

Over the next months I remained crazed, verbally combative, and violent. I injured many and scared more in these frenzies. I was a sick and wild animal of the most belligerent degree. To control me more straps and drugs were used. Some attendants made physical revenges on me while I was subdued.

In time I calmed. I graduated from caged isolation to the social rehabilitation unit. I was placed with ten other relatively sane patients. We were fed well and enjoyed many other comforts. Dr. Silkworth was happy to share with anyone who would listen that a wealthy businessman, sympathetic to the woes of alcoholic insanity, made a sizeable endowment to the asylum for the treatment of hopeless alcoholics and addicts.

I remained there in the facility for years. I was under the influence of a number of hard hypnotics and other tranquilizers. The drugs caused me to shuffle about and slurred my speech. I tried a few feeble escape attempts and acts of violence which only led to more shots and straps. The kindly Dr. Silkworth gave me chance after chance, believing my behavior to be a symptom of my greater condition. He thought the behavior was a product of my ailing brain.

I grew to love and respect Dr. Silkworth. Genuine concern bled from him. His hope and optimism crashed through the dank filter of the place. Each of his patients were only human in his eyes. His hope became my hope. His love for me became my love for myself.

Then my pathetic world came crashing down. The other patients and

I were brought to a conference room typically used for group therapy.

"Thank you for coming. There are some changes coming, unfortunate changes, but you must be strong. The hospital has informed me this unit will be closed. Patients who remain here in this hospital will be sent to the general psychiatric unit. This will be decided on a case by case basis," Dr. Silkworth said.

The patients rumbled. Many shed tears. More were angry.

"In consideration of this I have resigned and accepted a position at another facility. This is my last day with you."

True to his word he was gone the following day. His interim replacement had already arrived. The man was Dr. Stanley Horn and he would facilitate winding down the unit and determining which patients would remain.

A week later I was brought to Dr. Silkworth's office. His nameplate was removed from the door and a very different man waited for me inside. Two burly attendants stood strong to protect him.

He was short and squat. Thick glasses concealed most of his fatted face. His hair was black and oily. His chubby hands held a thick file folder.

"Sit," he said without a glance. He waited for me to sit in the seat across from him, "Simon Martotte. Is this your name today?" he asked.

"Yes, sir."

"Dr. Horn."

"Yes, Dr. Horn."

"It says here when you were admitted you claimed your name was Nathan Sorren. You claimed this was not your body, that you had tricked it from the real Simon Martotte."

I had no such memory of this confession.

"Morphine addict, violence, psychotic breaks, hallucinations, and delusions. Years with little improvement. Is this your body now?"

"Yes, sir. Yes, Dr. Horn."

"This is straightforward. And let me just say this. I am very different from Dr. Silkworth. His methodologies and views are, well just plain silly. Sensible people know there is no talking treatment for the addicted. It is weakness, moral and intellectual weakness. There is, though, a cure. It lies in confinement, medications, and electricity, electro-convulsive therapies. There are surgeries, too, that can be done."

I shifted in my chair.

"You have no reason to worry. I am transferring you to psychiatric. I cannot let somebody in your state leave here to do Lord knows what to the people out there. No, you will stay, but I will spare you the volts and knife if you walk straight and follow my rules. If there is any violence, or a threat of violence, I will give you the volts. Do you understand?"

I nodded. With that he waved me on to the waiting attendants in the hall. My things, mostly second hand clothing, were packed in boxes for me to carry to the unit of my transfer.

After all the years I still had monstrous cravings for the elixir. I tried to control my behavior. Sometimes I would comply with the mandates and injunctions, but then the fury would arise. Typically, I was not violent. This outer realm of self-control kept me from Dr. Horn's treatments.

One morning agitation devoured me. I watched another patient, a wet brain who had been with me on the other unit, drop to his knees. He slapped at imaginary bugs with his outstretched palms. He continued to do so over several hours. I attempted to convince the man that there were no bugs to be squashed, but to no avail. He drove me mad.

I begged Melvin to swab the floor with his mop to show the man that nothing infested the floor. The patient Melvin was given great freedoms and even held a paying job acting as custodian and gardener. He was not much for conversation, but did a wondrous job with the azaleas. He usually just mopped away at the floor mumbling unintelligibly to himself.

Melvin swiped his mop over the area, but the man would not cease. Crimson rage overtook me. I ran over to the wet brain and kicked him wholly in the ribs and then again in his abdomen. He fell face down on the floor coughing. As the attendants subdued me the wet brain smashed his palms on the floor. The attendants struck me about the back and head with fists and nightsticks until another needle was sunk into me.

Some time later I awoke held by the familiar straps of the cold metal table. This time I was not alone. Over me stood Dr. Horn scowling. "I have reached my end with you," he said. "It's time we try something new."

They pulled me into a small room. It was a dingy gray place, bright with white lights. Two held me down while another placed electrodes on my head and chest. A bit was placed in my mouth to prevent me from biting off my own tongue.

"You'll need this," the attendant said.

The current shot through me contracting every muscle. My back arched to breaking proportions. I clenched my jaw and made inhuman screams through the mouthpiece. Then came a familiar sensation. I felt the beginnings of the separation of my essence. As soon as the division occurred it ended. The jolts were not enough to set me free.

I recuperated from the fiery therapy with a compliant smile. I was carried away from that room with a new secret. There were no argumentative outbursts, no assaults of the staff or patients, and I attended all required functions. I earned their approval, especially from Dr. Horn.

After months of compliance came the reward of permissions to tour the hospital. I was allowed to travel throughout most of the facility. Once closed off doors and halls opened to me. I had hours and places to myself.

My first indulgence was the hospital library. As fortune would have it there was a small section devoted to the trades. I found a handbook for electricians. Electricity was somewhat of a mystery to me, but I quickly learned the basics of the discipline. I was competent enough to apply its science.

Armed with knowledge and makeshift tools, I watched. Each day Melvin made his rounds through our ward and then Dr. Horn's office. His last stop was the room where I was given the volts. I caught the door when he entered and covered the latch with a wadded paper. This would prevent the lock from engaging.

A short time after he left I entered the room. I removed four screws with a small slat of flat metal broken from the arm of a large door hinge. I located the voltage regulator and removed it from the machine. If my understanding was correct this would ensure unadulterated, raw electric power.

I returned to the day room and sat. In my hand I clenched the slat of metal. I waited for Dr. Horn to make his rounds. His pudgy frame passed the door. I confirmed Melvin was in the area and jumped to my feet. I rushed with the slat.

"Horn!" I shouted, slashing at him with the metal piece. One swipe cut into the white shirt covering his fleshy belly. Blood seeped into the material. His eyes widened behind the lenses.

The attendants and nurses piled down on me. Horn shouted commands and the blade was pulled from my hand. A nurse approached with an extended syringe.

"No," shouted Dr. Horn. The nurse stopped and turned away. "Bring him to E-T!"

They placed me in a restraint jacket. My arm was tucked within it. My legs were cuffed with chains. They dragged me forward across the floor. They brought me where I wanted to be.

"This will not hurt much Simon," he said holding a towel to his abdomen. I was too happy to say a thing to him. He turned the dial completely to its right. The first pain was immense. This was the severing of my tongue by my involuntarily clenching teeth. Then the smell of burning flesh filled the air. I was burning from within. Then the miracle.

I tore free from the prison flesh of Simon. It had been over a decade, trapped in both place and body. The cold wind from nowhere raged. I drifted up and out over the bewildered Horn and staff standing over the electrocuted one-armed body. I was a phantom roaming the halls of the institution. I drifted toward my last sighting of Melvin to the faint music of screaming madmen.

Then I saw him. Melvin was swinging the mop back and forth over the hard tiled floor of the dayroom. An elderly woman lashing her tongue about in a state of tortured dementia sat on a bench staring off into nothingness. Her eyes widened.

"Demon!" she hissed, pointing a long twisted finger at me.

I felt the creeping darkness overtaking the world and hurried my assault at Melvin.

As with Uncle James, I found it easy to expel Melvin from himself. The surge of his distorted thought and memories overcame me. I shuddered in ecstasy, absorbing his madness all in one flash.

In mockery, I mopped the floor in the same doped way Melvin performed the task. Melvin's mind was nothing short of a complete disconnect. It was difficult to enjoy the spoils of my brave experiment.

With an approving nod of a security guard I walked out the front door of the hospital. Though muted by medication, effort was still expended ignoring the barking rocks and carnivorous flowers along the path from the hospital. As I reached the public street I set down the trolley of gardener's tools. On a second thought, I pulled the spade and placed it in the band of my waist.

21

I traveled south to Virginia on the resource of an elderly couple. They erred in offering me their charity. With money and the auto I learned to drive after some folly I made way to the old plantation. My prayer that the root still flourished was answered.

After collecting much of the root, I boarded at a comfortable hotel suite. I brewed a batch of the drinkable liquid. I ignored the silverware barking commands at me. I ignored the patches in the lush carpeting that sought to swallow me whole. I drowned everything out with my elixir.

I wanted leave of Melvin and America. I considered only a return to Europe and decided upon Germany, the place of my second birth. Within days I was on a steel ship crossing the Atlantic.

With my senses heightened by the elixir, I found an English physician reminiscent of Addison. The man was relatively young, wealthy, and single. I met him at a mahogany carved bar where we spent most of the journey. It was nothing to fill him with the elixir as we talked of matters of medicine and the Great War. I was able to ignore the liquor bottles calling to me as we spoke.

We went for a late night smoke on the upper deck. The both of us were high on scotch and the elixir. I decided this was his end and took him there. Dazed, I easily pushed Melvin over the bow.

Questions arose on the ship where the odd, but pleasant black man went. Investigators made way to me and I told them my new friend proved quite depressed. I mentioned a failing grain concern and creditor demands. A bartender verified this false tale I offered during one of our drunks. It was suggested the poor sap was depressed and leapt from the ship. This became an official conclusion.

When I arrived I was awestruck. Germany was in ruins, both

mentally and physically. I had been shielded from it, but the Great War had raged throughout those lands laying a path of death and destruction. Peasants and the wealthy alike carried handfuls of metal coins to purchase small loafs of bread and powdered milk. The place was aimless and depressed. It was a perfect place for me.

I traveled to Heidelberg. The city sprawled, but I sought its oldest parts. A shadow of Faustus' home stood grand along the riverbanks where I witnessed his transfiguration. Time and rot were yet to lay the structure to total waste. The doors and windows were boarded in part, as if closing off the house had been interrupted halfway through.

I climbed through the aged broken glass of a shattered pane. Much of the furnishings remained, caked with ancient dust and mold. Brown seeping water stained those parts of the ceiling yet to fall. I took in the sight of decay and made my way to the basement. I saw the char of a raging fire that consumed the laboratory. No documents or other recordings were to be found. All the bottles were broken as were the instruments and glassware. I saw the vat, now little more than brittle rust, where I destroyed the boy I had been.

I traveled into that humble side room where Faustus and I sealed our fates. There on the stone floor, unchanged by time, was the very earth upon which those devilish footprints first appeared to me. No insights were to be yielded from this return trip to the place of my second origin. That White Devil did not appear to me, nor did the ghost of Faustus.

I remained in Germany, settling in the city of Berlin. Months became years, and I worked along as the Doctor, remaining recklessly inebriated by the elixir.

I found employment quite simply with his credentials. I took on fellowships at Universities and from there was offered work at small medical offices and the larger hospitals throughout the city. I lectured and treated the sick and injured for many maladies, innocent and grave. I ate fine foods and drank rich wines, always doctored with the precious elixir, and otherwise lived a luxurious functionality.

I did not return to the syringe during these years. The phantom aches of the arm long lost never did subside. I stood to be some ungodly combination of all those I devoured. It was a hell within my skin.

The German needed faith. The once proud, accomplished nation became bankrupt in spirit and resource. Small meetings held by a disgruntled political party began to grow. They were the Nation Socialist Party. They had a visionary leader in a standout boy from Vienna.

I attended rallies. Some were mundane, focused on matters of economic restoration and national pride. Other meetings moved to the paranormal where there was talk of a race of supermen, the would-be rulers of Germany and eventually all of the earth. These men, if purified gene lines could be laid, would possess great powers of the body and mind.

Hitler ascended to Chancellor and then Führer. I watched the burning of books and the enacting of their laws of hate and blame against their own Jewish people. Countless defectives were laid to waste in these years. The hatred I held for my original self was now the hatred of a whole people.

Germany's live-in outsiders left in great number. I was amongst them returning to England. I joined a practice of physicians there and left them for my own venture. I still marveled the Germans from afar. Then one came to me.

22

I awoke to a fugue. Keeping track was mind numbing. Life bled into life. Time was a meaningless lark. *Who was I?*

A uniform hung beside the bed. The gray-blue tunic was pressed so neatly, its accompanying schirmmutze cap sat on the nightstand. It was all coming back to me.

Officer Heinz entered my medical practice upon the referral of friends. He sought the treatment of my fabled remedy. This was my reintroduction of Cruikshank's elixir, not the Vella Root. Heinz was polished, scrubbed, and scraped clean of hair. His eyes were cold blue and his hair thinning blond.

I asked him to sit atop the mahogany examination table. The Nazi moved with the finest precision. Confidence and purpose ran deep within him.

I loosened my essence. It spread from my body and into his mind. The ethereal bonded the corporeal. I could taste his memories, his identity.

The man was no mere soldier. Heinz headed a special organization of Nazi academics bent on finding some relic or creature lost for the ages. I knew just what they were looking for.

From his mind's eye I saw the sketch. Its faux human face peered outward from the frayed page. It was that demon beast introduced to me by my Rosetta. The thing I chased across the globe with Hudson. The creature and I traveled through history.

Heinz's mystery was appealing. Here it would be so easy. He sought my magic potion and from there it would be easy for me to do the switch.

"Everything okay Doctor?" he asked through an obtuse German accent.

"Ja," I answered.

He drank heartily from the glass I prepared for him. Tinkering and added extracts lessened the offense of my elixir's odor and flavor. I conquered the rotted bitterness, giving it a sweet sugary smooth drink. He told me he would like a crate to bring home to his compatriots. I could only laugh.

"Crate upon crate you will bring with you," I said.

He sat back in his chair smoking. I drank from a cup of my own potion. We exchanged pleasantries and smoked German cigarettes from a silver case imprinted with the Swastika. The cigarette case would be mine. I only had to concentrate.

"I thank you for the remedy my good doctor. I must be meeting a plane in only a few hours from now," he said.

I focused first on separating from myself. The gross discomfort was essential. I felt that cold, falling terror as my essence broke from my physical being. I floated in the nowhere place. I then did an astral charge into the Nazi officer, unloading him easily. Like clockwork his lost essence traveled into the vacant physician.

The full taste of his mind became my reality. I saw his angry father beat his mother and brothers. I felt the terror of hiding from his father's whip underneath his bed. I knew the safety the camp for boys provided. I knew the sanctity in which he held the National Socialist Party and his position within its framework.

Always in my favor was the element of surprise. His body was in even better shape than what I had traded him for. His eyes held in wide open terror. I felt the flow of his life into my consciousness. I watched his mother help servants cook for his large family, his schooling at a German academy, his indoctrination, and all he read about that demon creature.

I pulled the Luger from my new hip and fired a square round into the forehead of the doctor. I fumbled in my pockets for that engraved cigarette case and lit another of the German cigarettes. They were remarkably delicious.

In the pocket I discovered a memo outlining the itinerary his of return trip to Germany. I recollected it all completely. I would follow his lead. The journey would afford me time to familiarize myself with the other memories and role of this Heinz. I left the office and never looked back.

When I arrived in Deutschland I was greeted by a stream of Nazi occultists and fanatics. The demon enthusiasts informed me that the creature of legend was found. It was then being smuggled out of the United States. I was informed by the most senior of the entourage that the itinerary changed. I was to meet directly with the Führer himself.

Adolph Hitler knew the complete gravity of an alliance with the creature. He knew the heart of the ceremony and dismissed it as a necessity to achieve the great powers to come. I looked forward to my reunion with it. I hoped for solace within the glory of the monster.

I was taken by motor car to an unassuming office complex in central Berlin. A masculine female secretary brought me to a small waiting area. I declined coffee. She turned her husky shoulders and left me waiting outside a white wooden door.

After a brief wait I was ushered in to meet him. There he stood before me, the modern monster, Adolph Hitler. This new body of mine was larger yet he possessed another quality entirely. He dominated the environment. He was clean and orderly.

"Greetings my good man," he said in hard German.

I nodded in deference. I sat in the single wooden chair before his modest desk. Behind him hung an aerial map of the German landscape with proposed annexations. No other decorative measures had been taken in the room. I gazed at him.

A familiar feeling overtook. I was spinning, no, falling from some dreadful height. I thought back to my meeting with the White Devil. Pure evil pervaded that room and this one. Fantasies of possessing his life did not even pass in thought. He would be unattainable.

"After a good much of searching our brothers have found the beast!" he exclaimed in maniacal excitement. "I am most pleased with the work of your group."

He was desperate for some advantage in the war he intended to wage throughout the world. It was his belief that the demon creature would give rise to a race of supermen.

"You will go now. Tomorrow a car will meet you at your hotel and return you to the airstrip. You will arrive at the designated destination within this day. From there, you will be taken to the site of the beast."

He ordered me to do all necessary to realize our vision for the creature. I promised him that I would do just that. He then continued, "Deutschland Forever!"

I raised my right hand and opened the palm to him. "Heil Hitler!" I boomed. He reciprocated the gesture before I pivoted and walked from the room.

This is where I awoke, wondering for a moment who I was. I needed to dress and ready for the driver would be there within the hour. Later in the morning I was aboard a plane again heading for the South Pacific.

The island was a nameless lot off the coast of the Philippine mainland. Though nobody knew, it was there the Japanese siege began. The island was uninhabited. It provided their German allies a secret and far isolated location.

The small airplane skidded to a halt before a small congregation of uniformed soldiers. Three large Jeeps covered in camouflage waited for my escorts and I.

23

These are the things his mother told him. As my Nazi caravan made its way to the hilly campsite a father was excluded from the bloody delivery of his son. He paced back and forth amongst the other nervous fathers. His wife's delivery was through a cesarean section three months premature.

Private First Class Thomas Dorean received word of his wife Natalie's auto accident. She crashed several miles from the fledgling Mojave army base where they lived. The day was rainy and the road slick. Considerable blood loss brought her to the nearest hospital rather than a risky return to the base and her treating physician.

His commanding officer allowed him a brief leave before his deployment to Spain. Adept abilities in the primitive electronics of the time anchored him stateside at the burgeoning base before the war, but the same skill now required his immediate presence at a budding Spanish outpost.

He continued back and forth, smoking and waiting for some word of his wife and their child's condition. First there had been the good news.

The child was removed successfully and was well enough developed for survival. In a short time Private Dorean would be permitted to observe his child in the incubator where he would remain for several weeks. Then there was the bad news.

Natalie's legs were crushed in the force of the accident. There was no avoidance of amputation. Private Dorean so loved his wife he heard only that she and their child lived, thinking not first of the psychological trauma inflicted upon his wife in the same crash.

They allowed Private Dorean access into the post-operating room where his wife lied unconscious. This she told the little Taxman. Each of her remnant legs were wrapped in thick bandaging darkened by red blood. He went to his wife and held her limp hand for all the hours of that day and the next.

He dismissed the calls from his superiors. He ignored a personal pleading for his return to the base. Private Dorean paced between his wife who awakened to the horror of her disfigurement and his tiny, blue son dependent upon the pumping and grinding machines.

When the military police arrived, Dorean had been awake for over two day's time. They stalled his arrest buying coffee in the hospital cafeteria. Tired and torn from within, he resisted as one of the officers pulled at his arm, causing the man to fall and dislocate his back. The other soldier knocked Dorean to the ground with a nightstick and took him into custody.

The birth announcement for Paul David Dorean would tell the world that the premature child weighed three and one half pounds and that lifesaving measures were employed. There was no mention of his father's arrest or the disfigurement of his mother.

Weeks later, Natalie and her child, Paul David Dorean, left the hospital and visited the stockade on the base. She cradled the premature baby on her lap as she sat in her wheeled chair. There she saw the spark in her husband's eye. It spoke to the love they shared. It was stronger than the worldly barriers placed between them.

The good Private told her the military court would be lenient under the circumstances. He would serve no more than sixty days of menial labors. Each accepted and looked forward to the day when their family could be together.

The day never came. Three days after the visit, a raging inmate attacked a guard in the rock yard. Private Dorean intervened. The man snuffed out Private Dorean with a large rock. He died a prisoner hero in custody under the California sun. A posthumous pardon cleared the dead father, but the baby Taxman and his mother would remain alone.

24

The jeeps withstood the treacheries of the journey. The diesel beasts arrived to the occultist stronghold. The largest tent stood dominant in the center of the camp.

Humming generators powered the illumination of the interior of the canvas-covered frame. The room was mostly empty, but for two time worn statues of lizard like creatures defiling smiling women. These were some of the same sculptures that filled the condemned church of my childhood. While the elements ran their course on the more detailed features, I could still clearly recognize them to be the same.

"Should the men bring in the box for your viewing?" asked an attractive young woman. She was strangely out of place in her Nazi officer uniform. She showed no signs she and Heinz copulated much of the preceding year. He was clear about that from the origin of the relationship.

"Please do so, Eva. Do it now." I asked her in a perfect German tongue. I remained cold and distant as he always was in his dealings with her.

Eva left and returned with two soldiers wearing soiled civilian clothes. Neither of the men exhibited any emotion. One of the men, Dolphie I recognized him to be, found the creature in its buried Catskill mountain prison.

On a dolly was the nearly plain wooden box the Nazis invested millions to find. The outside of the box could only be distinguished by the dialects branded upon it. There were no cracks or holes through which to view the beast. The first was hieroglyphics. The second was a chain of unrecognizable forms. The last in Latin, the language of science, was clear:

Ne aperi arcam, "Do Not Open This Box."

The simplest of instructions would be defied in that night. Much research had been done, much intelligence gathered. I offered none of my old knowledge of the creature. The warning should have been heeded.

The moon chased the sun from the sky. We were ready. Ten of us milled about inside the tent. Numerous others stood watch outside. It had been Eva and I, and three in civilian clothing. The others wore impeccable uniforms. The three men took their position over the crate with crow bars, hammers, and a saw.

"Bring them in!" Eva commanded. Heinz's ego scarred within me. It was I, the commanding officer, that should properly begin the ceremony. But in her excitement, her bloodlust, she called for commencement. My foreknowledge of what would happen to her, only some of which she knew, provided a basis for immediate forgiveness.

Eva stepped forward and tore the clothes from her body. She went down to her hands and knees. Two of the uniformed soldiers removed their clothing and violated Eva. I felt neither arousal nor jealousy over the matter. The spectacle brought back the old hurts of my Rosetta. Heinz prepared for the liaison from the day he met young Eva serving potatoes in some insignificant mess hall before the war.

The civilians pulled the lengthy spikes fastening the cover to the remainder of the crate. Much heaving and effort resulted in the removal of the first spike. I heard the thousand little agonies. Steadfast the men continued.

There was no sound or movement from within the box. If in fact the thing within the box still lived, it showed no sign. Every eye in the room aimed at the box as the second and third spikes were pulled from the dry crate.

Over the screaming metal and wood I heard a lovely voice. She sang softly, maintaining a firm tone. The tune escapes me though the half faces of the excited children never will.

They followed behind the portly woman with the honey voice. Each held the hand of the child both in front and behind them creating a chain of blindfolded Philippine children. None of the seven young ones were any older than ten years. The songstress led them as they giggled and laughed within steps of the crate.

"Now keep your eyes covered," she said interrupting her singing for the gentle command.

The last of the spikes was removed to the tune of the songstress. Two of the men gently lifted the top from the wooden crate and laid it on the dirt floor. Each of the men walked backward in opposite directions. We waited.

For seconds the adults save one remained silent. The blindfolded children still laughed as the fat woman sang to them. It was then two sets of fingers appeared and gripped the open edge of the box. The fat woman suspended her singing when she saw it, but resumed. Tension appeared in the fingers as the thing pulled itself from the crate.

There it was. Any doubt that the thing was not the demon monster of my youth vanished. Before me rose the creature with a human like face. That thing older than I gingerly climbed from the box scanning each of us.

Eva was the first to act. She stood naked and walked toward the singing woman. She grabbed the last child in the line and pulled him away from the bunch. She tore the blindfold off the child. The boy's eyes grew wide in terror and then wet with tears at the sight of the creature. He attempted to cling to Eva, but she shoved the child with great force toward the beast.

As the offering neared the monster became invigorated. It clamped its small jagged mouth onto the child's thin chest. Blood seeped onto the floor as the beast devoured the flesh. He moved about the body eating here and there. When it finished only a pile of gnawed bones remained.

Not all reactions were uniform. The gore first sickened some of the men, yet like good soldiers they turned it around. Others silently cheered it on. The portly woman sang through her smile to the oblivious children remaining.

Eva motioned to another soldier, pointing at first to the children and then to the beast. The message could not have been clearer. Without hesitation, the young soldier grabbed another child, removed its blindfold and threw the baby to the beast.

Ancient and weak when it came from the box, the creature looked more powerful by the moment. Defined muscle mass was growing within the creature. Its skin took on an elastic resilience and metallic sheen.

Eva and the duo continued defiling one another as the beast devoured the third and fourth child. I looked around the room. There was no agony or fright, only adoration for the abomination. Then the event took on a new dementia.

With force the creature approached the two naked men, one completely lost to the sex act. He was the first shunned away. The creature stood upright and lunged at him with a bold strike. The man went back several feet and landed in the dirt. He was not unconscious, but was too scared to move. The second naked man never removed his eyes from the creature and stepped away from Eva when it approached.

We watched as the creature mounted Eva. She was not scared. She welcomed the creature. The thing grew stronger with each thrust. Its sharp fingers pierced the flesh of Eva's shoulders. Blood dripped from the wounds, collecting in small sticky pools below her. The thing shuttered and then slinked off of her.

Eva remained face down on the ground for maybe a moment and then stood. Her eyes met mine and I saw the horror within her. She lost herself completely in the foregoing and now knew all. Tears fell as she ran from the tent naked clutching her womb. I felt no desire to aid her. In fact, a smile of sick satisfaction filled my face.

The creature returned to devouring the little defenseless ones.

The myth of the creature Heinz had known. Its legend told of great abilities that would be bestowed upon those present as the thing feasted on innocents and held intercourse with a human woman. I did not know whether this was formula or ritual. Heinz knew nothing of the science behind the claim. He knew only the legend. He read of men becoming impervious to pain and body damage. He heard of men running faster than deer and leaping over great canyons.

The island served as a testing ground. If the myth proved to be reality, then such ceremonies would take place on a grand scale. They would be an army of supermen. Hitler's fantastical beliefs would materialize to all as they conquered the world.

The creature suddenly paused in the carcass of the smallest child, a girl. It dropped her body to the floor and shifted its eyes around the room, from person to person, each one of us frozen in fright. A target was found.

Its eyes locked onto me. It slowly began to walk toward me, stopping less than one foot away. I saw the faint spark of human recognition within it.

"Boy!" the beast beckoned. It recognized me after all the years, all the bodies. It could see my essence.

I backed away from it in the horror of my exposure. As I did, I began to hear the retching. I felt a phantom pain where my hand had been marked by the demon.

"Be gone!" the creature screamed.

The first was the fat woman. She stopped singing for a hacking fit. She coughed deeply and vomited. A frothy green ran from her gaping mouth. Next one of the men coughed and vomited. Others followed. I felt a twisting in my belly as I turned and ran from the tent. I ran and ran, finding myself miles from the airstrip. I did not stop until I saw the small plane disappear into the pale blue sky. *Eva* I thought.

I did not vomit. I felt ill enough to crawl to the ground. I slept all the remainder of that day and well into the next. I awoke to chirping island birds. My head throbbed painfully and my vision clouded. I cautiously made my way back to the campsite. All were vanished.

The first bodies I should have found were those of the sentries. Nothing remained. The same was true inside of the tent. The smell was putrid, but the canvas dwelling was empty less the open crate. The thing was lost to both time and me again.

I went to another tent. I found communication equipment in order. I radioed out for aid. An investigatory team would be dispatched and I would be rescued. I gathered a collection of the root and bottles of elixir.

I was returned to despondent superiors. I stayed in rooms, a hostage to bureaucratic inquiry and disappointment. Piecemeal attempts to understand what happened on the island yielded no result. I was neither reassigned nor placed to any use. I stayed in a bureaucratic purgatory with sedatives, my elixir, and monstrous nightmares to comfort me.

I took the body and life of another officer who served as my overseer. The man, like I, remained in a nexus of nothingness. His sole role was to care for me. When I exchanged my doped-out shell with his, I fashioned a noose out of bed sheets and staged a suicide.

As my project seemingly failed, so had that of my majors. Adept armies of the allied forces wielded crushing defeats throughout Europe. I learned of the brilliant weapon that set Japanese cities to cinder. In one fiery flash incalculable numbers were dead. Then they did it again.

The Nazi party collapsed around me. Suicide, murder, and flight were everywhere. It was time for my exodus from old Germany. The war was over and things would change. I was no longer an officer. I was a war criminal, a rogue to human decency. There was no reason to remain.

I found escape through expertly forged identifications and traveling visas. I made my way to South America, landing in Brazil. While some like Mengele sought to fortify the remnants of the Reich, I was content to recede into worldly obscurity. Occasionally I would hear tales of a cruel scientist, like all those before him, but I never ventured to my former comrade.

Aside from the false papers, I made little effort in concealing my identity. I wore no disguise and went freely about my way. I ate and drank in public squares. It was there I saw my first motion picture, *Dracula*, and remain forever captivated. I followed with *It's Wonderful Life*. Sometimes the films were dubbed into Spanish and other times remaining in English. These wonderful films were my most cherished products of your budding America.

My conspicuousness led to an approach from an Argentinian businessman. The wealthy man searched the globe for the counsel of an insider to Hitler's occult tribunal. Methodical inquiries and blood money brought him to my door. All of the party's secrets had been available for purchase. For a fee, he too heard the age-old tales of that powerful demon-beast and believed he could buy it from the dying party.

"Cost is of no consideration," he said. I laughed inside. This man could never know what an encounter with me, let alone that beast, would cost.

I would provide him with a map leading to the haven of the beast. My service required the payment of one hundred thousand dollars in U.S. currency and first class travel tickets to the United States. I watched the place change from afar through film and flickering television. I was eager to partake in the spoils of their war victory and broadening culture.

I prepared my hotel room. I set forth a pitcher of water and bottles of compatriot smuggled German beer. A flask of the elixir was made handy to pour into any beverage selected. The curtains and glass doors to the balcony were opened wide.

When he arrived he brought a leather bag filled with the money. He also brought a local girl with whom his arms were locked. I insisted he dismiss her and he did so at once. She turned at the door with a pout mouth and sneer of contempt for me.

I curled the parchment in my hand. The sketch on its inside was broadly stroked and fanciful, meaningless lines and markers denoting nothing. He painstakingly counted each of the bills at my request. I reasoned that this would increase the likelihood he would accept my offer for a drink.

"Aqua?" I asked him.

"Si, senor. That would be most excellent," he affirmed as he counted the money. I filled his glass and watched him drink it down. I lunged into him right then, exchanging my Nazi shell for his suave filled three-piece tan suit.

The next day's *Diario de Pernambuco* headline read: NAZI COWARD THROWS HIMSELF FROM SUITE.

I folded the paper as my flight was called over the intercom. I found my comfortable seat in the first class section of the airship and ordered a fruity alcoholic drink. Into it I injected my elixir and sipped away.

I danced through his memories finding him to be of the drabbest sort. There was no passion or imagination within the confines of his mind. I quickly tired of his nagging greed. I would not remain for reasons of taste.

25

Paul Dorean was hungry. He knew how to make a peanut butter and jelly sandwich. His mother slept in her room for several days at a spell. She was doing it again. Sometimes he had to be independent.

She was not dead yet. He knew what dead was. His father went to heaven after he was born. Besides, he heard her call out in her sleep a number of times. She was just sick.

He loved his mother very much and she loved him. He did not even mind she was in a wheelchair. He withstood the incessant torments of the neighborhood children. Occasionally he found himself in fist fights over the subject. She told him that "if they don't like it that is on them." He understood what she meant and agreed with her.

He was worried for his mother, but was afraid to mention it at school. He heard a story about a boy whose mother and father got sick and the boy was sent to an aunt in another city. Paul liked Chicago and living with his mother. He would just keep trying to feed her a peanut butter sandwich and water until she woke up.

She never did. Paul stood at the head of her bed holding a plate and glass. Something happened he cannot still reconcile with reality. He sensed a change from living to death. He placed a hand on her leg and knew she was gone. Like I, he knew of the essence.

After another day of self-sufficiency Paul went to school crying his mother was dead. He said her spirit left. The teacher wanted more information. He elaborated she would not move and her room smelled like the boy's room at the school. It had been days since he last heard a feverish cry.

The police visited the home and found Paul's mother dead. A stroke brought on by diabetes ended her. Diabetes was one of the many illnesses that entered his mother in the eight years after the accident that took her legs. She was no longer for this world. Paul was removed from the home and placed in an orphanage.

Paul found he did not have any distant aunts in any other city. He found he did not have any known relatives at all. He was adjudicated a ward of the state and placed in foster care, taken in by an accountant and her husband who lived in suburban Chicago. He changed schools, but received new clothes, a number of new toys, and a brand new bicycle.

He never forgot his mother and he did not think the Thompsons intended for him to do so. They talked with him about his mother frequently. He told them the stories his mother passed on to him. He spoke of his father's arrest by the army and transformation into a hero inside the stockade. The Thompsons rubbed his head and told him they would love him as much as his parents loved him.

Soon the sadness of losing his mother faded away to a tolerable hurt. Paul excelled in school, advancing a grade in half a year's time. The Thompsons bought a bigger house and adopted Paul. He learned what infertility was overhearing Mr. and Mrs. Thompson before the adoption. He shed tears for Mrs. Thompson's unhappiness. He found contentment in making the loving couple happy by being there with them.

His second mother cried proud tears as he delivered the commencement address to his graduating class. He was the valedictorian. It seemed that the hardest days of his life passed and he was now blessed with all the possibilities the future held for him.

The Thompson accounting firm grew considerably over the passing years, leaving Paul with the benefit of selecting any of the schools to which he was accepted. Working in his adopted mother's firm exposed him to all the matters of finance. To her pleasure, he elected to pursue a degree in accounting at Harvard.

In only three years he graduated from the prestigious Ivy League School. While he returned to Chicago his first two summers to resume employment at the Thompson firm, he spent the summer after his graduation at the school purportedly to remain and study for the Certified Public Accountant Exam. This had only been partly true.

In his senior year he dated Rose. She was a sophomore at the school. The two met at a function of the student government where Paul served as the Treasurer. She came from a family of wealth and privilege. She selected Harvard as it was thousands of miles from the controlling grip of her father and mother. Since her birth they attempted to make each and every of her decisions in the same manner they ran the small chain of hotels they owned in southern California.

Rose secretly changed her major from business to the study of literature. She enjoyed the courses of philosophy and poetry and not the rigid rules of economics and finance. Until meeting Paul she dated only a few times, gravitating towards the young men of the arts. She acknowledged the irony that she found such joy in Paul, a man with no interest in the esoteric.

Paul decided he was going to continue his education. Before the relationship between the two deepened, he applied for admittance to Berkley's Law School and Harvard. He favored Berkley, but his commitment to Rose left him one choice, or so he thought.

During the summer, the two lived together in an upscale Boston apartment. With considerable monies at their disposal, they indulged in the culture of the city. Mundane employment could wait. Paul only left her side to study for his examination.

Wealth is no immunity to tragedy. The lesson came to Rose in the night. Her father purchased a small hobby plane a year prior and its remains washed ashore on a sandy bank of the Pacific Ocean. His body was never found.

Rose abruptly left. The next day she asked Paul to follow. His love for her was total. They set out from Boston the following day and never returned.

They both made arrangements to attend Berkley after all, Paul in its law school and Rose as a junior undergraduate. They lived in an apartment building near the school bequeathed to her. They continued their romance as Rose provided companionship to her mother and Paul passed the Certified Public Account exam while attending law school.

Rose's mother released the imaginary reins held over her only daughter and accepted her decisions. She accepted her pursuit of advanced studies in literature. She accepted her living with her boyfriend Paul. She accepted that her daughter was pregnant with the young man's child and the two would marry while both still students.

They wed in a private ceremony. Rose looked beautiful in the long and flowing white gown that did all but hide the bulging abdomen beneath it. Paul had never been happier in his life.

26

During those years of Dorean I, too, evolved. I had returned to a different America. I traveled up and down California, a magical place of drugs, love, and detached anonymity. I was eager to shed the Argentinian's skin. This led to the worst binge of identities, but beforehand there was a bit of business to be done.

The Argentinian accumulated great wealth. His material obsessions fueled a magnificent empire of riches of which I was the sole beneficiary. Such resource could not go to pass. Foolish mistakes of the past left me destitute and hungry. My problem was unique. I wanted to transfer wealth. Alone this was simple enough, but to an identity I yet did not know. I sought the advice of counsel.

The lawyer Skaggs sat back in his devil dark office. A bent and crooked man, greed filled the hollow of his bones. He and the Argentinian were carved from the same cold rock. He was most eager to assist me for a substantial fee. He drew the papers for an instrument he titled the *Gray Bearer Trust*. Any person in physical possession of a certain sealed certificate could access funds. To lose possession of the instrument was to lose all of the wealth at its ends. This was a solution for me, as I could pass the certificate from life to life, always with such great resource at my disposal.

Skaggs and I traveled by limousine to a large Los Angeles bank. I opened the account to deposit millions. What I thought to be prudent would be the foundation of my ends.

I parted from Skaggs with assurances that he would manage all affairs of the trust. He had limited power to withdraw funds, but was to receive a significant commission each year for his duties as trustee. On him would rest the burden of all public filings and tax payments. I was then free to roam, unencumbered by the law or depravation.

I know not how many lives I lived in this time. Some were for a few hours or days. I was deeply ill and my compulsion held me fast in its grip. I was a corrupt policeman and then his partner. I was a clergyman and then the altar boy he defiled. I was a utilities worker. I was the director of a funeral parlor. I changed bodies like clothing. I knew neither joy nor comfort in any of these skins, though each drank heartily from my elixir and cup of the trust fund.

Ultimately, I became Noel, a mangy twenty- something drifter. I first laid predatory eyes on the boy while he strummed a worn acoustic guitar. The instrument's open case sought the spare change of each passerby. There was much enjoyment in his carefree nature which I made my own.

Noel was all-too-trusting to take a ride and an offered drink from a friendly driver in formal wear and pale skin. I made the swap. His strength overpowered that of the gray man in the black suit. The parlor director was elderly, easily taken by the virulent youth. For good measure I planted the blade concealed under the passenger seat cleanly into the chest of the driver when the car came to its stop. Of course I removed the trust papers from the glove compartment before meeting the world in my newest form.

Noel proved to be an adequate haven. His body was healthy and fit despite his hand to mouth beatnik lifestyle. In time he proved his resilience by being most physically accommodating to my abuse of the elixir. He was tall and handsome, though in some secret, unassuming way. With no friends or family or employment it was an easy life to secretly slip inside and remain.

27

I found another love in Hollywood and the moving picture. The sets, the stories, and the acting evolved into heightened realism. Habitually, I attended the movies. Steadfast I sat in the padded plastic seats as Technicolor images splashed along the silver screen. I fell in love with the greats: Grant, Stewart, and Sansone.

I could identify. The medium was the closest thing to what I was on the earth. Through films anybody anywhere could travel to any place and be anybody. This could be done in the comfort of an air-conditioned theater. Through a fiery projector's beam, I traveled the world, the universe, and ultimately time itself. There were no boundaries.

I now had a context to judge my use of the dark science and determined I made a waste of it. I toppled no governments or ideologies. I founded no institutions or organizations. I made no contribution to medicine or science or society, save the death of the Ripper. That was then.

At the origins of this journey, at least its supernatural beginnings, I knew of a Devil. From that I concluded the existence of God. I know nothing of the Christ, but have seen the entry of both heaven and hell, choosing neither door. Looking back, I know all worldly things and had nowhere to go but this long way down.

As the beatnik Noel, I played a tattered guitar on the sunny city street corners for spare coins and worked a number of odd jobs. I found my way both in and out of communal living. I communed with The Family for a weekend, but could not tolerate Manson's religiosity despite the drugs and physical loves made possible through him. I knew nothing of his festering violence.

I shared the elixir with many in my new carefree world. I connected to the people and things around me. I stayed in Noel for over fifteen years. I killed no one. I went about simply absorbing the surrounding. I dare not say I was content in the man as I ever was. I found a manageable functionality living the life of this wandering, pleasure-tripping being.

I combined various drugs with my elixir and found new and nauseating highs. I grew to love the culture they inspired. I wanted to be Heston, McQueen, and Bronson. I wanted to fight intelligent apes, street thugs, and agents of dark fanatical dystopias. I wanted to make love to the women who splashed their naked bodies onto the giant screens. I wanted to break free.

Occasionally I would see a famous actor in Los Angeles. One would just cross before me from time to time. I followed Charles Bronson for a few blocks one Saturday, but lost him. There was never any real plan, but I imagined occupying his place in the world.

Through my wanderlust I would trade with John, a star of sorts, but it would also be in these latter years the greatest star would come to be.

28

My unknown enemy sat at his metal desk. There were colors and codes of meticulous organization. Photos of the Thompsons and his mother smiled out frozen in time. There, too, shining down on him were photographs of his wife and their son.

In the mirror that morning he recognized how much he had grown to look like his natural father. He was now a few years older than the man he never knew had never been.

His fingers perused the disconnected documents that would lead him down my path. He would discover what I was. He would stop me. He was the righteous one. He was the Taxman. He knew nothing of these things.

He graduated from Berkley's Law School over a decade earlier. The California bar exam was easy for him. He was pursued by a number of the larger Los Angeles law firms, but declined for a decent paying job in public service. His employment had been with the main southern California office of the Internal Revenue Service.

Originally it was for his resume, but the stability and hours of public service led him to stay. The foreboding tale of his own birth haunted his choice. He wanted as little as possible left to chance, knowing he would be home each night for dinner.

His deep understanding and seemingly unlimited memory found him in the position of investigations agent. The promotion was years earlier. He was a hero, if that bureau had such things. His colleagues admired him. Those he sought would pay. Stress had yet to take its toll and his alcoholic ways layed dormant.

There was the file, ominous and plain at the same time. Its mystery baffled the agents that seized it in the raid of the unscrupulous lawyer. In a fury of hacksaws and subpoenas the Service descended down upon the attorney for numerous crimes of finance. The lawyer's name was Skaggs.

It had not been Dorean or any other human eye detecting the irregularities and evasion. It had been the machine. The large mainframe hummed in unison with the massive fans cooling its core. While some agents called the computer HAL, Dorean considered it the Beast as it occupied two whole basement rooms. The innovative thing did what no human can do. Churning day and night, it matched and compared financial records of the banks of the world. In its mindless quest it uncovered my old lawyer and the bearer trust we created.

The file was delivered to the Taxman because much malice surrounded the so-called bearer trust. Its founder was without address or income. The principal came from a soon-after murdered businessman. He was not a citizen and held no connection to Noel. A preliminary look revealed the South American businessman was murdered in a seedy L.A. hotel. The literal dead-end only enticed the Taxman all the more.

Dorean became fascinated with the trail of blood that ran from the still significant wealth of the trust. Taxes had not been paid, nor had there been any justice for the murdered trail of individuals. They seemed so random yet all were connected to the unusual economic entity.

The machine was of limited use. Though it pointed its electric suspicions at the account and its founding counsel, it could do nothing in the way of solving the surrounding crimes. The FBI and local authorities were pursuing the matter, but it was the role of Dorean to make sure the delinquent taxes were paid and willful evaders prosecuted. Solving murders would be only incidental.

He dug his fingers into the mass of the file and came across the name of Noel. He was the only one to withdraw funds and live. This had been only hours after the bloody mess was left for a police photographer. Inside the envelope were all the glossy angles of death. It was the mortician. He looked just as I left him there on an inner city street.

Unable to find an address, he decided upon a risky venture. Standard procedure required a restraining of the account, disallowing any withdrawals from the *res* of the trust. Dorean petitioned the powers that be to prevent the restraint. This would be his means of finding Noel, or whoever held current power over the account. His wish was granted.

The pattern of withdrawals was basic. A few thousand here and there, all made from a handful of banks. Two in Los Angeles, one in San Francisco and another in the north of the state.

The Taxman visited each of the banks, personally speaking with bank managers of the highest rank. He was given assurances that he would be notified immediately if any party came to make a withdrawal. The account was flagged and no withdrawal could be made without the consent of a managing member of the bank.

With this plan he worked and waited. He spent much of the time investigating the list of all those who had gone to the bank, presented the trust instrument, and withdrew money from the account. He could find no sensible connection. He moved on to different cases and files, but never did let the interesting case of the bearer trust and its mystery stray from his thoughts.

29

A spell was spent in San Francisco. I was perusing *Inside View*. The aging actor Rolla Sansone had bloated to morbid proportions. Accompanying photographs were provided through the vengeful considerations of a terminated housemaid. She claimed the famously reclusive Sansone sent her to an adult theater with a camera to film pornographic movies. I recognized the place. The Mitchum was only a mile away.

I took to the cinema in that seedy district of San Francisco. I became engrossed. This visual art form brought me to new levels of arousal and intoxication. I would binge on the elixir and watch the beautiful people perform. This exhibitionism dwarfed all the orgies and drug parties of any commune.

The adult motion picture industry boomed and The Mitchum along with it. Special events were held at the theater heralding new films. Actors and actresses would come and meet fans for photos and autographs. The Mitchum likely did this as much to promote the films as to offend the protesting zealots marching feet from the theater's double glass doors.

I attended a few of these premieres. That last I saw was a sex riddled detective story. In San Francisco I returned to the needle and at the theater snuck away to a small custodian's closet. Privacy was necessary to fix my shot. I opened the door. Inside was John.

The man was crouched down, clicking away at the hissing butane lighter he held in a shaky fist. The flame ignited the far end of a long glass pipe extending from his pressed lips. The entirety of his body shook subtly as he pulled in the white smoke. He eyes slowly closed in waved ecstasy before realizing my interruption. The tuxedo-covered man startled back to the leaning mops and brooms.

"Mr. Holmes?" I asked. "I am Noel."

He extended a trembling hand. I shook back firmly, placing another hand atop his so as to say that his secret was safe with me. He held the pipe out and I accepted it. John set the fired torch to it as I placed the tool in my mouth. Dragging in I tasted the freebase rock cocaine.

It was by no means as powerful as the elixir, but it created within me a distinct, pleasant perspective over everything. I felt a great physical euphoria with an overpowering sense of self-confidence. The elixir removed and separated. This new substance seemed to embrace and encourage. Though the feeling was fleeting, I was impressed with the drug.

I saw John looking over me as he loosened his tie. He ran his jaw back and forth, clenching his teeth.

"You want to hit the town?" he asked.

At that time John Holmes was the most famous adult film actor in the world. Women, and some men, swooned for him. That night John and I went from club to party again and again. Food, drinks, drugs, and women were simply thrown to him and from him to me. We traveled to Los Angeles.

I was with a star and we enjoyed unlimited supplies of cocaine. My thoughts turned to coveting him. I never saw a person so wanted by the world. I did enjoy him too much and thought that maybe he could be my companion for the ages. For the time I was his friend.

Our one night on the town became six. I accompanied him to movie sets, the homes of his friends, and even his forays into high stakes prostitution.

I introduced him to the elixir, but he vomited violently when he drank from it. Terrified of needles, he would not try to inject it. I was desperate to share it with him, which led me back to experimentation for the first time in years.

After much tinkering, I yielded the elixir in a smokeable crystal form. It was hard and white like the cocaine, but with a slight tinge of green. One hit was potent enough to bring about all the affects of the elixir in its other forms.

I was eager to share it with John. He would come and go from my hotel. Sometimes to his youthful paramour; other times to the dealers and users who lived a life as we lived ours. I went to him at his hotel with a fresh pipe and loaded it for him. It gave a familiar crackle as he hit from the piece.

"I like it," he said plainly through his smoky exhale. We both laughed together. From there came a day full of smoking a combination of the cocaine and elixir. It was like nothing before.

The day became several weeks of festering about the rented room. We neither ate nor drank much of anything during the time, nor did we answer to any of the callers at his door. His little girl lover hounded us from time to time, but John ignored her. Paranoia overtook the both of us. We were each convinced police would storm the dwelling at any moment. I even suspected that John figured out what I truly was.

"You know John," I said to him.

"You know what?" he asked packing the pipe.

"What it is I am," I said. Curiosity fill his haggard face.

"Which is what? A fag?" he asked in a casual manner.

"No, John. I am the interloper."

He remained silent. From his questioning eyes I determined further elaboration would be helpful though never demanded.

"Interloper. The word, in its usual sense, describes a person who enters a situation or environment in which they do not belong and then participate in it. They are, well, 'butting in.' But I am able to do more. I can actually become somebody. I can steal bodies."

At this he laughed and said, "Steal mine," taking the briefest of breaks from the pipe.

Without another word I did just that. I forced him into Noel's body as I entered his. This had been only for his amusement.

The lies and truths of his life overwhelmed me. I felt his depravity. The alien warm member hung half-erect creeping down my thigh. I took steps forward, feeling it sway with my gait.

"Holy Fuck!" he exclaimed. He looked to the wall-sized mirror. He smoked more of the cocaine-elixir combo while watching himself in the mirror.

"This is fucking cool man!" He followed with a series of poses and postures.

I had still not lost focus on the heavy weight between my legs. I felt freakish and returned to the body of Noel and returned John to himself without incident.

"Fuck, that was cold. How did you do that?" he asked. I explained to him an abbreviated tale of the elixir, omitting my encounter with the White One. It was then the blood came. Just a trickle at first, I wiped it away before he even noticed.

"Amazing," he said as he took another hit from the pipe. I smiled a smile of appreciation and understanding. I remain fond of John to this day now despite of him. Then there was a real problem.

It came from my nose and then from my mouth. I felt an overwhelming, pulsating pain in my head and chest. I fell to the ground paralyzed. All the years of abuse came to fruition there in that place at that time.

"What's up, man?" John asked as I lied incapacitated on the floor. He pulled a pillow off of the bed and placed it underneath my head. I vomited as he took more and more hits from the pipe. My vision blurred and I closed my eyes.

"Oh fuck, man. No!" he shouted in perfect self-absorption. I heard the fumbling of a corded telephone. "Hey front desk, there's a guy up here in room thirty-seven. He's passed out and real sick. He needs a doctor!"

I found myself in a familiar, but unpalatable territory. I felt death seeping in upon me from all angles. Whether overdose or the culmination of the abuses the edges were closing in around me. My friend was leaving me to die. He would do no such thing.

Deep within myself I found all of my hate, all of my fear. I used these dark materials to fuel a desperate bolt from my dying body. Though he made it from the room, I extended the astral plane to its most finite. The push was my weakest, but it was enough to dislodge him from his body.

Now I stood outside the door of the hotel room. I turned and walked back in to the unconscious body of Noel. There was no evidence John actually made it. The shell looked comatose,though it breathed. Living or dead, it did not matter for I was no better a friend than he.

All the memories and emotions I tasted so briefly rushed through my mind once again. I felt all the sex, all the money, and all of the fame. I felt all of the drugs, all of the loss, and all of the shame. Lies had begotten more lies and there was little truth. I found it difficult to discern the man's falsities from reality.

I made it to another hotel blocks away. Within hours the freebase neared depletion. Action would be necessary.

What was the man's name? John introduced us and I was having great difficulty moving through the inventory of his mind. If it would not come I could find his precious waif. Her whereabouts I knew.

I smoked the combination cocaine and elixir. I could not pause for more than a few seconds until faced again with the irresistible urge to set the torch to the glass pipe. My lips and fingers burned. I walked on the tips of my toes around the room. I feared that the slightest noise would open the door to all the authorities of Los Angeles. It was madness. The only escape was the mere seconds after each hit of the drugs.

Nash. The Nash.

I remembered the name. Eddie Nash. He owned a nightclub where John and I drank before we isolated ourselves from the world around us. John introduced me to the man, but Nash offered only a dismissive wave. Now I was John and he liked John. He paid in drugs when John came to the parties held at his gated home.

I made my way to Nash where violent beats of music leaked into the surrounding street. Security in the form of two large black men stood at the door, but quickly ushered me through. The rooms of the home were filled with fine things, debauchery, and abuse. John's brain directed me to Nash within it.

Deep into the home I found a study. On the desk in the room were mounds of the drug I sought. Nash was in the company of a young girl put to an unspeakable chore.

"John my boy!" he shouted out waving to me with a hand clutching an amber liquor in his ice filled glass. I returned a smile and strutted towards him.

"John, do us a favor. Show the girls. Show the girls that monster cock!"

I felt humiliated, but began to unzip my trousers, full well knowing that my compliance would ensure a steady stream of the precious white I sought. The girls' eyes widened at the marvel. This time he allowed me to dress again without sexual performance. For that I was grateful. My hunger for the drugs was absolute.

"I had a call for you. Actually, it was a call from you," he laughed. "Some crazy guy at Ingleside called and said he was you."

John was alive.

He filled a glass pipe with the cooked cocaine and I discretely added flakes of the elixir to the mix. Thoughts of desire and craving, of guilt and fear evaporated into smoky solace. Nash left me to a pile of the drug and retired to a bedroom with the girl. I smoked in solitude for hours. As the sun rose, Nash returned. He was no longer jovial and appreciative.

"You pathetic piece of shit, John. Look at you!" he shouted over the music in disgust. "Take it and get out of my sight!" He threw a thick glass ashtray. From the darkness appeared a black giant sworn to protect the evil little man. I left the home without incident.

I walked the streets of Los Angeles. I watched the soundless images of televisions behind caged windows of a boutique storefront. I saw the faces of Ronald Reagan and a Pope, each of the men having drawn bullets from would-be assassins and lived. I was soon to know the violence of the era as my own.

30

As the new decade slouched into the second year of the shimmering eighties, Greg Whales, then still Greg Aberdine, would experience a loss not so different from the loss of my childhood. Greg and his brother Vincent slept while their mother consumed her ever-increasing dose of heroin and cocaine speedball.

That day Mrs. Aberdine again turned to tricks to support her desires. Shift workers from the surrounding industry proved insatiable over the preceding weeks. The laborers provided a steady stream of income. She had not slept in nearly three days and she would do all that she could to prevent the inevitable crash awaiting her. She chain-smoked long cigarettes and injected more drugs to stay afloat.

This did not sustain. Mrs. Aberdine lapsed into a deep sleep with her cigarette dangling loosely from her painted fingertips. The burning cigarette toppled into a pile of magazines where a bottle of nail polish remover also laid. The cigarette ignited the glossy paper; the paper fire melted the plastic bottle. The liquid poured out, spreading fire across the living room floor and under the door of the bedroom shared by the two boys.

The incident was reported in the *Daily* Gazette. The grainy inkblot of a photo showed the remaining ruin of the home. It did not show the raging red and orange that consumed the Spiderman pajamas his little brother wore. Only Whales would know the searing pain and terror in his brother's face inside the flames. But-for the action of a heroic fireman, Greg Whales would have never existed.

An enraged county prosecutor would focus on her conduct after the fire. Whether by heat or smoke, she awoke from her slumber and made a modest attempt to quash the sustained fire. Realizing futility, she left the apartment and crossed the street to a neighborhood deli where she phoned the city's emergency services.

In her sickening sadness, Mrs. Aberdine confessed to police that she had a drug problem and prostituted to support the problem. She told them about all the dope and all the coke. Feigning sympathy while taking notes, officers at the scene gathered enough incriminating statements and other evidence to charge her with negligent homicide. She was convicted and sent to state prison.

Greg's father let him attend the sentencing. He stood in the street waving the short-spanned good-byes of a child as the Sheriff's car took his mother away. She made no effort to contact Greg or his father. Through her twice, the third of our dark trinity was born.

31

"Yo! John?" said a rough voice.

I turned and saw a man I knew as David. Dave. He lived with a group John accompanied on and off. Like Nash, they took him in for the novelty. But in the end they, too, considered him a hapless clown.

I greeted the man who was friendly enough. Of course this is how it always started. I knew their game having yet to play it. John would be ridiculed and then make himself scarce only to be lulled back to be emasculated by them all over again. Dave invited me to the home on Wonderland Avenue. I really had no choice.

I spent weeks there in a perpetual state of intoxication. I contributed the elixir to the party and found it to be a success in that crowd. The bliss ended with the end of a supply of their conventional drugs.

John thought of it before. He only remained silent for fear of the plan's ramifications if caught.

"I know where we can get some cash and lots of stuff," I announced to the group of five sitting desperately around a maligned dining table. They looked ravenous.

"More bullshit, John!" echoed anonymously through the smoky room. I could not blame them as I myself was continuing to have difficulties discerning John's truth.

On a pizza box I sketched a schematic of the mansion owned by Nash. I showed them the room where the drugs and money were stored. I showed them the path from the door I would leave unlocked upon my visit to the house. I burned as I did this, each of his very humiliations of me replaying obsessively in my head.

There were no arguments. There were no rejections or objections posed. There was merely the silent assent of the desperate and depraved. I felt a charge of adrenaline fill me as I found my place of leadership in the group that considered John its jester.

"I can get in to leave this door unlocked," I said calmly, coolly.

Nash was receptive to my visit. The cyclic nature of the relationship returned to the arc of his open arms. He was excited to see me again, particularly eager to show off the prize between my legs. This time, I was quite happy to oblige.

My novelty wore after a time. Nash left me to smoke cocaine from a mound on the desk in his study. He left me to entertain and I was contentedly alone. I did partake in the freebase as John's will was not his own with the drug.

Then the moment came. I was able to steal away from the room and go to the back of the home. There I found the door held in the eye of John's mind. It was a simple locking device for such a grand place. I flipped the lock to allow our entry and returned to the office. I continued to freebase alone.

Nash returned and continued in his kindness to me. His hospitality and genuine fondness sent a small pang of guilt through my abdomen. In justification, I found all the incidents of mockery stored in Holmes' brain. He was sorry to see me leave, wishing me well and hoping for my return.

We could not be certain how long the lock would remain open and decided to strike that night. I would not be with them. My presence would no doubt lead Nash to our domain on Wonderland. I was filled with cowardice and contented to sit and wait.

Within hours, the gang returned with a great deal of money and drugs. They found hundreds of thousands of dollars, pounds of narcotics, and manufactured pills. For a moment there was enough to go around. It was then they returned me to the clown.

I was given a pittance of the cash and drugs. Less than a tenth of the booty was mine according to the majority rule. I immediately went to using the drugs and at its end found myself returning some of the money to buy more of the stolen cocaine.

I left the group. Their torments returned full swing and I was too angered to stay. I knew none would hesitate to silence my protest of dissatisfaction. With my head down I left with a little money in my pocket and less than half an ounce of the cocaine I purchased.

The resentment entered full bloom. I risked my life in tampering with the lock at the property. This risk would outlast any benefit from the money or drugs I held.

I tried to rest in my motel room, but could not. I continued to base and smoke the cocaine until it was gone. In desperation I conceived a new plan. I would go to Nash rather than wait for his inevitable visit to me.

I did just that. I went to the mansion and found him in his rage. They humiliated him, laughing at his desperate plea for life from his knees. Now Nash was on the offensive and I hoped he would accept me on his side of the battlefield.

"I know about the robbery," I said to him. I wondered if that alone would merit a death sentence.

His large black bodyguard stepped closer to me, close enough to reach me if the tale was not told in the speed and degree Nash demanded. I told him everything other than my role in opening the door. Nash never knew I facilitated the crime. He did, though, question my allegiance.

With the massive hands of his bodyguard at my throat, I agreed to show him where he could find the crew. Further, that I would ensure that his men would get inside. I told him that I was more than happy to do so.

Four, Nash not amongst us, climbed into a large Cadillac and made our way to the Wonderland address. With the black bodyguard at my back, I rang the electric buzzer and requested entry into that den of iniquity.

"It's John," I said into the squawking wall box.

Another buzzer shouted as the door was opened to me. Two of the three men pushed me aside, each with a metallic pipe in hand. A third led me from behind.

I heard the first thuds from whoever was unfortunate enough to open the door. By the time I entered, the man's face was so badly beaten I knew not which of the members he was. The anonymous man was dead in a collecting pool of his own blood and tissue.

The armed men entered separate rooms and began to club the sleeping bodies in each bed. Completely vulnerable, the horrid job was done in less than ten minutes. I never made one strike. My role was limited to confirmatory nods toward the sleeping culprits. We recovered what remained of the money and drugs in the dwelling and left into the night.

32

The electronic media devoured the crime. Each channel of the dial offered coverage. The television hung from a wall brace. The vertical hold was failing causing the image of the Wonderland dwelling to roll continuously on the screen. Paul Dorean's eyes were fixed on the box, but he saw nothing.

His wife drove home alone in despair over the imminent death of their only child. Less than a year earlier, a kind doctor told them of the leukemia in the boy's blood while prescribing Mrs. Dorean a significant dose of tranquilizers. The small round pills became her world. She clutched the bottle in a fist walking from Dorean and out of the hospital. The Taxman believed at the time she could be fixed, later. Then he had to focus on his dying child.

The doctors and staff effected yet another transfusion in futility. The light of this world was closing to the boy and there was no magic or medicine powerful enough to stop the killer cells. His father was taking a rare break from the death chamber disguised as a hospital room.

Paul's heart tore in two as he waited for the grueling agony to finally overtake his long ago happy child. His bright eyes were fading fast. His child, Danny, was a child of privilege. In so, the boy once appreciated the wonders of food and his mother denied him nothing. At six he stood twenty percent overweight. At seven years, only five. He now laid an emaciated bag of bones, trying to understand why God had let him enter the world at all.

Dorean was beyond such questioning. There was only a cruel and wicked nature at work. Though once a man of faith, he was now a man of rage and contempt. The second act had yet to play, but he knew then that his marriage was also in its own death chamber. There could be no marriage when one of the parties is lost to the world. Here, they both were in some way.

The doctor walked slowly. This was the end of emergency. Nothing more would be done. The machine tolled its familiar flat tone of death and the child was no more.

33

Nash was satisfied with word of the assaults and recovery. He offered me money and some of the drugs with an insistence that I leave the city. There was nothing I wanted more in that moment than escape. I had greater plans than a mere geographic change. It was time to return a borrowed item to an old friend.

I found him quite easily. Though society locked him away in a hospital ward for the mentally disturbed, he was docile and compliant. His fits of identity ceased. He was allowed to have visitors and even eat lunch with them. His caretakers believed a visit from a friend could lift his spirits. I was happy to oblige.

I filled a thermos with the elixir and purchased two sandwiches at a deli neighboring the facility. An elevator lifted me to the secure ward where I was no doubt recognized in the sneers and giggles my entry received. They placed me in a small visitation room.

John, in my old frame of Noel, shuffled through the door in a worn pair of pajamas. The vacancy in his eyes left when he saw himself sitting there with a bagged lunch.

"I'm so sorry, John," I said with all the sincerity I could muster. Surprisingly, he was not angry. To the contrary, he showed glee.

"I'm not fucking crazy, am I?"

"No John, not at all. I have come to undo the wrong I have done." With that I slid forward a cup of the elixir. He drank greedily from the cup. His body acted violently yet he kept it down. This was now a matter of necessity that I consume the drink. With great force, I swallowed the beverage and contained the fury within my innards long enough to enter him.

Now I was in the pajamas across from the true John Holmes. I saw first satisfaction. I then saw the horror of the preceding events fill his mind. He vomited onto the table.

"My God," he offered.

"I am sorry, my friend."

He stood and walked backward from the visiting room. He turned and walked briskly to the desk. That was the last I would personally see of John Holmes. I was sorry to hear of the trouble I caused him and his ultimate fate. I consider it something more than another anecdote for my damnation.

I am still uncertain why I agreed to replace him in the institution. Perhaps it was my own plea for sanity. Perhaps it was obligation to a friend. It is probably something of both.

Noel proved a difficult path to rehabilitation. They labeled him some form of psychotic and it took time for me to convince the staff I was addicted to drugs rather than organically unfit. In time I proved this to them and was offered a release into a substance abuse rehabilitation center.

My hopes rose yet again for the chance of a new beginning. I was tired, and sick of being so. I lowered my fists and went forward.

34

Then there were two. The Aberdine males moved into a small flat in the Stockade, the oldest section of Schenectady. Greg was given his own room. A perk once sought, it was now loathed. His dreams swelled with images of his brother in Spiderman pajamas engulfed in flame. The burning child walked the halls of Greg's mind carrying a ragtag stuffed bear. His father shrugged away Greg's terrorizing dreams.

Mr. Aberdine continued his employment with General Electric for a time. The smile and charms burned in the fire, leaving only an automaton. Each day after his shift, Greg's father would land in some anonymous city bar and peck away at the suicide waltz of alcohol.

First, he remained responsible, arriving home in the early hours of the evening to eat the dinner his remaining son prepared. A factory layoff found Aberdine unable to find an equivalent wage.

Greg watched the metamorphosis of his father through the drink. The boy, silently shy, made his way through the smoky neon lit rooms finding his father to sign papers for school, for a pittance to buy house staples, and in some way to know that the man was still alive.

Most nights his father returned home late. He was rarely alone. Greg slept through the rumblings until the laughter and music shook the apartment. He then would awake and go to the living room. Drunken men and woman danced about kissing and sloppily fondling one another. One such night, he found his father wrapped around a heavy woman in the corner of the room.

"What the fuck do you want?" his father asked.

Greg froze in time. Aberdine offered a cruel, cold stare up and down the boy.

"Look at him. My son, Look at him!" said his father pulling the needle up from the spinning rock and roll record. Greg stood small and nearly naked before the drunken adults. Some remained silent while others giggled. They all looked him down. He felt the shaky heat of unwanted attention.

"Prancing around this apartment and playing with dolls. Dolls!" he said with his hands full of the small jointed soldiers of plastic and screws.

"Faggot!" his father shouted twisting and turning the men, snapping the internal bands of rubber holding the toys together. Tears erupted in Greg's eyes as he ran to the sanctity of his bedroom in a dart. There he felt insulated from the world. He clutched his knees and drifted back to the nightmare world of his burning brother.

35

I escaped Inglewood Psychiatric without the elixir. Evaluations and papers were sent back and forth between facilities and I was finally transferred to Pleasant Creek Addiction Treatment Center. It was a ninety-day program with aftercare options.

First I went to a detoxification unit. This was mandatory though the acute withdrawal symptoms had long passed. As for the obsession of the mind, that is eternal. I walked from the detox to the resident unit. I lived there with sixty others.

I attended daily meetings of Narcotics Anonymous held in the building. Addicts filled the room smoking and drinking coffee. They shared their stories and spoke of a life without drugs. I listened. I tried in vain to apply their principles to my unique dependence.

Oblivious to my pursuer Dorean, I followed the recommendation of the counselors. I was referred to a yearlong community residence. We did chores and attended therapy groups. Through bitter fights with temptation I remained. I, the antique monster, sought the counsel of ordinary mortals.

The year passed and I continued to attend Narcotics Anonymous meetings each day. I engaged a sponsor, a mentor of sorts, to guide me in the program. His name was Chris. He was a kind old man. I told him nothing of the elixir. I practiced the twelve steps of the program, applying it to my addiction. This worked for a time.

I completed treatment. One morning they provided me a certificate and a filled plastic bag. I looked inside and found the clothes I wore the day of my admission to the emergency room, the day I had left John to die in my stead.

The bus rode along the run down streets of downtown Los Angeles.

The streets I once roamed were now alien. I fingered through the pockets of the clothes and felt the unmistakable rocks. They were loose, but there all the same. It was my smokeable, hardened elixir.

The bus dropped me a block from the apartment secured by the program. The first month was paid, but I was expected to find my own employment. It was furnished and awful, but it would be my home.

Having put away the few articles of clothing and personal effects I searched for a secret place. I should have thrown them from the bus or into the toilet, but I did not. I wanted nothing more of the elixir, yet allowed this reservation to remain. I pried the baseboard of a bedroom wall and within it crammed a cigarette cellophane containing the elixir rocks.

I humbled myself by working at a shoe factory. By day I sewed leather pieces into shoes. By night I cleaned my tiny studio apartment. The Higher Power I came to believe in once again shone down on me. I nearly loved my life there. Of course, something was still missing.

I actually saw myself aging again. The once pitch-black head of hair yielded to coarse hairs of gray. Sinking skin darkened under my eyes. The resilient body of Noel was in decay. This troubled me a little more each morning. For me, physical age and death were not absolutes, but for Noel's body they were.

I was part of something more than myself. I made friends with varying degrees of commitment to living a life of sobriety. Some voluntarily attended the Narcotics Anonymous meetings. Others were directed there by a forceful push from the agencies of criminal justice. One of these men was Walter Gigbe. I took to him yet knew that he continued a pattern of abuse despite his parole. He was honest to me with his struggle to stay abstinent from heroin. He thought himself unable to live without the substance though he desperately wanted to do so. He asked that I become his sponsor. I agreed to help him.

We forged a friendship with one another. I was continually amazed by the irony of finding myself in a position to aid another human being. Perhaps in some small way I believed in atonement or could repay the program.

We worked into the later hours of many nights. Gigbe shed tears and offered his confessions. I provided him counsel and instruction. Despite my best efforts, he could remain clean no more than two days at a time. We would have weeks with no contact and then he would return. I would not give up on the man as I, too, knew the stranglehold of addiction and the futility of battle against it.

36

For the Taxman these years passed, too. He constructed no image of the man he pursued. Imagery was a device used in the youth of his career to pass the countless hours of drab file reviews and cross-checking. Now he was practical. The man he sought was a human blank, nameless and faceless.

Others in the agency opined that the perpetrator was not a lone man. He knew, deep inside his innards, that it was a solitary doing. The mystery would not be simple. The many assumptions were a myriad of subtleties strewn together. Occam's Razor could not apply.

His legs ached, but no pleasure or purpose drained from the chase. The mystery filled the void in his heart and home. Noel had vanished. The trust fund, with its hearty millions, was virtually untouched. The last withdrawal was not from Noel at all. It was I as Holmes. That was seven years earlier.

Dorean's plan had failed. Only an internal audit revealed Holmes' withdrawal. Further human error delayed receipt of the envelope. A negligent misfiling delayed the accompanying evidence. An apologetic clerk arrived at the desk of the Taxman with the item that should have been delivered earlier. The Taxman had an indecipherable scrawl completing the withdrawal slip. It was these errors that called for the machines.

The envelope contained a grainy image corresponding with the withdrawal. The man was tall and thin with curly hair and a modest mustache. An intern identified the man in the photograph. The intern, fresh from the debauchery of modern American college life, immediately recognized the wall print composite cleaved from the bank footage.

"That's Johnny Wadd!" he exclaimed.

The name held no meaning for a man of prudence such as Dorean. He knew only the value of methodical, personal control. There had been his time with alcohol after the death of his son and his wife's abandonment, but that passed with his own recognition of the signs.

From this, the intern described both the man and the myth of John Holmes. He described his ascension and collapse in the world of adult entertainment under the weight of drugs and sex. With that Dorean was armed with information to study and then locate the man.

With a few calls he found the then address of Holmes. Superficially, it was all there: Holmes' withdrawal, the murders, and the decadence. It still did not fit. He did not suspect that Holmes was the evader he sought. *Where had Noel gone?* There was no body and no missing person reported. He hoped Holmes could give him more.

He was a short drive. Upon entering the building, his nostrils flared to the scent of the institutional antiseptic. It was also the colors, the lights, and the uniformed staff. This ward was particularly grim; it being designated as the last song for those labeled terminal. In these spaces he learned of the cancer devouring his son as his marriage unraveled. He now fought this battle against his own renegade cells, but that had to wait. He was on to something.

John was paying for his limitless debauchery in the years before and after me. He was wasting away only yards from the seat of the Taxman. Somewhere he contracted the invisible invaders that set fear and bigotry into the stone heart of the turning world. Within him a losing war waged its course. Dorean watched as a somber nurse left the room and motioned that he could now see the dying man.

With a slow controlled series of breaths, the Taxman prepared himself for the ghastly state in which he was sure to see Holmes. Dorean had no personal knowledge of the virus, but the media provided increasingly graphic reports of its devastation. There was no real preparation for what he was going to see.

Holmes was a skeleton sheathed in dead-gray skin. His face and eyes were receding into the darkness of his skull. He had no motion, no energy.

"Why won't you just leave me the fuck alone!" Holmes snarled through an oxygen mask of transparent plastic. It did not escape Dorean that Holmes' believed him to be yet another Los Angeles Police detective. The sick man was tormented by a number of policemen seeking a deathbed confession. The acquittal ensured his dying freedom, but cold case curiosity kept the police on a vigil.

"No," said the Taxman, "and I am not a cop. I am an IRS agent."

The statement caught the attention of Holmes. Through the haze of dripping morphine and the pain the drug could not mask, Holmes was curious.

"I'm not paying them!" John offered with a hoarse laugh.

"No, this has nothing to do with you, John. At least I don't think it does."

"What then?"

"I want to know what you can tell me about a mister Noel Garrison," said the Taxman, "Garrison was the last to access a certain trust, the Gray Trust, before you. Who is he? Where is he?"

"You wouldn't believe me if I told you."

"Please try me. I have an open mind in the matter."

With this consent, John told the Taxman of our adventures. He spoke of the elixir and the switch performed thrice between us. The first had been for amusement. The second for survival. The last out of love.

Dorean listened and cast no judgment. He asked more questions, but remained distracted by Holmes' original proposition. His meticulous notes would compensate. He could think only of what Holmes referred to as the "switch."

The Taxman left the hospital major in an arthritic fog, his aching bones shrieking out. With each painstaking step, he sank deeper into confusion. He knew not which concept was the more maddening, the astral drivel of body switching or how neatly it fit the case as he understood it.

He drove from the parking garage telling himself that he did not believe, that he could not believe. Yet he did. He was chasing something beyond reason.

37

I memorized the article in *Gentlemen's Quarterly*. Greg was well liked, athletic, and strong academically. He worked part-time as a delivery driver for a hardware store. He saved enough money to purchase a worn sedan. His greatest acting was the hiding of his sadness.

On a wet fall day, he hit a large road puddle sending his car into a tree. Unbelted, Greg was thrown violently into the steering wheel fracturing a number of his ribs. This ended both football and basketball for the year.

Greg would not be idle. He searched for other activities to fill the void the accident created. Others noticed his discomfort in standing idle. An English teacher suggested a hand at acting.

Greg was tall, darkly featured, and exceptionally handsome. He was cut and masculine and showed an immediate aptitude for memorizing and delivering lines. He auditioned for a supporting role in the play *Guest House* written by an ambitious classmate. Based on the audition he was chosen for the lead. He received praise from his teachers, peers, and the local media. His father remained silent.

That same English teacher invited Greg to meet a drama professor at a nearby university. Greg and this professor became friends. He encouraged Greg to audition for an agent.

The agent specialized in actors for commercials. He advised Greg to move to New York City. Greg was happy to leave both his father and Schenectady behind.

Greg became nationally known for his appearance in a series of humorous car insurance advertisements. This exposure led to a supporting role on the critically acclaimed situation comedy *Guys Like Us* that was cancelled after just one season.

With a new agent and name, Greg Whales was given his first starring feature film role. At nineteen he starred in the teen romance comedy *If Only When,* which became a runaway hit despite a meager production budget.

Greg became a cultural icon. Teen magazines proudly displayed his symmetric grin month after month. Movie roles were offered and every feature made was an assured hit. This was merely a beginning.

Then came *Beyond the Jaded Sun*. He was offered the starring role of Gynn. The intergalactic vigilante searched for the aliens responsible for the destruction of his home world. He hated the blue screen work, but injected himself into the franchise. The movie and its two sequels created a worldwide hysteria.

Fans waited in line for each edition at the theater, subsequent releases for home viewing, action figures, and video games. They were there around the world, a row of fanatical fools in the costume of their favorite characters. Greg took a portion of it all. At twenty-six, Greg Whales was nearly a billionaire.

Despite the success of the franchise, critics largely ignored or denounced his contributions. The series was considered "increasingly bloated," "lacking in originality and vision," and "using CGI slight of hand to deceive its audience into believing it was watching a story rather than explosions and spaceships."

Greg married actress Gloria Wright who co-starred in the first *Jaded Sun* sequel. Their chemistry proved to be limited and the pair divorced in less than two years. The tabloids suggested all the usual explanations. *Inside View* opined Greg was incapable of human connection.

Greg and his agent, Max Whitman, sought roles to satisfy his detractors. The first of these films was *Blood and Ink*. He portrayed Canadian author Randal Sands aiding Americans in avoiding the Vietnam draft. Whales was nominated for an Academy Award, but did not win. He received a Golden Globe and a series of lesser acknowledgements. He made a few more serious films, most successful, but never enough.

While the world fell into greater love with the star, Greg became more and more reclusive. He purchased a sprawling Malibu estate. Eight-foot high brick walls assured no easy entry for would-be trespassers and blocked his view of the sunny hills. His security staff of ten was trained in the martial arts, combat firearms, and a number of defensive technologies and techniques.

The proverbial straw would come the day Greg's second to last picture premiered at Mann's Chinese Theater on Hollywood Boulevard. Early reviews for *Rift* were lukewarm, one calling Whales a "wooden faced has-been who never really was."

He appeared from a silver limousine of bulletproof armor with two bodyguards at each of his sides. Next to appear from the vehicle was none other than the beautiful Vanessa Dane, co-star in the film and Whales' current love interest. She had only one bodyguard. Whales and Ms. Dane locked arms and stepped onto the flowing red carpet.

Behind the velvet ropes, which were chains custom tailored to mimic a particularly gruesome torture scene in the film, stood all the fans and all the paparazzi the street could hold. Camera bulbs provided a continuous stream of bright white light at the star. His entourage paused for them all. Somehow above all the clicks, screams, and cheers he heard her.

"I love you Greg!" she shrieked in a bloodcurdling pledge.

In his dreams, she would whisper, but there in that moment she screamed. She squeezed the trigger of the forty-five placed to her right temple. Greg bore witness to the change the instant their eyes locked.

The crowd moved from the girl in a sickening lurch, leaping from the splatter of blood and mind. Photographers aimed their cameras first at the dead girl and then back on the star covered in a crashing wave of blood and tissue.

The last sliver of Greg Whales that enjoyed his celebrity fell away. His slow progression towards complete isolation would magnify its pace a thousand fold. It was by no means immediate, like reflex, but his was coming to its chronic end.

Inside View purchased exclusive rights to the funeral from the girl's insolvent parents. They provided the magazine with an interview and a most uncomfortable display of the Greg Whales temple her bedroom had become. Based on legal advice, Whales offered no condolence or visit to the family.

Within a week of the suicide and its nearly instantaneous coverage, another fifteen year old girl took her own life. Greg's lawyers told him to worry not since they could prove the second girl had an extensive history of self-abuse and mental health treatment.

Greg Whales was seemingly the antitheses of my original self. Where he was handsome, I was ugly. Where he was globally loved and adored, I was a hated mistake of birth. He was successful. I was nothing. He was everything I ever wanted to be.

38

Then came our first intersection. Dorean pursued the case of Noel Garrison from the sterile confines of the Internal Revenue Service files to the deathbed of John Holmes. The results were nil. Other cases came and went, but he remained bent on finding the elusive me.

He declined numerous promotions to supervisory capacities in all of his years. He was obsessed with the puzzle of my life. The bearer trust certificate was a passing torch of death. The Internal Revenue Service wanted money and justice. He wanted answers.

I lived my humbled life oblivious to my pursuer. I did not go to the well of the trust for reasons of my own sobriety. I lived off my own earned dollars, ate off my own broken back.

I assumed the knock on my door to be Gigbe, my troubled protégé. He usually joined me for coffee on his sober mornings. It was not. Through the fish-eye keyhole I saw him. The lines of his face told a tale of age and torment. He looked pained to stand there. I opened up to the harmless chap.

"Good morning," the old man said.

"Good morning to you," I responded.

"My name is Paul Dorean. I am with the Internal Revenue Service. Noel Garrison?" he asked as he handed me a tiny white card.

"Yes."

"I need a moment of your time."

My world fell from beneath me. In that moment the life I had come to know would end. The interest of one governmental entity would surely bring another. Some part of my secret escaped from its bottle. The placidity of life vanished in that moment.

"I have been looking for you for some time. May I come in?"

"Of course, please do."

He passed the archway and stood centered in the room. He looked from here to there, but his eyes returned to me.

"Mr. Garrison, I am here to ask you about the trust, the Gray Trust."

My eyes deceived me. Ancient and evil I stood there, trembling at the sight of him.

"Yes."

"Do you know Juan Marquez?"

I denied it.

"Martin Provost?"

I denied this.

The list continued and my denials followed. All the names were once mine, stolen from others, but then mine. He sought commonalities. I hijacked each of them, and then drank heartily from the trust in their form.

"What of John Holmes?"

He knew.

"Yes, I know John. In a different life he was my friend," I answered, "but I am sober now."

"Well then no better time to deal with this. I am going to need you in my office."

"Mr. Dorean, I am more than willing to help you. I want this behind me, whatever consequence I must suffer."

The phrase surprised Dorean. He did not expect Noel Garrison to speak in such a way.

"Then please come with me," he said and placed a hand on my arm.

"Am I under arrest?"

"No."

"Then I would like to meet you after my shift. I am late for work."

The Taxman silently considered.

"I am not hiding. I am right here," I said.

The Taxman stepped away from me. He ran his finger over a side table. On its edge he stopped and looked back to me.

"That is not to say you couldn't be charged. Tax evasion and obstruction of justice are possibilities. I could get a federal arrest warrant. The agents would swarm in and throw you to the ground."

"I have a life," I said.

He held his notepad out displaying all the names. I looked over his wrinkling flesh. From the abyss rose the old haunt. I craved the elixir.

"These people all had lives."

"Please, I will cooperate. I'll do anything!"

"I cannot. You will have to come with me."

In him I found my adversary. Instincts returned and I rushed at him. He was old and frail, easily falling to the floor. He cried out in agony as I shattered his hip. His eyes closed and I should have killed him there. The decency of my new way of living saved the aged agent.

He would recover and others would certainly follow. I had assaulted a federal authority. His masters would not stop until they captured me. I went to the cramped study. I descended to the floor and pried the old loose board where my material reservation laid. There within the space were the bits of elixir I tucked away. Damnation lied within.

39

I traveled by public transit the many blocks to the flop house of my troubled protégé. I pounded on his door. He finally answered, haggard-faced and worn. Gigbe was a young man, but the abuses of his living aged him considerably.

"It has been awhile." I said, "Consider this a wellness check."

The apartment was in squalor. I saw no direct proof of his return to heroin, but the circumstantial evidence overwhelmed. Gigbe was pale, moving in constant ticks of motion.

"Clean yourself up and I will make coffee," I said.

He went into the bathroom and the shower faucet ran. I hunched over the counter of the room's kitchenette and rolled two tobacco cigarettes. In each I placed the crushed elixir rocks. A few drags would serve my purpose. I found a can of instant coffee and boiled water.

He came from the bathroom in a tattered robe. The distinct eagle insignia of the Bryson hotel chain was barely visible. I handed him a coffee.

I took the cup and walked to the littered nightstand. Among the empty packs he found his cigarettes.

"Man, I am in some trouble," he said.

I went towards him extending the cigarette I freshly rolled. "No, no try one of these. I insist," I said.

He nodded and took one. I placed a lighter to its tip and then placed the other cigarette to my lips. The faint crackle of his burning cigarette sounded as I lit mine. I saw the question in his eye as I inhaled.

I was again in the cold space. The time away had no bearing on the experience. One could never become accustomed to that plane of being.

I forced myself inside his body. The assault of his mind was blistering, but I braved through. I struck Noel's head hard with the thick glass ashtray before Gigbe could acquaint himself inside. It took a second and third blow to knock him to the ground.

I tried to stay calm. I told myself the shell was only temporary. This did not suffice. The pain was too much to bear. I wanted heroin. I felt a creeping, crawling sensation over the new skin. My nose ran viscous mucus. I was entirely sick and entirely sore.

Searching his pilfered mind I learned a bag of the substance was in the nightstand drawer. I pulled it open to the glossy image of Greg Whales on the cover of *People*. Underneath it was the stained white powder. My mouth salivated. I found his works there, too, and a small pistol which I placed into my pocket.

His residual mind directed me to fix the shot. I thought back to my gangrenous arm long removed. I thought of the pain. I shot the dope and melted into silky warm euphoria. The room, the city, and the world simply dissolved. I fell back on the unmade bed and stared up at the cracked plaster ceiling. My eyes lazily rolled to the needle that still dangled from my arm.

His thoughts drifted aimlessly through my consciousness. I thought of his first dance with the needle. I remembered the origin of the bag in the drawer. A man named Randy had not been paid for it, but that was okay. I would take care of it the next day. I thought of the parole warrant for my arrest. That was okay, too.

The effects of the drug reached their zenith and then descent. I started to feel alert and anxious. Then came an impending sense of doom. The man named Randy, a violent man, was looking for his money. He knew where Gigbe lived and would be there soon. The bag was a tenth of what I had been "fronted" and not a solitary granule was sold. I shot more of the dope and waited for my doom.

The fateful knock came to pass. By then I had crawled under the bed and pulled the pistol from my pocket.

"One, two!" came gruffly through the flimsy door. The door flew off the top hinge, coming to a limp hanging toward the ground.

It was Randy. He was intrusively large with the mallet hands of Father. I waited as he walked into the small bathroom, tore the moldy shower curtain from its rings, and then turned and opened a small cloak closet. He muttered and swore.

Inevitably, he lowered himself to look under the bed. I fired the pistol into his forehead. Little of his head remained after the blast. I sickened, but went through his pockets. There was a roll of hundred dollar bills, more heroin, and car keys.

I tossed some soiled clothing into a duffle bag and then threw the bag back to the floor. I grabbed the remaining heroin and his cash and left the room, propping the unhinged door up to seal off Randy's budget crypt.

I found the old mustang matching the taken keys. The vehicle roared to life and I exited the parking lot navigating traffic to a train station only a few miles away.

40

His hip healed enough to resume the chase. Each step was a new agony, but he had to know.

The body of Noel Garrison was cremated. An autopsy revealed "remarkable" scar tissue covering every organ, including his brain. Had the man not been murdered, he was soon to die. The family held limited calling hours in a Connecticut Funeral Parlor. Only family attended the small Catholic service.

The Taxman contacted Noel's family out of methodology rather than solace. He heard only the things he already knew. Garrison was deeply involved in drugs and wanted to be a star guitarist. He was aimless and no one could explain his association with the Gray Trust. They knew nothing of the missing parolee Gigbe.

It was another oblong piece that did not seem to fit the puzzle. There was no discernible pattern in the madness. It was as if anyone could rise up and come forward with the instrument to extract from the trust.

Ultimately, the asset was frozen. This proved meaningless. There were no attempts to access the trust at any bank. It was as if the bearer decided to forgo the millions within or the certificate was no longer in human possession.

The Taxman went to the Los Angeles police and notified them of his contact with Noel before the murder. He told them an edited tale of the trust, and provided them with names of those withdrawing funds. A keen police detective, Rogers I think, recognized names of some deceased from cold case files including the late John Holmes.

Gigbe was the obvious subject. His parole officer was notified of his involvement in the deaths of Noel Garrison and Randy Bloch. The connection to all the other murders was unfathomable. The police did not see them as connected. They thanked Dorean and agreed to share information with him.

The Taxman was not satisfied. He prepared a chart, a genealogy of death. Murder begot murder and so on and so forth. He watched the blood flow down the walls of his home. The trust did not exist until the nineteen fifties, but the murders went back further. He connected the Argentinian and suspected his involvement in the so-called suicide of the Nazi jumper.

Dorean could not dismiss the words of the dying Holmes. He desperately wanted things to be simple. He could not believe it this time. There was an explanation. He thought of his mother and the change within her at the moment of death.

Modern science was catching up with me. The Taxman and Los Angeles police collected evidence from the apartment of Noel. They found trace amounts of the elixir in a discarded bottle and a like substance in our cups of coffee. Gigbe's fingerprints were on everything, even the bloody ashtray that ended the life of Noel.

A warrant was issued for Gigbe's arrest. I was no fool; this I knew would come. The Taxman abandoned the case of Noel Garrison. His estate was worthless. He moved on to the fugitive Gigbe. Superiors were puzzled, but all he needed to do was show him the chain of the trust. Gigbe was the new man. The Taxman believed this so only for a time. He knew soon Gigbe's body would be found and the chase would continue.

41

The set was desolate. Many of the structures were real, built by union laborers on a bed of sand. Most of the buildings were façade, needing only to convince the camera frame of their reality. The desert heat sweltered the little artificial town.

A producer pounded on the trailer door. It was an outlandish rolling home, dragged through the dunes by a powerful diesel. The thing stood tall, two stories so. Inside rocked Greg Whales. He listened, waiting for the rapping at his door to stop. It always did. Everyone always gave him more time.

It had been this way for the entire shoot of *Manifest Destiny*. Whales headlined the western thriller. The trade papers reported an interesting reversal of fortune. While Whales was originally cast as the honest lawman Hank Rutherford, he now played the villain Lind. Writers burned the midnight oil to rewrite the script for extended screen time for the ruthless killer. When Bruce Willis, the original Lind, agreed to the swap, the picture seemed set in precious stone.

Variety reported Whales to be unhappy over the script and refused to film key scenes. *Inside View* reported a different tale. Undisclosed sources claimed Whales was afraid of desert creatures and refused to leave his trailer. We now all know the truth, but then nobody did.

Willis eventually left the picture gracefully, citing commitments to other projects. The studio had no choice but to let him go. There were talks of recasting the picture or filming it on a studio lot, but these ideas, like the movie became dry as the desert air.

Executives, agents, and media pundits cast about threats of lawsuits and numerous dispersions. Nothing really happened. The picture exiled back to development. Of course it was made a year or two later, without Greg

Whales or Willis, to a modest success.

Greg returned to his estate, refusing to comment. Greg's omissions receded into the annals of useless history. He would simply sit and wait for something better to come along. He secretly hoped nothing would.

42

I traveled east by rail. Leaving California, I fixed a shot of the heroin and nodded off for nearly an entire day. This vicious cycle continued until I reached Virginia. Even the heroin could not quash my desire. I would not stay, pausing only long enough to acquire more of the Vella Root from my old farm. From there, I traveled north.

I took Manhattan by hazy storm. I found a room for rent and went about the business of cooking the elixir for injection and then the smokeable rock form. I would inject the unholy combination of the elixir and the heroin which was quite pleasant. I enjoyed the velvety seduction of the heroin and the elixir divorced me from the weariness of the trip. I cared about nothing and was master of my meaningless universe.

I roamed the streets, senses heightened. I watched the Wall Street crowds descend upon the nightlife bars. They ate pills and snorted cocaine and brought home both the willing and unwilling.

The day came when I had no heroin left. I licked the bag clean and found minor solace in the elixir I was drinking, smoking, and shooting throughout the grind of the first hours apart from the drug. Then returned the sickness.

My body ached and the elixir proved not enough. I gathered what remained of my cash and walked out onto the urban street. I was lost, but eventually came upon a man selling bundles of the drug in a small run-down tavern. I bought what he had left, but found myself desperate in a matter of days. I had to escape from the body.

I returned into the night with a glass pipe and several rocks of the crystallized elixir. In the same tavern I met a man. He had striking blonde hair and piercing green eyes. His face told the tale of happiness. His physically fit frame was that of a thirty-year-old though he was edging forty. The man's name was Stephen, as was my eldest brother's name, and he worked for Con Edison as a young executive.

Stephen was searching to heighten his success with some cocaine. He told me he was a "weekend dabbler" and nothing about him stirred disbelief in me. I told him that I had in hand some rocks of cocaine and would smoke with him.

I packed it and placed the glass to my lips. Stephen looked curiously as the ignited crystal bubbled and boiled in the pipe. He reached out for the loaded pipe from me. His life was to be mine. He drew deeply. Then the world came crashing down.

A spotlight captured the two of us. Stephen ran, but was taken to the ground by an officer strategically placed behind us. I fell to the ground without force.

The New York Police Department's Central Booking was zoo-like. I sat chained, while the drunken and drugged raged about. Jail overcrowding left me on the bench until processing and transportation to another facility.

I was photographed and my fingerprints were taken. These measures would tear through the Dobson alias I gave them. The computer provided them a lengthy printout of Gigbe's indiscretions. Somehow, the murder warrants did not show. As far as they were concerned, Gigbe was merely a parole violator.

Then their error. Due to the crowding they placed me on the same bench with Stephen who had also been charged with possession of an "unidentified narcotic." Worse for him they found a small stash of a pharmacy within his jacket, nothing of which he held a prescription for. I took my chance then.

With the concentration of the elixir diminishing by the moment, I battled my way out of Gigbe's shell. The aching pain of withdrawal ceased and I was in the oppressive space between us all again. I made my spectral charge into his body and jarred him loose enough to take control. Floods of his accomplishments were followed by the agony of his parents' divorce and rejection by his father.

"What the fuck?" the man Gigbe started to scream. He looked in horror at his codefendant. I nestled in the body and life of Stephen. I looked away, indifferent to the chained madman beside me. Ultimately his thrashing and wailing resulted in being led away.

I was brought to a small run-down courtroom where I met Edwin Sarrow, the most recently hired attorney from Stephen's retained lawyer's firm. He was young with a high-pitched voice. This was not the man Stephen would have expected to see. He offered bittersweet news.

"Archie is on vacation in Italy. I was on call tonight so they sent me over," he said.

"What am I looking at with this?"

"Well this is pretty serious. All the substances have to be tested but they are charging you with possession of crack cocaine and other narcotics."

"Prison?"

"Could be two to seven years," he affirmed, "but there is a chance I could get you released if you are willing to go to a drug treatment facility. I'm going to go to bat for you."

God I wanted the elixir.

After several weeks in a holding cell I was brought to a rehabilitation center in the mountains far north from the City. The facility, named after the patron saint Joseph, was perched away in isolation. The Tudor stood proud on the mountain top.

I was greeted by a rotund black man named Elliot. He showed me to my room. It was there I figured I could reach the Vella Root and achieve another exodus. I knew I would have to bear the place until an opportune time. I laid back into the bed and slept the sleep of a free man.

The next morning came and I awoke to the rumblings of my neighbors showering and dressing. I laid there in drifting defiance and then back to sleep.

A resident woke me. He said I would be discharged if I overslept. The place was more rigorous than Pleasant Creek had been. Fearful of going back to that forsaken jail, I stood up and dressed. I followed a group of men down a stairwell until we reached a line of mostly young people. I smelled the simple delight of fried eggs and sausage.

After the hearty breakfast I was directed to an assigned group for therapy. Eight of us waited for a counselor to arrive. He did. His name was Teddy. He was dressed in a plain white dress shirt with faded jeans and Indian moccasins.

I was welcomed to the group and introduced through pleasantries and a much-abbreviated story of what brought each man to the facility. My turn then came, and I told them a combination history of myself and stolen Stephen. They did not judge me. I was welcomed into their fold.

Teddy then asked another of the group members, Patrick, to amplify a comment he had made regarding his childhood. He told us of the horrible actions of Stan, his stepfather, who placed his hand over a burning stove for spilling cola on the living room sofa.

Tears swelled in his eyes. His voice became choppy as he elaborated further on the violence and deprivations he endured. My eyes began to leak and my hands trembled. I desperately craved the elixir in any form. I wanted to run, to hide, or die. Teddy would not let me.

The group focus turned to me as each observed the dramatic sadness overtaking me. I never uttered a word, to anyone, about Father and the things that happened at the table of my childhood. I told them of the beatings, the lamp oil, and the vicious violence that opened the doors of heaven to me. I did not mention it happened over four hundred years before.

In a kind and gentle voice,Teddy told me that it was my decision to leave my pain there. I could let the turmoil of my youth free in that room. It would remain though I would be free to go. The cold hatred, contempt, and cynicism melted away and I returned to Nathan Sorren, the ugly hapless boy. I knew I was accepted wholeheartedly by this man Teddy and the place.

In that moment I no longer wanted to escape. I wanted no elixir. I wanted to recover again. I came so close before. Perhaps this was my time for redemption.

43

The flowers and fragrance could not conceal the truth of the place. It appeared as a place of help and healing, but it was equally a place of cold death. Dorean thumbed through a dated magazine, not so much reading and looking at pictures than pretending he was not there. He could only think of his dead son and the dead porn star.

Cancer had taken to his body as it had his son. The aching bones were no longer just arthritis or the hip broken in my escape from him, but a festering bloom of malignant cells. He was amidst a grueling infusion of toxic chemicals and a surgery, battling the disease to fleeting remissions.

Today was a good day. He told his office a dental appointment would take his afternoon. He could not tolerate a flock of well-wishers in every cubicle. If he were going to live or die he would do so in private. The Taxman did not want them to know he was contemplating surrender.

The electric box on his waist chirped. He pulled it up to him and saw the number was from his office. He rushed to the reception desk and was permitted by the girl at her post to use the phone despite her rolling eyes. Gigbe was captured and locked away in an asylum.

"There is something else," said the ominous office chained agent at the other end of the phone.

"What?"

"Well it's crazy babble, but Gigbe claims somebody stole his body. He thinks he's possessed. I already talked to his treating physician. The guy is a certified lunatic."

Somebody had stolen his body. The Taxman placed the phone on its cradle and looked to the receptionist.

"I need to reschedule."

Within the hour he was boarding a plane to New York. His mind raced through his conversation with Holmes, a conversation he believed. He denied himself too much reflection in the matter, but here it was again. The thing, this creature, was moving again. It remained his secret theory. To share such with his superiors would result in immediate retirement. He would be another worn old one on his way out of the world.

He could justify the trip. Gigbe was now subject prime. From the air phone he called the Los Angeles police to find they already had wind of the arrest and commitment. They were sending detectives and a forensic psychiatrist. The Taxman would arrive first.

He detested being inside yet another institution. They were all so much the same. Whether in the intensive care ward of a hospital, a jail, or the center for oncology, there was that lingering smell of antiseptic and the chorus of screams and tears.

That bright Con Edison executive was there, locked away in the body of Gigbe and a cage for madmen. He did not know he was lucky to survive his encounter with me. He only knew that his body and life were pilfered. He was not going to be alone in his belief.

"My name is Paul Dorean and I know you are not crazy," the Taxman said, "but I need you to tell me everything."

From within the drugged daze Dorean saw the man's relief. The muted rage and desperation yielded to a pleasant acceptance. Recognition was all the man needed in the world.

Then the brief, but fantastic story came. The Taxman now held two accounts of my existence, albeit one from a dying liar and the other from an incompetent felon. These were the companies we kept.

Dorean decided then to come forward with his theory on the tale. If they called him crazy there was nothing he could do. "That was on them," as his mother once said. He would reveal the facts: the elixir, the murders, the Gray Trust, and the claims of body transference. What else could he call it?

44

I had fallen far in my short relapse with the elixir. Over the months of treatment I poured myself into all they offered. I cried. I confessed, in part. I failed to disclose my supernatural knowledge or abilities, but I was as honest as I could be at the time. They say that it is your secrets that keep you sick.

In addition to the group therapy and individual counseling I returned to Narcotics Anonymous. A man from outside the facility agreed to be my sponsor, but I mostly shared with Teddy.

Teddy directed me to complete a fourth step. I set forth a "fearless and searching moral inventory of myself." The list should contain the entire harm caused to others. He assured me it was confidential regardless of content.

Weeks later I handed him two tablets full of my writings. I omitted my ability and the uses of it, but included much of the incidental murders and thieving, which I found to be unbearable burdens in sobriety. He dismissed me.

Another week passed and he brought me to his messy office. I was certain that he would only see a monster. His eyes, however, failed to betray him. Teddy projected that same accepting kindness.

"You have lived a wicked life," he said calmly, "but that was not you. That was the animal, deranged from a life of drug abuse, and a horrid childhood," he said. He placed a firm grip on my knee. "In this office, at this moment, you will let this all go. Forgive yourself for your God already has done so."

This simple step worked. Instantly, I felt the weight of four hundred and fifty years of evil release me from its crushing mass. Perhaps there still could have been heaven for me. Perhaps there was no destiny in that enveloping dark place.

The relief was fleeting. A very real concern reached the surface of my thoughts. It was only a time before that wretched old Taxman, or a successor, would find his way to Stephen Dade. This was a certainty.

This reservation remained. I no longer wanted to steal lives or kill, but the transformation was incomplete. I would need to change just one more time. This would be the last. Control was possible with a plan. I would live, grow old, and die just as the mortals did. These things I told myself.

I needed to find the perfect body and life. I erred not in my desire to live like other people do, but I set my sights too low. Perhaps I needed to find a life of resource and privilege. If it were to work, me remaining as one man, then it would have to be a great one with power and wealth. I would have to be loved. There could be no questions.

This epiphany did come complete with the fear that one drink of the elixir would send me on a binge lasting decades. Yet no other decision remained.

Cosmic relief of this choice freed me. I would remain Stephen until sure. There was time to look and think. Only when the moment was right would I roam one final time.

I graduated the program. Next was a halfway house in urban Queens. The choice benefited me two-fold. I could stay committed to my sobriety and avoid detection under confidentiality. The residence afforded me eighteen months to find my mark. Temptation ebbed and flowed, but I remained steadfast. Self-help meetings and counseling perpetuated my abstinence. I even made friends again. No longer some fairy tale beast. I was a man with a life, hope, and dreams. I remained a man with a secret.

45

He wrestled his aching hands as he waited for Roberts to enter the office. Dorean needed to share the facts. The delay was eternal.

"Good morning," Roberts said. He offered a worn, but pleasant face. He removed his sport coat and loosened his tie.

"Hello Marty," the Taxman responded.

"I have this memo and quite frankly I want to know what it is you are getting at."

The Taxman cited the file number and told him all of the sparse fruits of his investigation into the Gray Trust, its enigmatic creator, and its beneficiaries. The elusive man, or men, raised the eyebrows of Roberts. Dorean refrained from sharing his belief in the otherworldly claims made along the way. He was prepared to say the words "body snatcher."

"My primary person of interest is now Stephen Dade," the Taxman offered.

"Stephen Dade. Dade, oh yes, this was the identity your maniac Gigbe claims?"

"Yes, sir."

"Leads from the psych wards of New York?" he asked through a smile.

"In a way. There is something remarkable happening here, Marty. I have followed disappearing people over four decades and never once has anything been like this. Assets and people shift and change. In the end they are always the same people, always the same things. Nobody in these pages had anything to do with one another before the transfers. They meet, give up millions to the next, end up dead or insane, and it goes on like this."

"What are you proposing?" he asked.

"A body snatcher, for lack of a better term."

Roberts buried his face in his hands and rubbed his eyes. He looked back to the Taxman, perhaps surveying him for hints of dementia. Unexpectedly Roberts stood and turned away.

"Anything is possible," he said.

This declaration was unsettling to the Taxman. To him it meant either his superior believed his conclusion to some degree or Roberts was figuring how to pacify him. He dared to go forward.

"Is that so?" the Taxman inquired.

Without turning back, Roberts said, "I know a story, well part of a story, from when I was an agent. It must have been twenty years ago. Something caught old HAL's magnetic eye."

"What was it?"

"Something unusual, indeed, not unlike your suggestion here. You see, there was a man, Kneids, Dobri Kneids, who faithfully paid his taxes each year of his life. He was wealthy, a keen investor, really."

"Is that the unusual part? A rich man paying his taxes?"

"Funny. No, he paid them for eighty years."

"I pay my taxes and I'm getting there myself."

"The sixteenth amendment was ratified in nineteen thirteen. From our best intelligence Dobri Kneids was already forty-five years old when he filed his first return in nineteen fifteen."

"He lived to be one hundred and thirty years old?"

"Well there is more to it than that."

"In nineteen eighty-two Jim Banks, a field agent, went on a routine audit call to his home. Kneids lived in Baltimore at the time. His finances were immaculate to the half-penny."

"Jim killed himself in nineteen eighty-three," I recalled.

"Jim reported then that the man he audited was about six feet tall with brown hair and eyes. He guessed him to weigh one hundred and eighty pounds. He estimated his age to be forty."

"My God."

"Of course we checked and rechecked, running it through HAL and agents. There was no mistake. It was the same man."

Roberts finally turned and looked to the Taxman. Without breaking eye contact he lowered himself and pulled a leather portfolio from a bottom drawer in his desk. He slid it across.

"I took these from Jim's desk when he died. Nobody knows I made these copies."

The Taxman opened the folder and saw some notes on yellowed white paper. His eyes went to some cryptic comment.

December 12, 1982 – went again to Kneids. He was friendly and receptive to my visit. Sometime inside he put something into my head. It won't leave.

Behind the notes were two photo static copies of photographs. The first was from the Department of Immigration and Naturalization. He showed a photo of Kneids when he entered the United States from Bulgaria. He was the proverbial tall, dark, and handsome man. The second copied photograph was taken at the audit. The picture showed the very same man unaltered by the passed time. The realization sent an aching chill through Dorean's arthritic, dying bones.

"There are things in this world we just will never understand. This is one of those things. Keep this to yourself, but do not stop. I will be in touch," Roberts said turning away from the Taxman again. With that Paul Dorean left the office.

The matter did not end there. Instructions were in place for such circumstances like those Dorean exposed. Like his superior in the time of Jim Banks, Roberts dialed a number never used. The act ignited a spur of activity inconspicuous to the Taxman. Not even Roberts knew where these things went from there.

46

He was the one. We watched him fill the screen in the latter decade of the twentieth century. He brought us to the ancient battles of the earth, beyond the stars of our galaxy, and into deep recesses of the human condition. It was not just the films of Greg Whales that drew me.

His image was everywhere. The man was all things. His celebrity was detained by no earthly bounds. He was beamed around the world to television and computer screens. Crisp high definition amplified the perfection of his face and body to the plane of gods.

My obsession formed in all of the works described herein before. The compulsion to become Greg Whales solidified in *Bouquet*. Filmed before the false start of *Manifest Destiny*, it was there he showed me that he was all I could ever want.

The film centered on an arrogant businessman who cheated his partners, his wife, and all of a large city as he fell into the throws of a gambling addiction. The pain he carried through the egotistical shell of his character, Mitchell Morgan, was layered beyond human doings. He was the best that ever lived.

I sat in the dark theater. Whales looked down. His pain was my pain. I believed he could understand the night cries my victims launched in my dreams. He could know on the inside I was human, like he, and the both of us went through life pretending to be somebody else. He was my mark; in him I would lead a life worth living.

For months I read all I could find on the man. I found the trade journals and all of the gossip surrounding him. I learned his favorite foods and wines.

In the night I crept away from the halfway house with the significant monies taken from Dade's retirement account. I traveled by bus to Virginia and then off to California. The New York authorities may have sought me out, but I did not plan on remaining Stephen Dade very much longer.

For days and nights I parked a short distance from his home in a tricked out rented Humvee. The vehicle was absorbed in the glamour and desperate photographers around Whales' neighborhood. I watched his deliveries and shift changes. I watched medical professionals come and go to the estate. Then I saw my entry.

Weekly, Whales received a delivery from India House. His love of curried dishes and the flat breads of the cuisine had been the subject of idiot interviews. India House catered only to upscale clientele, but I found it relatively easy to reach inside.

I followed the driver back to the store. Its owner had been the hardworking son of immigrated parents who built three stores. His parents graciously gave him one of the outlets upon his graduation from business school. Veejay, a young Indian man, proved capable in both his marketing and lifestyle. He began to socialize in higher and higher circles, finding himself supplying the swankiest Hollywood eateries.

Veejay gambled and drank, but worked from his offices every day I watched. In his shadow I found his haunts. I brewed a new batch of elixir as I determined the place I would know the man.

I sat across from Veejay at a Los Angeles Casino. The game was poker. I watched for a time and saw my advantage. From within, I knew how the shrewdest thinkers thought. The game and he were no exception.

I chased the man into a number of pots, allowing him his victories here and there. I played his confidence while I sipped the elixir and read his mind. He was a fine gentleman. His biggest secret was his women, kept not from a wife, but from his mother and father who frowned greatly on both promiscuity and interracial intercourse.

As the night drew along, the alcohol and excitement merged into a melancholy atmosphere. Only he and I survived the steady stream of bankrolls gone bust. This had not gone unnoticed by him.

"What's your name, man?" he asked.

I told him my name and that I was trying to become a full time player, a dream he would admire. He complimented my game. I told him I was doing well but was looking for a steady paycheck during daylight hours. He had taken an interest in me.

"What line of work are you in?" he asked as he spied at the cards he lifted slightly off of the felt table. He threw them to the muck before I had a chance to answer.

"I worked for Con Ed in New York, but left to open a catering business. I couldn't make a go of it," I said.

"Interesting," he said. He rubbed the stubble under his chin. "Here's my card. I like you. Maybe I have got something for you."

It was that easy. I was in consideration for employment by a man with direct access to the home of Greg Whales. All this in a blink of time. Opportunity was pounding on the gates of my hell.

After more drinks he told me that he delivered the finest of foods to celebrities throughout Los Angeles and the surrounding territories. He mentioned no names. I only cared about the one. We enjoyed each other's company for another hour or so and parted with a friendly handshake.

I called him the following day and set a time to meet with him later in that week. At our meeting I brought all of those things required for one to find employment. We talked little of the job and much about the game of poker. The application proved a mere formality and I started employment with his firm the following week.

I worked hard for the man each day and night. I remained in his favor with my knowledge of his products and the camaraderie we shared with one another. I sought and received all the shifts available so I would eventually deliver to Whales.

I continued to study the life of the actor. There was much speculation about his mental stability. *Inside View* cast its dispersions that Whales was receding from the public into his own small world. I ignored this, believing the man simply needed a break from being Greg Whales. This would be my way to tempt him. I could provide him the anonymity he so desperately desired.

47

Imagine the loneliest man, a castaway inside a creation of stone. Servants whirled about cleaning and primping the palace to perfection. The staff, like the contents of the home, were just things. Greg Whales made no connections to things.

I knew only the rumors of his mental demise. Enveloping darkness surrounded Whales. It was not the real hell I knew to follow this life, but it was the same to him all the less. I continued my belief that Whales was fine, just tired of the barrier fame had placed between him and the world. Denial runs deep.

He sat in a throwaway room drinking scotch and fighting away the creeping tiredness his medicines made. Watching television was of no use. He could not concentrate on the images.

Greg fell out of contact with his handlers. Calls from his agent, business managers, and publicists went unanswered. Many visited, yet none were granted admittance to the estate. His staff followed orders without question. He wished he could do without them as well.

Time was beginning to lay its marks upon him. Whales' skin subtly wrinkled at his eyes and brow. His hair was colored. He was consulting with a surgeon specializing in follicle transplantation to fill the receding arches of his temples. Even his body, perfectly honed and trained to invisible degrees of specificity, was starting to fill and expand ever so slightly.

The fears racing through his mind were incoherent. There was no logic or reason within. Bursts of adrenaline rushed through him when he thought of the world outside. There still were moments of rash lucidity, but they were fleeting.

The adoration of the world was nothing. The years within the public eye were not a capital to spend against the progression of his illness. Nothing could halt the amplifying madness.

This is how I imagine him now, pathetic and worn. Then my candle still burned for his life. Through him I would become a man, a defrocked human returning to his race. I did not appreciate the deviations inside him.

48

"It is important for you to keep these appointments," said the physician. The man championed Dorean's battle with the disease and was eager to fight. Dorean was not; he was lowering his dukes to the malaise of infirmity and old age.

Death was now his only secret. His theory of the body tripper was underdeveloped, but out there all the same.

"I know, I know," said the Taxman.

"There are advancements coming down the pipe all the time. My friends at U.C.L.A. should be your friends, too. Please, take this referral."

The Taxman assented to placate the caring physician. He felt he owed the man. He accepted the card with the intention of seeing what they offered.

With that he left. His mind repressed his condition and returned to mine. Roberts not only encouraged his pursuit, but also demanded it. He received word that all of his other cases were reassigned. His sole purpose at the Service was to craft my doom.

He reviewed the old notes and followed the old leads. Again he was in the uncomfortable position of waiting for my next move. Laws of confidentiality and the reality of anonymity protected Stephen Dade. Again, there was nowhere to begin.

49

In the sack I placed the stuffed parathas and lobia; on top of it a copy of the novel *Tale of the Body Thief* by Anne Rice. In the novel a bored centuries old vampire is offered the same gift I was to offer Whales. The night creature swapped his immortal body for one of flesh and blood. The creature learned what it was to enjoy the sun, the physical love of a woman, and the pleasure of eating foods and drinking wine.

On the inside of the paperback's cover I wrote:

> *I, too, know the pain of living in the world of our choices. Take comfort in the fact that I can offer to you an escape from your life, either temporary or permanent. Know me by my true name.*
>
> *Sorren*

I considered other methods of enticement, though none proved to be necessary. I needed to draw him in. Some mystery and hope could trump the absurdity of my claim. I would leave it up to Greg Whales.

Following the suggested exercise of his spiritual therapist, Gi, Whales braved through a side door of his home. He walked within the outdoor confines and made way to the tower to receive the two bags of delivered groceries. The small turret-topped building was the guardhouse at the front and only gate.

He took the bag and set it upon a small marble-top table serving one of the many side entrances into the home. From the satchel he removed the book placed on top. He read the book before. He was even offered the lead role in a proposed adaptation of the work, but declined before the production all-together ceased. This, of course, I knew.

Whales enjoyed the story and fantasized even then about slipping out of his celebrity and into the open spaces of normality and anonymity. He carried the book out and away from his body as though he was barely accepting the strange gift.

His library was elaborate. The books on the mahogany shelves were purchased throughout the world. Experts of literature consulted and returned a list of the prize works that would "make the room," or so the interior designer told him. Original printings of *Quixote* nestled beside a second and third century's bibles. Whales read none of his priceless works.

In a distant corner rested those he fancied. Some were popular horror stories written within the last thirty years. There were King's *The Dead Zone*, Koontz's representative works, and an embarrassing number of self-help books. Then there were the books of Rice.

He compared the delivered copy to his. They were identical in every respect, though I gave him an edition from its second printing and he owned the first. Also lacking was the clever note inside from the author that she believed Whales would have made a better Lestat.

During the comparison, he came upon my inscription. As he read it a cold wind brushed his back. He knew not whether this was a simple offering from another unstable fan or the idea that somebody knew of the maddening discomfort he was feeling living his much-envied life. His frontal mind asked that he dismiss the note's suggestion as the psychosis of yet another of the disturbed enthusiasts. The core of his mind wanted desperately to believe that such possibilities exist.

When I returned to the store and learned that there had been no phone call from the estate, no complaint over the delivery of a book gift, I was certain the man had been intrigued. It was all I could ask for and the most I could expect. I wanted to drive back to his estate and offer him the knowledge both then and there, but did no such thing. I resolved a patient approach to this finest catch and I would not hinder my efforts with the impetuous nature that had so often been my fall.

India House delivered to the place no less than once a week and through trick and trade I was assured I would be the one. It was my belief that this time he would be waiting for me.

The following day an assistant of Whales called and asked that a collection of spices and our specialty curry be delivered post haste. I smiled, loading the purchase orders for that day. My last stop would be at his home. I wanted him to wait so he would want it all the more.

I arrived at the guarded gate in the delivery van. The vehicle was marked "India House" leaving no mistake as to my identity as I neared. The familiar faced guard, branded by the metal plate pinned to his shirt as Hanson, offered the most splendid news.

"Mr. Whales asked that you deliver the goods directly to the main house," he said in an official soldier tone. "After, of course, I inspect the vehicle and the contents of any and all packages within the vehicle."

I was happy to oblige. I exited the van and placed my hands on its hood. Hanson frisked my person and indulged in each of my pockets. There was nothing but my wallet with a license, a bottle of the elixir, and thirteen dollars. He wrinkled his nose at the bottle, but returned it. He inspected my vehicle. Hanson waved me forward toward the house.

The double door of the stone home was grand indeed. It was made of a dark stained wood surrounded by a recessed casing of carved granite. In its grooves small angels and devils encircled a branch of thorn and leaves. The entrance looked as though plucked from some ambitious castle of my youth.

Those antiquated times were served by little else. Perched over the door was a menacing camera making small humming noises as it focused itself on me. The door had both a pad were one could place a palm for immediate access and a button activating the bell. The home was a technological wonder concealed in the cold architecture of ancient times.

I depressed the doorbell and became enchanted by its tone, an arrangement composed for Whales by John Williams. As the music completed, the door opened to an elderly woman wearing black and white. Her eyes held knowing intelligence and order.

"Good evening, sir. Mister Whales has asked if you would be so kind as to make delivery in his study," she said.

I nodded and showed her the bags to be delivered. She asked me to follow her into the study, a large open room off from the library. In the distance I heard running water. At a broad desk sat the most famous actor in the world, Greg Whales.

"Sorren," he said as our eyes met. Whales motioned with a nod of his head, dismissing his house servant. I offered him a pleasant smile. "Please sit," he directed.

I sat in the chair pushed back from the front of his desk. I scanned the man and found no evidence of the claims of *Inside View* and the other scandal sheets. His eyes told a tale of confidence and shrewd mental health. I did not expand my consciousness as I was not under the influence of the elixir. One premature drink of the beverage could send me out of control and I could not risk this with such a delicate plan.

"Very good, but I am not interested," he said with a congratulatory smile of his white and perfect teeth. I did not understand and told him just that.

"The book. Don't get me wrong. It's a great book. I enjoyed it, but it's just not something I hold in interest. I do not regret passing on the character before and do not wish to play it now. I take it you are its producer. Elaborate, indeed."

"No, I am nothing of the sort," I responded. I understood what he thought but was not prepared for this perception of me. I fumbled forward through the moment.

50

Then it came. Only days passed since the Taxman left his concession with the doctor trying to save his life. He did make the call as he promised, but did not care if he lived or died in the moment. They scheduled him an appointment. He pondered how history was defined with people while the present was defined by its institutions.

Phones rang and paper was shuffled around. The Taxman was oblivious to it all. He stood outside of time. He stared down at a photograph of Stephen Dade wondering what was inside of him. He thought of a movie he watched after his divorce. It was *The Hidden*, the story of a malevolent alien overtaking the bodies of earthlings for its own pleasure seeking ends. I had seen the film, too.

The rumbling machine beside him sounded. From it came what he was waiting for. Again, I fell victim to the infernal wage reporting laws. This was not my error. I did it on purpose, thinking I could get to Whales before the information was processed. The machines advanced under Moore's Laws and I was largely ignorant to their speed and efficiency.

Within the hour he held the name, address, and number for the India House. He folded it and informed Roberts he was going to perform a perfunctory check. Roberts called the secret number again.

51

"What I have to offer you is something grand, indeed. It is not what you believe it to be," I said.

"Look, I am just not interested. I'll give you credit. I have been offered some parts before-"

"I want to offer you a gift, a reprieve if you will," I said to him calmly.

"A reprieve?"

"Yes, the greatest reprieve. This gift would allow you a brief escape from yourself."

"I admit this is an ingenious way to get my attention. You're very convincing, but I just don't have the time. It's not something I am interested in doing," he answered.

"No, it is not a script or a commercial or anything of the sort. You do not understand what it is I wish to offer you."

"What is it then?" he asked.

"Your life. Your freedom. Your anonymity."

His eyes changed. He calculated me as a lunatic, not some ambitious writer or producer set out to impress a star. I did not need to expand to know this of his thoughts.

"Well, regardless, I am not interested. I will have to ask you to leave. Thank you."

"Oh, but give me one more moment to explain. Let me show you I can do what it is I will propose. I will allow you to enter this body. You will have your consciousness inside of this body for any length of time you choose." I hurried this out of my mouth. In doing so I lost much of the cool confidence I enjoyed when I arrived.

"Right. Like I said, I am just not interested."

"I suggest a week."

He motioned to a member of his security staff appearing behind me and placing a gentle hand on my shoulder.

I continued, "It would be you. You would be you, but disguised in a body where nobody would recognize you. You would be in this exact body I am in now!"

"I have listened to your proposal and decline it. I am finished. Now, Reid here will show you out the front gate."

"Take my number then. Do not dismiss this so readily. Consider it. You could leave this place, any place, with no mobs, no photographers shouting out to you. I know this to be what you want. I will give you time to be!"

With that I walked from the room. Both his personal assistant and the one called Reid dismissed me with grim looks.

"Oh, Mr. Whales, one more thing." I reached into my topcoat and held out a small glass bottle of the elixir. "Drink this and see."

"Absolutely not!" piped out Reid. I did not let his objection stop my motion of placing the drink on the table. Whales did not fail to notice this.

I walked from the room. I heard his footsteps coming behind me. He held out the flask.

"I do not want this!" he shouted.

I saw that as Whales bellowed in protest his fingers clutched the elixir ever the tighter. I was excited by his personal involvement. It was not Reid or a servant rejecting me.

"Drink it," I whispered.

Our eyes met and I saw him as I knew him to be all the long. Whales was hungry. He would first know the escape and separation of the elixir and then he would desire our exchange.

52

That unassuming fellow, the old man rife with surface pleasantry, arrived at India House. Dorean learned I was on a lengthy run and would likely not return until the next workday. I did not answer calls to my company phone.

The infernal ringing box on my waist alerted me to his presence. Vijay called for me. A dark skinned foreigner could ill afford a standoff with any federal bureau.

The Taxman was aloof. He claimed a confidential investigation required that he speak with Stephen Dade. The man looked pale, "like he was dying painfully," Vijay said. Remember, as Dade I never withdrew from the trust or committed any act. He was a simple person of interest, an interest held by the Taxman alone.

Dorean had my address. The elderly man raced the motor. He arrived at the rented home. The grass was overgrown and mail crowded the simple black box bolted to the side of the front door. I had never been particularly reliable in matters of upkeep and maintenance. My obsession with Whales was everything.

He looked up and down the street and thumbed through the mail. It was all glossy advertisements. The top one read "To: Stephen Dade or Current Resident." With some force, he tried the front door. It was unlocked. This was my oversight. He stepped into the dwelling with great caution.

The old man lived a rigid code of conduct. He did not speed on the roadways. In the dissolution of his marriage he gave his wife everything. He did not even gossip at work. His obsession got the better of him. It was now he, too, afoul of the law.

"Hello?" the old one asked into the dark stillness of the house.

No response. He continued about, lifting little things here and there, but found nothing. He pulled a small pad and pen from the breast of his jacket. He scribbled a note requesting contact and included his business card. His resourcefulness was further proved by the small roll of tape he kept in his pocket. It was handy to fasten notices and cards to the doors and windows of those eluding him.

He then drove out of the driveway and parked his car across the street. He looked down to the sandwich on the passenger seat. The Taxman could eat nothing other than the pills that masked the pain of his aching frame.

Dorean would stay there all night for a glimpse.

53

The offer was a tangible shard in the physical world. Though without color, texture, or mass it was as much a fixture of his home as any other article. I left it there with him. He would doubt and question as he should. Then would come fanciful consideration. Seeded deep within him was all he would need to come to believe in me. The world delivered Greg Whales to me in that way.

He stood alone in the foyer. His eyes traced the intricate pattern of the white and cream ceramic. He looked up the long winding double staircase. He browsed the art of unspeakable value hanging flat on the bright white walls. His watch was worth more than most homes. Yet, he had nothing.

Somewhere in his mind he heard the mockery of his father. "Faggot." "Pussy." "Queer bait." He remembered the wreckage of the last photograph of his family before it turned on itself. His mother was worn, but still beautiful. Manly kindness rested in the eyes of his father holding his brother with his free hand on Greg's shoulder.

Phantom blood of the suicide fan crept slowly over him. He felt the warmth and salty viscous. Everything dissolved within the flashes and screams. He thought of Rolla Sansone and knew how close he approached Rolla's state of being. Greg was alone on his descent to madness. Everybody is. Once within, there is more company than one can bear. A handful of different pills would ready him for the journey.

The lines of the two men's lives ran parallel, Sansone having only the benefit of departing on his own road to madness before the conception of Greg Aberdine. There were others too, but Greg lacked access to the withdrawn. Sansone would receive him on the side opposite of sanity.

The eccentric recluse lived in the house central to the cluster of an isolated group of homes. This tiny neighborhood once was an enclave for entertaining people of Malibu. His estate occupied the entire three square miles. His brick Tudor was by no means the most extravagant of the homes on the parcel, but it did rest in the center hidden by the other dwellings.

Some of the other buildings were used as staff lodging. Most were empty, but not lifeless. Any one of them could accommodate a large family at any time. Over the years these homes filled with star struck employees of Sansone until they were subjected to his bizarre demands.

Rolla had risen to stardom in the late nineteen fifties in a series of westerns. He was handsome, large, and powerful with the grizzled looks of a middle-aged man while only in his twenties. He sprang from the cowboy pictures into a number of genres. Somewhere between *Gravel Road* and *Aliens Amongst Us* the tremors began.

The shaking was mild. He considered the possibility that the scotch took a bad turn somewhere. He stopped drinking it after lunch. Nothing changed at best; maybe it was worse. Sansone stopped drinking all together to no avail.

He found when the cameras were off he could barely muster a word when amongst a group of people. He felt a powerful constriction in his throat though his personal physician found no physical explanation. His powerful connections afforded him a delay to the start of *Stone or Steel.* Sansone spent the time consulting with psychiatrists and other doctors. He settled on the prescription of a strong sedative that arrested the tremors and eased the mounting anxiety.

Sansone somehow made way to the location set of *Stone or Steel* in Brazil. The shoot was disastrous. The medication left him tired and irritable. He was incapable of remembering dialogue beyond a sentence or two, let alone delivering effectively. He slept into each afternoon despite the director and crew hammering on his trailer door.

The actor then disappeared for a number of days without explanation according to the *Unauthorized Biography of the Great Sansone.* He returned to the set demanding that no inquiries be made. Having put down the pills, Sansone improved and filming was completed. Critics remarked that never had Sansone achieved such believability in any role. His "terror was so genuine it left them crawling out of their seat..." Hollywood rumor circulated that Rolla received counsel of a supernatural nature to aid him.

He returned to Malibu, to the neighborhood he would one day own. When he walked outside the door of the home the first time, the tremors returned. His heart raced and his throat tightened. He could barely walk, but found when he went back inside the house he was fine. He braved his way to yet another psychiatrist who diagnosed agoraphobia. Soon Sansone would not leave his home for days, then weeks, and then years at a time.

Rather than fade into oblivion during this decline, he parlayed his significant earnings into his own finance-production company. He worked over the telephone from his house. The venture immediately scored with successive box office champions. I loved his work on the screen, but he proved to be an even more heralded producer. His last great achievement was the first of the *Jaded Sun* pictures. Whispers of his supernatural entanglements continued.

It was only natural for Greg Whales to seek the counsel of Rolla. They had grown close during preproduction. Greg, still young and eager, visited Sansone frequently in those days. His dealings with the supernatural were limited to bogus spiritual advisers and the latex and CGI creatures he befriended and battled in his films. He had been a Christian, an agnostic, a low level scientologist, a Brother of Kenu, and all combinations of the four, but knew of no magic in the world.

When Greg Whales walked to the giant double doors of his home, Rolla had not worked in any fashion for eleven years. The man continued to make millions through residuals and licensing deals, lifting nary a finger. Sansone grew morbidly obese, addicted to powerful hypnotics, and did nothing other than watch syndicated television repeats and the security cameras that monitored his property.

Whales walked ginger steps towards the door of the home. The exterior was maintained yet stood as lifeless as the surrounding structures. The door opened to him before he sounded the chimes.

There were two reasons Greg Whales traveled to see Rolla that day. The first was the speculation surrounding Sansone's disappearance and bettered reemergence on the set in Brazil. The second reason was more primal. Whales knew that his life was coming undone and thought Sansone offered a speculative glance into his own bleak future.

Whales found Rolla in the study. The room was filled with litter and filth. Sansone sat in an oversized chair, wearing only a soiled bathrobe and ancient slippers. The withdrawn actor emitted a foul odor of onion and sweat. The air in the room filled with the ammonia stench of urine.

Whales scanned the room to consider the source. He found it. Along the top of an antique bookcase were jars filled with a cloudy yellow liquid. The jars sat aged and open. Dividing them was an aged photo of Rolla and his equally famous screen partner Leone.

"Greg Whales," the fat actor said. The throaty voice crackled under the stress of non-use. His eyes remained on the television testimonials for users of a wrinkle lifting facial cream.

"Rolla."

Greg sat on the sofa. A blanket and pillow bunched at the opposite end of the couch implied that it also served as a bed for Sansone. Whales ignored the dampness beneath him.

"To what do I owe the pleasure of your visit?"

"Something is happening to me. I need your help."

"What is happening?"

"This," Greg said with tears swelling in his eyes. He motioned to the surrounding room

"I apologize for the disarray. It is my own fault. I do not permit the help in this room for any reason. I am today unable to tend to such affairs."

The room looked to Greg as if years passed with no intervention to the accumulating filth. He saw no benefit in trying to understand the reasons for Sansone's exile. He simply wanted to see it, to know where he was descending.

"Tell me of Brazil," Greg said.

Through the haze of all the pills, Greg saw a shimmering terror in Sansone's dopey eyes. The request could not be revoked. He had to have his answer.

"Please tell."

A rogue tear leaked from the aged actor's eye. Greg found himself within Sansone's pain.

"Much of the story is known, the truth of it imbedded in the bits and pieces of those rag papers I despised in those days. When they weren't spilling lies about Leone and I as lovers, they were paying waiters to eavesdrop on my dinners. These are some of those papers that now haunt you. Not to say that they've left me. No. They sit and wait, hoping for some photograph of me in this way I now am, or even better, me on that cold table that awaits each of us."

He paused for a labored breath. "My condition started before Brazil. It came on like a summer storm, a sprinkle and then full rain. In Brazil the loudest thunderclaps sounded. The fear unraveled there. I could do nothing but remain in the trailer set for me."

He adjusted his girth and swallowed a few powder blue pills without the benefit of a beverage to wash them down.

"I could not leave let alone work. After a few days, I enticed my physician to travel there and examine me. He found no physical malady, but suggested I suffered from agoraphobia. Are you familiar with this disorder?"

"Of course," Greg answered.

"The director presented me with time, filming the scenes I did not appear in. This afforded some weeks to try a number of prescriptions. It was settled on a powerful hypnotic. The drug subdued the terror, which still boiled beneath the thin membrane of the substance's design. Celebration of the arrived upon "cure" proved fleeting. I became able to exit the trailer and walk about the set, but was of no functional value to the production. I could remember no lines or marks. In this you would understand my embarrassment."

Here Sansone transformed. As his tale grew in momentum, he returned to the being he'd once been. He was now illuminated, but in no pleasant way.

"In my arrogance I abandoned my physician and sought a more primordial counsel. A crewman, one plucked from the nearest village of the shoot, directed me to an old woman, Mathula. According to the man, Mathula was skilled in the art of medicine, seemingly able to resolve all matters of ailment. I sent the crewman to her."

Sansone readjusted his position on the seat. His eyes closed. His face winced before his eyes opened.

"Of course I could not go to her. In dark irony she would not come to me. With this a bizarre arrangement became. The liaison crewman went with a small bundle of American dollars and a note offering a suggestion to our dilemma. I would consume enough of the pills to render me unconscious and hired men would bring me to her."

There was the same break in his continence.

"Within the hour the crewman returned with her response. 'Yes.' She gave the crewman a powder held in a small leather satchel. She said I would consume the powder and her aides would come for me."

"You took the powder?"

"Of course. Acting was my life, my identity. It was everything and I could feel it fading into the air outside me. I mixed the powder with water and drank it down. Within moments I was unconscious. I awoke to the sweltering stench of the medicine woman's hut of baked mud and straw. I was certain of this without inquiry. Some unidentifiable blackened animal spun on a spit feeding smoke through the open center of the hut's roof. Her plump gray hand turned the stick handle. 'Almost,' she said.

"Her face was turned from me as she peppered the meat with pinches of this and that. My skin crawled outside of the comforts of my trailer, yet I stayed hypnotized by the rotating flesh.

"More time passed and she pulled meat from the bone and motioned for me to take and eat. I devoured the flesh.

"You see, I did not see this to be the ritual. I thought the meat to be mere sustenance, but was wholly in error. In my last bites the room trembled. The clay pots and plants shook, some of them falling to the dirt floor on their sides. The disturbance seemed to emanate from the fire burning in the center of the room. I looked to it. No, I looked into it.

"From its direct center I saw a void. It was not a hole. It was a space in the world. It was a place without matter. At first it was no larger than a quarter. Then it expanded to the size of my fist.

"The room darkened and from the void burst forth a thing I can describe only as an energy. It had both shape and form, but it was transparent and malleable. It first grew man sized, and then up and through the roof of the hut.

"It was a monstrous tower shooting to skyward infinity. Then it returned, an arch of energy high above the woman's patchwork home with a descending return to the earth. The energy sought not the void. It entered me fully and completely.

"I said little to the woman and ignored surfacing thoughts that the meat I had eaten was human. I cannot tell you to this day why I drew such inference. Perhaps it came from some ancient innate guilt. I have no proof to either end.

"I walked from the hut and found transportation to the set where I commanded the director to begin with me. I carried through the production bold and confident, perhaps more so than ever. But I was filled with the fear of what entered me. I knew then that the thing took as much as it gave."

Sansone paused to close his eyes. He swayed slightly to some imagined chord and then returned to the present.

"Now that I have been forthright into your confidences, tell me why you ask."

Greg lowered his eyes to the matted carpet beneath his feet. He suffered greatly just being from his home, but still felt embarrassed in what he was about to tell Sansone.

"I believe you. That is I want to believe in such things," he said without lifting his head. "Someone has made an offer to me. They have offered to rid me of a condition very real and personal. I don't know, maybe I came here to hear myself out loud."

"What is this offer?" Sansone asked.

"A man has come to me telling me he can rid me of this," Greg said spreading out his arms. "He tells me he can give me a new body and a new life."

"This man, what makes you think he can even accomplish such a feat?" Rolla asked. The appearance of the obese actor changed again, his face drained of the little color that had braved forth.

"I know that he can. I am certain. He gave me a drink, a potion, and I tried it. I felt such a sensation, a feeling like drifting away, like I could leave myself, leave my body!"

"You drank this potion he offered?" Sansone asked.

"I did drink it. I did, and I loved it. His offer, the way about him, I loved it all. Him, however, I did not like. But I believe he can do what he says he can do!"

"Why then? Let me assume he can do this as you have assumed. Why would you do such a thing? You have everything!"

Greg replied, "As do you." With that he stood and turned to leave. The great old actor would not be outstaged.

"Stop!" he shouted. Sansone stood, which was an event more than a behavior. "This man plays with the unnatural forces of this world. These forces are powerful indeed. Listen to me when I tell you to not consider this. Decline and shut the man out."

"Why? So I can live like this, like you?"

Sansone sat back in the chair. Greg meant to apologize, but the actor abated him with a wave. "You came here asking to know that such things could exist. They do. Yet you also come as a voyeur to your future. The former is prudent, the latter unreliable at best. Each man owns his road and no two are the same. The man with his trick will, too, take more than he will give."

This angered Greg. He thought Sansone, knowing the pain of his condition, would appease him. He turned and walked from the room. Rolla Sansone was not done with his warning.

"I dream of my creature every night! I dream of it when I am awake! It will never stop taking from me! Never!"

Despite the warning, Greg left the grounds more ambitious than when he arrived. This unique and magical offer churned in his mind. He was desperate to leave his self-fashioned prison. He witnessed the rank isolation that awaited him. He thought of his suicidal fan, the flashing cameras, and desperately needed to recede. He could not be Greg Whales anymore.

The days after he left me he did many of the things I anticipated he would do. He sought medical advice and conferenced with his lawyers. The professionals objected to the half-truth plan he described. He paid no mind.

54

I left the delivery van in a mall lot, trading it for an old sedan purchased for the remainder of my journey. I took a room at a bedraggled Los Angeles motel and postured for the wait.

Then his call came.

"Sorren," said the famous voice, "I will do it."

"It is the right decision. You will see. When would you like to try?"

"Try?" he asked.

"A figure of speech. I have done it without fail, more times than I care to speak of. I offer this to you only because I myself respect and admire you. Admittedly, I want to see the world through your eyes, to know your perspective."

"What assurances do I have that you will give me my body back when I am through?" he asked. I was convinced that he did not care if he ever went back.

"You have my word and my history. You know not how old I truly am. Through centuries I have roamed this earth trying to find some meaning in my ability. I have concluded that this is all that there is for me to do."

"Tomorrow. Come and tell no one." He said this with the same composure and confidence displayed in his C.I.A. picture *Battleground West.*

"I was going to recommend the same to you. No doubt you have consulted with others. I advise that you not tell them, but I leave that entirely to your discretion."

With that the call ended. I was excited, already living and lost in his celebrity dream world. The ugly child would finally know what it was like to be embraced by the world around. I discounted all the things learned and lived while I was Gigbe and then Dade, believing that this next change would be my last.

I went to the junky sedan. I was so eager to switch with the actor I began my preparations for the vehicle. There were things to be done.

As I did this Greg Whales was attempting to walk out the front door of his home. It was getting harder with every try. In frustration, he began to drink scotch and take the powerful pills.

He swallowed hard and sat back in a lounge chair. He closed his eyes and prayed to an undefined god for strength to fight through, but his prayer was unanswered. He drifted off into sleep in anticipation of his chance to live as ordinary men do. He did not like or trust the stranger, but I was the key from the confines of his will.

Eternity passed. The sun rose and I rolled the old vehicle through the guarded gates. The guard greeted me by name as he simultaneously approved a list pressed to a clipboard of gold and marble.

I drove slowly, enjoying the excitement of all the possibilities. I wanted to savor this and every moment after for I found the one I would remain. I would know stability like never before.

He arranged it so that only he and I would be present in the serenity of his library. Greens and bright flowers filled the room. Greg motioned for me to sit back in an oversized brown leather chair while he sat across from me in a like furnishing.

"Is the table okay there?" he asked in his role as humble host. My response was light laughter.

"Yes. You will soon see the humor in your question, Mr. Whales," I said, tickling the petals of an African violet.

Whales was anxious to proceed. I revealed to him the bottles harbored within my long coat. They were smoked glass, each full of the precious beverage. I opened one, placed it before me, and placed the other in front of him on the table that divided us.

"I cannot completely explain to you what is about to happen here in this room between us, but I will do so to the very best of my ability. Rest assured, however, that no effort of yours is necessary other than sitting here in this room with me and drinking from the elixir there in that bottle," I said.

"Do feel free to drink it in its entirety if you wish. From that you will feel, well, you know. I trust you sampled from the small bottle I gifted to you on my last visit."

I waited for his gentle nod.

"The feeling of separation, for lack of a better description, is quite real. It is then that you will be vulnerable. By that I mean open for my entrance into your physical body. Once this has happened you will find yourself in a distinctly different place. I must tell you it is not a pleasant place by any means, but it is a necessary evil of this process. You will find you are still within this same room, with all of its furnishings and our two bodies, but it will appear quite alien to you. Nearly all color will have faded. Each object will appear dull and unworldly. Be certain that your time in this void will be brief indeed. It may seem unbearable, but simply tell yourself that it shall pass." I paused.

His eyes were still opened wide in amazement, though his body maintained the relaxed posture of a man who heard it all before. I enjoyed this cool, calm shell he exhibited. He needed to believe.

"There is also an invisible wind. It is furious and ever so cold. The wind is powerful, but it will not hinder your movement. As I enter and occupy your body, you will be immediately drawn toward and into the vacant shell I will leave behind in this chair. This is where you will experience the linking of your spiritual being, your essence as I have come to call it, with this physical mind," I said, pointing to my temple for greater effect. "And there you will know all of this body's memory, emotions, abilities, and limitations. They will pour down over you as a pleasant onslaught to your senses. Trust me to that degree. You will enjoy it as much, or more, than you will enjoy the feeling the elixir provides."

I reached out and drank from my flask casually. He, only with a slight tick of hesitation, did the same. He did so slowly, delaying his full commitment to me.

"After this rush, you will see through the eyes of this figure I now occupy. You will see me inside of your body having just experienced the sensations set forth to you. You and I will know each other after this experience greater than any two human beings on this earth.

"I must tell you, Mr. Whales, there is some shock in seeing one's self from the perspective of another. Perhaps your profession has better prepared you for such an experience in some ways, constantly seeing yourself as someone else on the screen. You will also find a second voice from within. This is merely the brain of this body making its associations and conclusions from the stimuli around you. This is a physicality remaining of the former essence of the body. These messages have no control over you. You will make your own decisions. With some practice you will even learn to completely ignore these remnant signals. Have any of your questions been left unanswered?"

"Yes, but I would rather just get going with it if we could," he said. I smiled and raised my bottle to him.

"I toast to our new and temporary lives," I said. He motioned his bottle in toast to me and slugged from it. I followed his lead consuming my own at a frantic pace. Then I reached out.

I separated from myself and rammed at his body with full force. I easily extricated his essence.

When I entered, the first of his feelings was of great loss. I felt the heat and burning of the fire that engulfed his young brother. I watched through his little boy eyes the broadcast of his mother being sent to the penitentiary for the negligent homicide. I read a great deal about it, but the event devoured him.

I felt his isolation and pain. I felt his escape when he first stepped on a stage. I felt the exhilaration of millions of fans throughout the world. I felt his love and gratitude for the opportunities his gods bestowed upon him. Then it was pain again. Slow at first, but next racing through me, controlling me, turning and churning into a raw fear. The fear was great and black and senseless, but it dominated him. I shook and then looked across to my body left behind. I saw him fill it.

He took it well. He smiled and looked down at his fingers and feet, moving all of them, reveling in his control of the new human body. He stood and danced and then stopped. This was my cue.

"Security! Security!" I shouted in repetition as I slinked back over the chair, knocking it over to the floor. I took the bottle that Whales drank from, sealed it, and placed it in my pant waist. I ran to the far side of the elaborate fountain as he gazed on with a combination of contempt and confusion.

The door burst open and through it came two security men

"Call the police immediately. He tried to drug me! He has assaulted me!" I shouted into the air. Within moments the enriched library of flowering greens and books was filled with more security and house staff. Whales, in my most recently vacated form, was thrown and pinned to the ground. Each of the guards held out guns of electricity aimed at the subdued man.

He screamed in protest. "What are you doing? It's me! I am Greg Whales!"

They pulled him from the room while others surrounded me in a wall of human protection. He was removed from the room and I was carried to what the chief guard Reid referred to as the "safe room." Whales' mind told me the room was ordered at the onset of his paranoia, a place of complete safety from bullets, bombs, poisons, and the like.

I stayed in there for some time. Reid asked me a number of questions about the detained man. I described him as a prospective spiritual advisor. I told him I was conversing with the man and he went insane in his attempt to attack and molest me. He assured me I was safe and went back to the captive Stephen Dade. He also reminded me of his attempt to dissuade me from the man days earlier.

Soon thereafter I was interviewed by a Detective Watts from the Los Angeles County Sheriff's Department. He was a gruff man, unshaven and large. He treated me gently and kindly, recognizing me to be the victim of a hoax and assault. I thanked him for the County's assistance in the matter and pleaded with him to support an issuance of an order of restraint against my assailant.

He gave his assurances the "swami" would be taken to a county jail if fit and if unfit to a psychiatric center. Another detective, a masculine woman named Shelts, returned to the mansion after inspecting the assailant's vehicle. She found all the ragtag photographs of Whales strewn throughout the vehicle. They had largely been cut from the pages of tabloid magazines, personalized them with identifying fluids.

The evidence was collected and the car impounded. Dade was removed from the estate in handcuffs and shackles. He shouted out as they pulled him from the place. He knew names of the staff and details of objects in the house. Nobody cared.

"He says your an imposter," Shelts said.

When they considered me safe I left the panic room and went to a large window outlooking the main drive. I watched as the line of police vehicles drove out of the property. I accomplished that which I had set out to do, but felt queasy and quite ill. This was nothing some of the elixir could not cure.

Hours later I received a phone call from Detective Shelts who told me Dade was involuntarily committed to a psychiatric hospital. His claims continued into the courthouse, leading the judge to believe he was neither safe to be in the jail or out on the streets of Los Angeles.

55

I was then free to live his life of my dreams. For a short while this was remarkably easy. Whales' world had been organized, categorized, and scheduled by a small armada of agents, business managers, and other handlers. The better part of two years was set forth. It was my inclination to follow his agenda so no suspicions would be raised.

The order and structure could have been positive. I recommitted to refraining from the elixir, but the old lies returned. I would not make up my mind. If I did I would not inject it. I would definitely not smoke it. These are the things I told myself. But Greg had not been following the scripts.

My publicist Nancy called and recommended a public interview to explain the brush with my stalker. She thanked me for taking the call. Whales' remnant mind commanded me to hold it in my home, a place no member of the media had ever set foot. The new Greg Whales was going to be different. It was the time to be open, honest, and inviting. No more secrets. I did not want to leave.

Nancy was jovial, speaking in a thick Manhattan accent though she lived on the west coast for nearly a decade. She agreed an interview in my home was ideal. We ran through the big name interviewers: Barbara Walters, Nancy Grace, or Larry King. We settled on Ellen Degeneres. She would facilitate telling the world of my harrowing experience with my stalker and keep it light, entertaining.

Within hours, Nancy called and said Ellen was excited and willing to do it within the week. She told Nancy she felt a great deal of empathy for me and was eager to help. The interview required the cancellation of a trip to Japan to film a beer commercial. It was for a staggering sum, but I did not need the money. It was an overwhelming relief.

In the days before the interview I was quite careful in my interactions with my management and the house staff. Though I controlled the body and mind of Whales, it was all subject to my interpretations. He was the most watched man in human history. I did not want to raise suspicions with my awkwardness in his form.

I accomplished this mostly by withdrawing into my bedroom and living area in the manor. This afforded time to practice being Whales. I probed his thoughts and memories. I found he suffered from the onset of his unnameable psychiatric condition. Some may have superficially called it agoraphobia, but that did not completely explain what it was. Over the following days, I attempted to understand the symptoms. I wanted to know why he had become so afraid of the world outside his home. *Inside View* was right.

The day arrived for Ellen's visit to my estate. I was crippled by earth shattering anxiety. She would, in fact, bring the world inside my home with nowhere left to hide. I spent the morning studying my reflection in a lavish mirror. This offered no solace.

I received word that she was approaching the house with a small caravan of her crew. I collected myself and made my way to greet her. I opened the door and was taken back. The larger than life quality surrounded her. She held reverence for me. Though it took over four hundred years, I had arrived.

We spoke first of my stalker and his fate. The perpetrator would likely never leave the institute. If he did, he would be prosecuted to the fullest extent of the law. We moved on to discuss my recently failed marriage to the model and actress Olivia Barnes and the tabloid fallout from it. We discussed my current love life, which was nonexistent. Then came the rumors of my exile.

Whales pushed this from his thoughts. I had to look for them in response to her questions of a rumor that I left my home only a handful of times over the last year. It was completely true, but I denied it saying I was trying to keep a low profile, my stalker providing both reason and rhyme for this course of action.

To prove I was capable of leaving my home, I suggested we conclude the interview at the large Koi pond in the citrus garden. We made our way to the western exit of the manor when she paused and turned to me in a hushed tone:

"How are you handling that little girl's suicide?"

It was more than I could bear. I began to tremble as we made our approach. Her inquiry coupled with attempting to venture outside proved crippling. I froze in panic. My fear raced, my eyes watered, and my palms dampened. My legs gave way beneath me and a cloudy, dizzying spell overtook me right there with Ellen and all the cameras.

Hans, my personal assistant, rushed and caught me in his arms. He helped me to the stone bench beside the double-paned doors. The world spun around me and I could focus on nothing. I felt the blood. I wiped my face, but could not stop feeling the smoldering tissues engulfing me. I could not repress it. The cameras were rolling.

Ellen was asking me something but I did not know what. I stood against the advice of Hans and my other handlers. I tried to stop at the doors, which were opened for me to receive fresh air. I found the first step the only one possible. Though I regained composure, I could not leave the room to the world outside. The doors may as well have been bricked closed. At the thought of such a feat, my legs turned to iron and my vision obscured through a menacing gray fog. This phobia of Whales' was like nothing I had ever experienced.

My handlers ordered the film crew to stop taping, but the damage had been done. The world's suspicion of Whales' mental decline was confirmed. I heard the chatter of my handlers erupt after Ellen and her crew gave us all pleasantly guarded good-byes. They spoke with publicists, magazines, television producers, and the studio executives controlling the lucrative contracts keeping the Whales empire afloat.

I was carried to my quarters and placed in bed like a child. Faint outlines of all the beautiful women who loved Whales I felt there beside me as I drifted in and then out of my thoughts. Hans opened my nightstand which revealed a number of prescription sedatives and pain killers. I greedily took the pills from Hans.

I vowed to never consume any drug after entering Whales and I already violated that covenant. Minutes later I did not care, swimming in a warm bath of relaxation. I basked in the memories and emotions of Greg's life, able to avoid his horrors while under the influence. I convinced myself that I was part of some master plan. Suffering was only a state of mind. So were both love and guilt.

I drifted into sleep until the following morning. When I awoke, I reached for a remote control and scrolled the channels of a large screen hanging on the wall. I saw my embarrassing spell on a number of the stations. My wobbling legs and rolling eyes made me quite the fool. Media pundits dismissed my handlers' excuses. Exhaustion. A medication change. They heard it all before and they would not accept the explanations. I was a nut, mentally unbalanced, and slipping into greater madness. I was yet another celebrity whose mind teetered under the pressures of the continuous spotlight. The rumors had been proven.

How far I fell in such a short time. I was groggy and my tongue was thick. My thoughts turned to the sweet elixir and I would not deny myself. With the phone next to my bed, I called for the trusted Hans.

Hans proved resourceful. He obtained all the necessary works. With all the hardware placed in my room, I began to mix and cook and bottle the elixir. I would allow no one inside.

As I mixed, then heated, then bottled, I obsessed over my image and what it was the world now thought of me. I became some tragic, comic clown. I knew the elixir held the strength for me to move forward. I would not inject it. I would not smoke it. I would only use it long enough to rise above my current problem and would then wean myself away from it yet again. It was merely an impasse to be overcome.

After a day I had an ample supply of the elixir bottled. I stored away all but one of the bottles. I would drink it and then brave the perimeter of the house. When it worked I would stage some event to show TMZ had it all wrong. They would know again that their star, the immortal Greg Whales, was as great as he ever was. He was still the handsome everyman star he had been for two decades.

I returned to the television and found it still projected my fainting spell. The experts traveled closer to the mark by recognizing the condition of Whales as agoraphobia. A symptom of his condition, it was quite accurate, but I was now Whales. I would return him to his center place in the universe.

I began to drink the elixir. I separated my essence, unlocking from the physical being of Whales, but remaining within it. I dared not leave his shell for those cold winds and the sense of fright and falling were too much to bear where no gain stood. The drink made me fearless and free with lightening for my energy. I was Greg Whales and belonged atop of the upside down world.

I rang down to Hans and commanded him to my bedroom. He confusedly agreed.

"I need some things," I explained opening the door to his soft knock.

"These things, I need them now," I said handing him a list. From there I had no choice but to wait for his return, consuming the liquid elixir. After two more bottles of the elixir he returned with all that I had requested.

He stayed and watched me transform the liquid into a potent, injectable form. He was in awe, but declined my offer to inject him with the elixir. He remained in my company.

The bedroom phone rang. Reporters were flooding the house with calls. I was quite high from my shot but could still not imagine leaving the confines of my room.

I transformed the elixir yet again, this time into the hardened smokeable crystals that my dead friend John and I so enjoyed. This process only took a few moments. I then began to hit from the pipe that Hans procured.

I encouraged him to drag from the pipe. That he was willing to do, though he needed to sit down after his first hit. I could see his joy. I could see his euphoria.

I thought of escape into this Hans. The servant could truly become the master! Perhaps this life of Whales would not improve, but I thought the better of the switch. I smoked deeply from the pipe and felt a renewed optimism in the life of Whales.

"Okay," he managed out of his mouth. It was ages since I felt those first waves of pleasure. Perhaps in Hans I found a companion. Maybe I would share the dark science.

The next several days were spent in my bedroom with Hans smoking away at the elixir. I had not broached the subject of my abilities with him, but taught him how to transform the elixir into its smokeable form. In time perhaps he would become my apprentice.

Eventually there was a knock on the door of my bedroom. It was my agent, Max Warren. He stood there with a dumbfounded look in his dark blue Armani sans tie. He was not pleased.

"Where the fuck have you been?" he demanded. Greg's memories assured me Warren did not withhold opinions or expletives. He knew exactly where I had been. His eyes disapprovingly scanned the disarray of the bedroom. The look landed on Hans who after four days in the bedroom was quite spiraled out.

"Leave him alone!" I shouted.

Max stood hurt and sorry. He had been with Whales since the beginning, landing him his breakout role in *If Only When*, and the lucrative *Jaded Sun Trilogy*. However, he could not question the will of Greg Whales.

"Alright, alright, I'm sorry. It's just that you had all that bad stuff on the tube and now you've been, well, unavailable. We've got things to do. Have you looked at either of the scripts?"

Greg's mind told me he had not. Each time he had tried to read them, his anxiety overwhelmed him, leaving him unable to focus on the text on the page. I again contemplated the nightmare I had stolen.

"No, not yet. Care for some?" I asked with a smile, holding the pipe out to Warren.

"Of course not," he said, stroking the medallion hanging from his neck. On it I could see the Serenity Prayer.

The memories came forth. After their mutual success, Whales sunk into further weirdness while Warren lost himself to cocaine, but returned. I thought about falling to my knees and begging for his help and understanding. I knew the chaos that would follow this relapse and did not want it. I took another hit.

"Maybe you should take a break. You're looking a little haggard there, Greg. I didn't even know you were into this shit." With that he turned. "I'll call you in a day or two. Put that down and pick up a script before then, okay bud?"

He was gone and we remained. His breach of the lair unsettled us. It seemed his entry encouraged others to come. My managers, assistants, and house staff came calling one by one. This we could not have. We had work to do. I told the last of the callers, a maid named Jennifer or Jeanie, that the next person to disturb us would be fired.

I asked Hans to review the two scripts halfheartedly. I knew that Whales, in this current state of mental minutia, was never going to work again. And this is how we went for a time. We rarely ate or did anything other than smoke the elixir. The only persons allowed in the room were those delivering us our infrequent meals.

I could wait no longer.

"There is quite some trick I know, Hans," I said.

He responded to me with a most curious look. I could see that he was taken by the elixir, perhaps as devoted a servant to it as I, and the toll it was taking on his physicality was not insignificant. I knew he would be willing to travel with me into infinity if I asked him to go. He could be immortal, in a sense, shedding his worldly shell for unadulterated freedom. He, too, would know the end of consequence.

"Soon Hans, I will show you eternal life," I said.

So deluded from the elixir, he nodded to this maniacal statement. He would have gladly accepted an end to gravity. I had become his god, the elixir his sacrament.

We smoked for days further, resting only when we collapsed. Soon the day arrived when I showed him the power. I asked him to close his eyes and concentrate on the feeling of separation. He answered in the affirmative when I asked if he could feel the expansion beyond his physical body.

Battering him in surprise was out of the question. I did not want to frighten him like the others.

I watched him as he changed, just for a few seconds, but change nonetheless. I could see that he left his physical being into the cold, frantic world between us all. He then returned to himself and opened his eyes. I saw his terror.

He began to grasp for elusive air. I went to him befuddled. Never had I seen such incident with myself or any of the others before him. He stood there dying before me. Slumping to the ground, he was dead. I was alone again.

I stopped watching the inane coverage of the Greg Whales meltdown. The spell was nothing compared to what would erupt from this new tragedy. I would be odder than ever with a drug related death in my bedroom. The questions no doubt would arise. They would want to know what it was we were doing. There before me lied the beginnings of a greater scandal. I dragged deeply from the pipe, calling Max Warren and my publicist. Max told me to wait and I did. Just me and my dead friend Hans.

56

His hands ached and his belly burned with hot fire. The tremors were great. Only the tips of the modest brown dye still showed, a chemical segue to the white-gray hair beneath. The Taxman sat uncomfortably in an orthopedic chair at his bulky metal desk leafing through pages held in a large accordion file.

He had waited patiently at the home of Stephen Dade. He waited so long he suffered a spell. Without eating or drinking, he went out and was spotted by a patrolling police car. They could not wake him and an ambulance brought him away. Somehow he kept this from his employer.

Less than a year remained between that day and the best estimates of the U.C.L.A. cancer specialist. His life was coming to a close. He hoped to work until the last tick of his clock, or at least until he found me.

The Internal Revenue Service was large with nearly unlimited resource. An entity as such could not miss a solitary man, but the same solitary man could miss the entity. The Taxman had no family, no religion, and his only friends for the most part were employed by the same behemoth as he.

As he threw an antacid tablet into his mouth and crunched down on it, a rap came to his office door. It was Roberts.

"This will interest you," said Roberts. He tossed the week's cheap paper rag *Inside View*. The Taxman's reflexes proved untrue. The pages fell to the ground at his feet.

"What is it?" he asked as he bent forward in concealed pain.

"Start at page four."

Roberts left him. Dorean examined the cover. He did not follow tabloid television, and lately did not even watch the news. Incidents concerning celebrities did not interest him, though he was familiar with Greg Whales.

The article inside told of a reclusive Whales shut away from the world at large. A stalker was arrested at the estate. No name was given though it was believed the man was committed to a local Los Angeles hospital for the insane.

An undisclosed source provided the catch: "He screamed, 'I am Greg Whales! I am Greg Whales!' as police led the man out of the home."

57

He sat patiently amidst the pungent smell of institutional sanitary cleaner and stale cigarette smoke. He watched an aged patient mop the worn pale green tile covering the reception area floor. The patient mumbled on to himself. A middle aged heavyset woman with frizzy hair typed rapidly onto a keyboard while speaking into the microphone of her headset.

After several more minutes he heard the buzzing release of the magnetic lock securing the facility. The door opened to the rattling keys hanging from the health attendant. The man in white came to escort him to an interview room.

"Mr. Dorean?" the short, muscle-bound attendant inquired. Paul had been the only person in the waiting area save the mopping patient. He stood and acknowledged the inquiry.

"Right this way sir," said the attendant.

They walked together down a decaying corridor of imitation stone. Each wall had a number of doors, many of which were opened to the small windowless offices inside. The loud compressor circulated dead and heavy air.

A uniformed guard sat at the desk, lifting his eyes only to see the identification Paul displayed to him. A familiar buzz sounded signifying the guard had unlocked and opened yet another door. This next door led to the maximum-security ward where Stephen Dade was imprisoned.

The attendant led him to a dingy interview room with a metal table and chairs bolted tightly to the stained cement floor. The Taxman sat and waited for the interviewee to arrive.

Moments later a highly medicated man shuffled his feet to the jingling chains that bound his hands and ankles. The man's dull eyes looked up to those of the Taxman, displaying a helpless case without one word. The attendant led him to the chair to sit, helped him down, and then fastened his chains to metal struts that were imbedded in the floor.

"You okay with him alone?" the attendant asked.

"Yes," the Taxman responded. Dorean scanned the chained man sitting before him. He knew from the photograph it was the right man. The limited background data he could find was that the man had been a successful young executive in New York. He learned of the man's disappearance after a drug related arrest. His obsession with the actor Greg Whales seemed recent. The man had no real criminal record. Once again things just did not make sense.

"Can you please tell me your name?" Paul asked.

"My name is a Greg Whales," slurred the man. The agitation in his voice was audible despite the psychotropics.

"I know you are Greg," replied the Taxman.

For weeks Whales pleaded his identity to lawyers, doctors, nurses, and even custodians. He then tried saying he knew he was not. He was now not alone.

"I need you to tell me everything you know about what has happened."

The shackled man lightened. Greg told him about the book within his grocery delivery, his meeting with the strange man he now resided within, the proposition, the elixir and the switch. Paul Dorean believed the unknowable. This elusive creature, whatever I was, became revealed.

The Taxman drove away from the institution. He wondered if his fragile body and acid bones were up for the task. He wondered whether his mind was slipping away from him to believe such a thing was even happening.

58

My lawyer and the two defense attorneys fired their questions. I could answer most with lies and half-truths. The Los Angeles County Coroner's Office removed Hans from the room. My ever-faithful maid had removed the empty elixir bottles, paraphernalia, and residues of our days in the room before the police intervention.

The toxicity tests would be conducted and findings would fuel the gossip flames of speculation. I had preemptive visions of the experts and their opinions. Yet worse, I could not seem to leave the room without an overwhelming terror. The connection established with the physical world through Hans was ripped away and I was alone. Then it came over the intercom.

"There is a man from the Internal Revenue Service here to see you, Mr. Whales."

"My accountant has power of attorney," I said.

"I told him that, Mr. Whales. He needs to speak with you as part of an investigation concerning the man that was arrested here on the property," the box squawked.

"Send him in," I retorted in disgust against the messenger. "Does this agent have a name?"

"Paul. Paul Dorean," squelched the wall speaker.

I saw his aged face in the security monitor. His hair, which was nearly all gray, was clipped neatly but not as short as it had been in our first meeting. I traveled down the staircase sipping from a freshly opened bottle of the elixir.

I opened the door to him. My eyes betrayed me in a brief flash. He honed in on the Judas spark of recognition. I wondered then if he knew of my true nature. If this were so I would have to flee no matter how cushioned the life I had stolen was. With a secret such as mine, I could not risk the prying nature of the government and their probing tools.

Though the supernatural had been viewed with skepticism, it still had been viewed. I would not become some mystical genie in a test tube for study. That was the first time I thought of it. I could take the old man. Surely, he would exchange his aged flesh for the body of Whales or what other body I could provide him. This would afford me an opportunity to end all the inquiries.

"Mr. Whales?" he asked.

"Why yes, Mister?" I responded.

"Dorean. Paul Dorean, I am with the Internal Revenue Service."

"Yes. As I told the gate guard to tell you, I have an accountant with power of attorney to discuss and manage all of my tax affairs."

"Yes, you do, of course, but this is not about your taxes."

"Oh, well then," I questioned, "what may I ask is this about?"

He paused and looked me over.

"Mr. Dorean?"

"Have we met before, Mr. Whales?"

"No," I answered.

"You're right. You must get that a lot. Well, privacy laws prevent me from revealing many aspects of this investigation, but I can tell you I was looking for Stephen Dade," he said.

"Yes. Well you could not have gone too far into this investigation without knowing that he is in an asylum," I responded.

"Of course. Well, maybe you will have the answers for more questions if I ask the right ones. Please, I would consider your assistance a personal favor, as would the IRS."

"Of course."

He asked if I recognized any persons contained in a long list of names. I denied all of them but, in fact, had lived the many of them. The man had done much research and exposed the haphazard trail left through my darkest years. He spoke of forensics and its fruitful yield at a number of crime scenes. Successions of murders were carried out with suspect becoming victim, so on and so forth. Monies had been transferred with no transfer taxes paid, but this was clearly no longer about the money. This was when the real questions came.

"Did you observe Mr. Dade partaking in the use of any drugs while in your presence?"

I denied it.

"Did Mr. Dade speak to you of any unusual abilities?"

"Abilities?" I asked.

"Did he make any claims about being able to leave his body, that is have his spirit leave his body? I think it's called astral projection."

I denied this.

"Did he tell you he could leap from his body and possess the body of another?"

I laughed aloud, "No sir and I must say this is an odd line of questioning for the Internal Revenue Service. Sounds more like something for the X-Files. What would it have mattered if he said such things anyway? Wasn't he raving mad?" There was no crowing cock, but my third denial weighted the air around us.

"I know, I know. We were just trying to figure things out."

"Perhaps these questions should be directed to some fortune teller rather than his victim. This whole thing is done in extremely poor taste," I said. I wanted to smoke the elixir. The urge was irresistible.

"Yes, I am sorry, yes. I do need a moment," he said.

"Well then, if you must, I must first use the restroom before we continue," I said. "Should the staff bring you a beverage? How about a spring water?"

"Yes, thank you."

"Spring water it is," I said walking up the stairs.

From my bedroom I phoned the maid and told her to prepare a pitcher of spring water with lemon twist and two chilled glasses. I requested it be brought to my room rather than directly to my guest. I began to smoke away at the crystals while I waited.

I looked to the closed-circuit monitor. I watched that decrepit fig casually inspecting the room while flipping through an open file, looking as though he was not looking.

The maid arrived with her silver tray delivery. I dumped half of the pitcher of water into the toilet, replacing it to the brim with the elixir, and squeezing the lemon into it as I stirred.

I called back the maid and asked her to deliver it to the Taxman. I instructed her to tell the old one that an urgent family phone call would delay me only momentarily. She had no choice but to oblige.

I smoked and watched her glide down to deliver the water plus to my *nemesis*. That is what he was.

I watched as he poured himself a nearly full glass of water. He fumbled through his jacket and produced a small reddish pill bottle. He opened it, placed one or two in his mouth, and then drank from the glass. I smoked more of the elixir and then left the room.

As I reached the bottom of the stairs, the Taxman stood to greet me and in doing so spilled the remainder of his drink all over his shirt and pants.

"Oh my. I'm sorry, so sorry," he said wiping the floor with his handkerchief. "My coordination is not what it used to be."

"Are you feeling okay, Mr. Dorean?" I asked, aware that a wicked hope passed from mind to air.

"Yes, well, I am a bit light-headed. May I use the washroom?" he asked feebly.

"Please, be my guest."

When he stepped forward he stumbled slightly, but caught his balance. Impulsively, I leapt from the body of Whales into that cold netherworld. I felt the same combination terror of drowning and falling known since the beginning. I bolted at him, but was repelled back.

I hovered there, inches above the marble floor, looking at the man. He tricked me! His essence remained firmly planted within his decaying ancient body.

He saw the inanimate, soulless shell of Whales slump to the floor before I reclaimed it.

I was doomed. For centuries I was damned, had flashes of redemption to only watch them slip away. One day there would be a final judgment and I would have nowhere to run. I felt the icy cold of hell with its heatless flames. I saw the end result of the brutality, the hatred, and the apathy. This was a new sensation, though, for my reign on earth was coming to its conclusion.

"You know, Mr. Whales, I think I have enough for now," he said.

I walked towards the door to follow him out, but the new terror overwhelmed me. My throat dried and closed. My knees buckled. I desperately wanted to vomit. There was nothing I could do other than know the procession of my fate.

59

Through my agents, I retained the investigator that assisted in the preparation of Whales' most recent divorce. The man, Stan Mitchell, proved adept at trailing the infidelities of the second Mrs. Whales, even onto the closed set of her flop *The Nowhere Train.*

Days later Mitchell arrived at my estate. He brought a number of photographs and an impressive detailed report summarizing the three days following and observing the activities of Paul Dorean. There was much to work with.

I knew he was old. What I did not know was that he was also sick, very sick. Mitchell followed him to work and waited several hours. That afternoon he left the Federal Building where Dorean's office was located and traveled to U.C.L.A.'s Jonsson Comprehensive Cancer Center.

Mitchell then followed him into the building. He walked into a waiting area to find the Taxman there reading. He poked around until he heard the confirmatory call.

"Mr. Dorean," the nurse said through a half opened door.

Mitchell watched the Taxman go to her. With that he left. It was then Mitchell went to work at his real specialty.

Mitchell had an eye for the desperate. The young nurse was broke and bitter. He needed information. The next morning he had Dorean's file from the oncologist's office. The figure appeared on Mitchell's bill as a general expense.

Inside was a trove of information. The Taxman was losing the fight for his life and had all but given up on it. The man seemed resolved to die. I found some hope.

Deep in the pages of his file, I found reference to his repeated visits to a psychiatrist in the same facility. I found notes summarizing a phone call between the psychiatrist and the cancer doctor regarding Dorean's chronic depression, and a recent mention of suicide.

The Taxman was prescribed mood elevators and narcotics for pain, but the pain was worsening. Not even the most potent of the substances could dull the agony below the point of insanity at times.

The pain led to his mention of suicide. He assured both of his doctors he would never engage in such a practice as he found it morally repugnant. He wished, though, that there were some other way for him to deal with the pain of the cancer. I had an avenue for him.

60

He returned to me. The Taxman may have known my secret, but I now knew his. I opened the door to him. The aged figure standing before me was burning in the fires of time faster than I. His end was soon.

"I know what you are," he said.

"And I you," I responded. "You are old and you are dying," I professed. "Youth. I want to give you back your youth. I can give that to you," I said. The man whom I feared to be so righteous and good would prove no different than I. His obsession soured to satisfy his own selfish ends. He, like I, wanted only to defy his God given fate and form.

"And how is it that you could do such a thing?"

"I know of a formula, a powerful elixir, that could free you. No doubt the man claiming to be Whales told you, only confirming what you had come to believe, since you met me the first time."

"Gigbe," he said.

"You know it to be true."

"It was then, really, that first time I saw you that I knew that something was different. I cannot describe as anything, but other-worldly," he said.

"You were correct, Mr. Dorean. I am sorry about your fall. I do hold certain knowledge. Special knowledge. This knowledge bestows upon me a special ability, but this ability is one of science and not individuality. Any person with the proper knowledge can reproduce it. I could give you that knowledge and you could use it to your advantage," I said.

"Tell me please. Tell me. I will do anything to escape this pain," he said in his old man frailty. His eyes closed as he shuddered from hope.

"I will tell you, but I must have your assurance that you will, in fact, carry it out. From there you and I will be of no debt to one another."

"Anything."

I then went about explaining to him the power and freedom of elixir, without revelation of its true nature and source of my knowledge. I told him of my true birth date and of the hundreds of years I lived. He was open. He was willing.

It then came time to explain he would need another to become. Confused, I explained to him through the analogy of Whales and I. Leaving one's body racked with pain would offer immediate benefit; he needed to find another human being to occupy. The occupant would need to be willing or tricked. This caused him some pause.

"Do you mean to say that this other whom I entice to exchange will have this body along with all of its pain and suffering?"

"Yes," I said, watching his eyes for registration, "there is no other way."

He paused further, but finally said, "It will be Whales then. The real Whales. He has known a full life of love and success and look what he did with it. He locked himself away from the world, shunning those that made him the great figure he had become. I believe this exchange with you has driven him insane. Why should I not enjoy the health and life he has taken for granted?"

I was amazed by the selfish deviousness that his cancer had allowed to grow within him. In the moment all my debauchery was forgiven.

"What of Whales then? After, you understand, he will be in your body and you will be he locked away in that asylum."

"Well, you could help me with that. As Whales, you could ask that I be released. You could tell the police that you do not wish to prosecute. We would then never need see one another again."

"How then will we do this? I certainly cannot go to the facility," I said.

"It is true then, what the rags say? You cannot leave here?"

"It is true," I said.

"I know a judge. I might be able to get an immediate release. I could bring him here, do this switch, and then murder this body," he said pointing hatefully at himself.

"Murder? That would only draw attention to me and certainly you. They would likely shoot you on sight."

"No, not really murder. Suicide. I could take a number of my pain pills, enough to kill me several times over. We can do the switch before the capsules dissolve in my stomach, and then watch from his perspective as this body dies."

His mind was wicked. His plan could work. It required my trust, but I saw no other way out of my predicament. Perhaps through him I would find the companion I sought for centuries.

"I will assist you in every way I can," I said.

He said nothing more. He turned to me in a painful wince. The intelligent, charming old man was as hungry as I once was. His eyes were teary and soulful. The art of our lives was the avoiding of pain.

"Bring him to us." I last said.

61

"Exigent circumstances, Your Honor," the Taxman said. He extended a proposed order to release Stephen Dade into the custody of the IRS, namely Paul Dorean. Judge Fredrick slowly removed both of his golf gloves using the last removed to wipe away the beaded perspiration from his forehead.

"Well, Paul, this is a highly unusual request," he said. He scratched the sun-drenched dome where hair had once grown. "With no provisions for a hearing, or service of notice upon the Sheriff or the District Attorney's Office, I must say, I am extremely reluctant to proceed in this manner, at least so abruptly."

The man accompanying Judge Fredrick on the course, a former legal partner and classmate, was short and squat. He hacked away at the golf ball yards off the fairway between two tall pine trees.

The Judge squinted his eyes, smiling at the folly in the rough. "Is there something more to this, something you can tell me which would justify such a gross deviation?"

"Your Honor, this man is critical to understanding one of the most complex tax fraud cases seen in all my years with the Service. I need him in person, now, or this case will die in my arms. I interviewed him and found him to be lucid and completely cooperative. I assure you he will be in my complete control and custody for no more than forty-eight hours and will then be returned to the facility."

"Paul, this man is dangerous from what you tell me. He somehow broke through the security of Greg Whales!"

"Please, Judge."

"There is no other way?"

"None, Your Honor."

"Forty-eight hours," he said as he gave his scrawling signature across the bottom of the instrument. "And we are now even."

"Yes."

Fredrick required reassurance that Dorean's familiarities with indiscretions of the past would be forgotten. When finished, he placed the gloves back on his hands. He selected an iron from his bag, and lofted his ball high in the air. It crashed down to the earth just shy of the green. He nodded a good-bye to Paul Dorean who returned a small wave.

The winding drive back to the institution was a blink of road for the Taxman. He arrived in the afternoon. After only a brief delay for verification Greg Whales, in the body of another man, was released from the institution. He walked from the place in chains with Paul Dorean at the helm.

Before the two even made it to the parking lot, a ten year employed nurse of the facility placed a call to Mitchell informing him that the IRS agent and his charge were on the way from the hospital. Mitchell did not know that the two were on their way to me.

62

The man in shackles was neither the commanding object of adoration, nor the hysteric dragged away by his own security staff. The chained man was quiet and passive. His will had been devoured by the steady stream of psychiatric medications and institutional conditioning. The handsome face I traded to him ran pasty white and ragged. His triangular physique was now lumpy and misaligned. His walk was a shuffle.

I myself did no maintenance on the frame embezzled from Whales. My negligence in the matter was pronounced through the bulging tummy and sagging posture. Glimpses into the many mirrors of the house offered the beginnings of a sagged and cracking face filled with yellowing pearls. The elixir took its toll again.

Then there stood the Taxman. Slouching and emaciated, he transmitted the odor and image of death. He was willing to become a monster, like I, to dodge the natural order of things. What a haggard lot we were. The three of us there, each doomed in our own unique fashion.

I did feel a renewal of sorts. The dark compulsion within me buzzed to the conquering of his virtue. Like I, this Taxman was to now and forever foreclose all paths leading to the good of heaven. His faith in my drink would damn him to a life eternal on earth, endlessly wandering the world in search of evasive peace and acceptance.

Freedom, euphoria, vanity, intellect, and now fame: all I found and none were enough to complete the void within me. My sickness sought the company of another uncovered in the decrepit old creature there before me. He would soon be a traitor to nature and God himself, defying the fate laid before him. I filled their cups in silence. For effect, I selected a remarkable pair of gem studded golden goblets. With the elaborate cups I offered the Taxman a ceremonial ritual of sorts, an unholy communion.

"I offer to you the cup of life. With it you will know a new freedom. You will know escape from death," I offered.

Whales put forth a nearly undetectable resistance to the goblet as I placed it to his mouth. His inarticulate mumblings gave way to a sip and swallow of the elixir. I saw no sign of his recognition of the blessed beverage. He was in a stupor, unable to appreciate the trade which was about to take place.

My eyes stayed upon the Taxman throughout. He focused intently on the chained man in a gaze of greed. He chewed and swallowed large white morphine tablets, washing each down with a healthy dose of the elixir. Any doubts of his commitment to the endeavor faded away. He, like I, would show the greatest faith through the necessity of the murder.

Then there was something, some pause of the moment, some suspension of the rotating earth, some thing that was different. It was palpable in the California air, but by then it was too late.

I felt the force of his assault. In another body at another time I may have been able to resist the battery. I would likely have fought it away with considerable glee to the challenge. Imagine it, if you can, the sheer arrogance required to challenge me at my own game and win.

Removed to the netherworld I found myself not directed to the chained man. I did not know where I was. I just know that excruciating bright pain consumed me from within whatever I was.

I had been evicted from the cold and dull space and planted within a temple of pain. Each cell of the body burned in anguish. Each breath carried in it a band of razor daggers, jointly and severely piercing and prodding the aged heart. The legs, shaky and unsteady, could not support me. With that recognition, I fell hard to the marble floor. I had been deceived out of the body of Whales, and led to the horrible predicament that was the Taxman.

I looked up to the chained man. He looked down on me with a smiling satisfaction. It was Dorean inside. That was all he could muster through the heavy curtain of hypnotics and anti-psychotics coming part and parcel with the body.

With great force, I tried assaulting the now chained Taxman with my essence, but he remained steadfast. No sooner did I leave the aching body than I returned to it for another grueling bolt of anguish. I tried then again at Whales, but found more rejection. Each of the men remained with a continence I could not disturb.

My thoughts turned to desperate violence. I thought of the gun I suddenly knew the Taxman to carry. In my rage, I was bound to use it on the both of them. The weak search of my body yielded nothing. It was not to be found, nor were the keys for the handcuffs or ankle bracelets the Taxman now wore. He had thought of this all.

At that realization the dreamy, floating sensation raptured me. I felt like those days when I had plunged needles into my arms and injected the hope and peace never known to me in life. Suddenly, my predicament was meaningless yet completely manageable. A warmth fell over me. I became confident I would resolve this and all things in some favorable way.

I soon found it was not only the three of us in the mansion. From the sides, the top, and underneath came a swarm of armed men. Each looked the same, covered in black night cloth and armored vests. I did not recognize the anachronisms on their patched arms. These clandestine warriors took hold of the surrounding area and me. Two of the men carried strange electronic instruments. The things chirped and buzzed in electronic confusion.

They separated the three of us and immediately capped and bagged the bottled and poured elixir. The goblets were placed in plastic containers, carefully held upright so as to not spill the remaining liquids within each.

I caught only a brief glimpse of Whales as he was escorted from the room. He turned to me in horror as they led him away. His return to the body of Greg Whales solved nothing.

An explosion of pain burst from within my new feeble frame. The hurt was slowly masked by the overdose of white morphine tablets. Despite great effort, my eyes closed. In the darkness there was a dying woman. I reached out with little boy hands to place a messy sandwich into her mouth. The Taxman's sadness was my sadness. This was my last of the free world.

63

I awoke again committed to an institution. Again, I was bound with a connected series of chains and leather straps. Ominous beeping and buzzing sounds emanated from the surrounding equipment, much of it being things never before seen. The room was asylum gray, lacking windows or decorative measures.

A burly armed man stood strong before the metal door. He stared straight, non-responsive to my inquiries. He was not there for my safety.

I inched and wormed through the sheets pressed over the restraint devices, but could find no further comfort. There was no television or visible intercom speaker in the walls. It was unlike any of the other modern institutions I had found myself.

My head remained clouded from the morphine overdose, but the events at Whales' home returned. I was able to view the liver spots covering my exposed arms and hands as I recalled I was in the body of the Taxman. I took no pleasure in his memories and at the time ignored his reflections entirely.

I had been duped in my own game. The pain had graciously been managed, whether by further medical intervention or the continued presence of overdose in my system, I do not know. I was not in the shooting agony felt after the switch.

After some time, a large male attendant with bulging arms and another older man in a lab coat entered the room. Neither addressed nor greeted me in any fashion. Their silence drowned out all of the other beeps and buzzers that had moments before filled the air of the room.

The large man went to my side. He lifted me slightly into the air and crouched to look underneath. The older man produced a squeeze tube from his pocket and handed it to the large man. The attendant squirted an ointment onto the tips of his gloved finger and rubbed it into my back. It was a decubitus ulcer, a bedsore. I attempted to speak, but only released a hoarse, senseless cry.

The men continued movement throughout the room, looking between me and the digital machine capturing quantifiable aspects of the human body. My vision faded seconds before consciousness and I was lost in sleep again.

I was in and out of dreamless darkness. I had no reckoning of time. Even the crude use of facial hair growth was eliminated by a shave as I slept.

I was visited by different faces each day, but they studied me only as some inanimate find. They saw me as an ancient relic of silver and gold to be cleaned, polished, and observed with no place left in human hands. Blood was taken as was skin and other painfully acquired tissues. No reasons or results were shared with me.

At some juncture the cravings for the elixir returned. I push and pulled against the bindings holding me firm to no avail. Half mad with desperate desire, I screamed out into empty darkness for my elixir, for my sweet Vella Root. I would have told them anything if it could bring me closer to acquiring the elixir.

Perhaps it was there they first spoke to me. He asked me to identify myself. He was a surly fellow named Agent Gaines who never identified in what agency he held his rank. I thought deceit to be my only means of escape.

"My name is Paul Dorean," I told this Gaines over and over again. I recited facts that were easily drawn from the mind of the Taxman: dates, places, professional accolades. None of these were accepted from me.

"We have strong reason to believe that you are not in fact Paul Dorean," Gaines said. "We believe that you are a perfect replica, but you are not that man. Want to tell me about that?"

Accepting that Gaines was a man who could believe in such a feat was difficult. His generic dark blue suit and plain tie suggested a man bound to the most basic of all explanations. That is, any person claiming that another had possessed their body was simply insane. Surely this was the way he would see it. I was tired, worn, and had fallen into the worst of pain. I conceded to the inquiry.

"I do not know what claims have exactly been made, but they are likely true," I said.

Agent Gaines opened his jacket and brought forth a small leather covered notepad and scribbled. I told him of the agreement between Whales and I. I disclosed the elixir. I told him of my powers when under its influence.

I gave him my long and colored history on the earth.

The interview lasted over four hours, much of which is the same details I offer to you in this instrument. Gaines treated me respectfully and courteously throughout the conversation. The horrific story changed nothing in his expression or posture. I sensed no judgment of my character or the veracity of my statements to him.

At our conclusion Gaines authorized another shot of morphine. My blood was filled with a mighty narcotic that excised the unbearable pain. I receded into myself, accepting all that had happened and believing that everything would ultimately prove to be manageable.

The doses were continued day in and day out. I was unable to tell whether I was awake or asleep, but I did not care either way. Occasionally, Gaines or some other agent would come and ask more questions. I answered openly and honestly. I was beginning to know the catharsis of turning the light on in the darkness that consumed me.

One day, a group came before me. They wore protective gear and carried visible firearms. They chained and strapped me to a transport cart. They wheeled me from the room and traveled down several floors in a service elevator. I felt the last rays of the sunshine on me as I was carried into the rear of a large, waiting van that quickly sped off from the facility.

The rear of the vehicle had no windows. Two guards remained there with me, firearms drawn. I closed my eyes and drifted away.

I awoke inside a windowless room with a large metal locked door. I was chained to a series of bars within the room, but was able to sit on a long bench of slats firmly bolted to the wall.

I heard nothing until there came the rattling of jailor's keys. I was escorted into a courtroom of sorts. Lacking were the typical accommodations for reporters and the public. There were two tables placed before an elevated bench. There were two well polished federal lawyers at a table and then me alone at mine. A handful of others filled the small plain room, all of them dressed in the garb of authority.

"You may be seated, counselors," said the Judge as he moved things about on his bench. "This is in the matter of case 7C-2007. Let the record reflect I have been provided with a photograph and physical description of the detained and will take judicial notice that this individual is present here in the courtroom. From that let us proceed."

With that both of the lawyers nodded, each giving me their own glance of shameful disapproval. The older of the two men lifted pages from a voluminous open accordion file and stood.

"Your Honor, I am William Mier senior assistant U.S. attorney and this is my colleague, assistant U.S. attorney Lawrence Cartwright, appearing here on behalf of the United States of America. We are here in the matter of 7C-2007 seeking the continued temporary detention of the subject until the date of the permanent detention hearing. We can prove that the detained is an unnaturally dangerous subject pursuant to Executive Order 7834A."

"In what way is this man dangerous?" the Judge asked.

"We are aware he does not look so, Your Honor. We do not completely understand the extent and nature of this man's abilities ourselves. We do know that he is able to supplant his consciousness into the body of another. We believe we have a significant trail of both U.S. and foreign citizens who were overtaken by this man for the purpose of theft, a complete theft unknown before in our world," responded the elder attorney.

"Is it fair to say you are claiming him to be some form of body snatcher?" the Judge questioned causing a subtle stir of laughter within the courtroom. The reference sparked a fading memory in the mind of the Taxman. Someone said this before.

"That is our claim, Your Honor. This man is not the man you see before you. The physical presence here is a lifetime employee of the Internal Revenue Service, agent Paul Dorean. We believe Mr. Dorean identified the abilities of this subject during an ongoing investigation and in an attempt to subvert exposure, the subject overtook Paul Dorean's body."

None of these outrageous statements were dismissed. This secret court heard a plethora of inexplicable phenomena. My life, all the things of it, were reduced to a number in this forum and I had every reason to believe that I would be detained forever in the end of it all.

Several more hours passed. During the time there was much talk of a secret formula, a small quantity that was discovered at Whales' estate. This I would not accommodate. The Court was assured that government scientists were working tirelessly to uncover the mysteries of the elixir.

For a time I was returned to the holding cell in order for testimony to be taken of unnamed witnesses. Likely it was at a minimum Greg Whales and the Taxman in his resilient cancer free form of youth.

Then at last, after all the statements, the arguments, the testimony, and the evidence, I was afforded an opportunity to refute the supernatural claims against me. I did no such thing, bowing to the will of authority.

"Your Honor, my true name, if a being such as I has a name, is Nathan Sorren. I was born in the year of our Lord fifteen hundred and twenty-nine to a wealthy land baron in England. I studied under the tutelage of a Doctor Johannes Faustus in my early adulthood where I fashioned a mighty elixir that permitted me a great ability. I then became this body snatcher that you speak of. It is all true, all nearly five hundred years of this. I have no count of the lives stolen away or the murders. I am the most vicious of beings and deserve far worse than any punishment available on this earth. I look forward to the end of it all."

With those solemn words I conceded to the State. The Judge and my persecutors seemed satisfied with my confession. His Honor announced a date upon which I would return to the Court for a *pro forma* permanent conclusion to the matter.

The pain returned as the proceedings ended. Though I was mercifully medicated, the effects seemed to lessen and lessen with each administration. I prayed to my enemy God that he take me from the world and send me to the Dark Place for eternity.

64

And now this prison place. There was no jury or trial, just their unofficial, secretive damnation. Here I sit day in and out, alone. There are few comforts to hide me from the deep river aches of this dying frame. Sometimes my cell darkens at its edges and I hear a distant bell, but then return to life again. The resilience of the Taxman's frame despite the filling death within proves to be another harsh coincidence.

My captors keep my concrete room cold. Each morning I watch the steamed air flow from my mouth wishing that it was my essence escaping into freedom. I sometimes dare to imagine my old lives, but am quickly brought to this present.

I have been subject to the obligatory pushing and prodding of government scientists. There have been biopsies, EKG's, EEG's, CAT scans, blood tests, MRI's, and x-rays. My blood, hair, skin, and bones tricked upon me are used for their curiosities. To them I am just some jarred thing to be quantified and understood.

There are no sharp objects in this room, or anywhere to affix my bed sheet. These things they thought of, too. I lack the fortitude to chew away at my own wrists or swallow my tongue. Perhaps such strengths will come.

I am impotent without the elixir, a prisoner of aged and aching flesh. My desperate childhood brought forth no such desolation. Not even in that dank, dark basement where Father left me to die.

I tell you all of these things perhaps from boredom, perhaps to enlighten you, but I think mostly to remember that I did once exist. I think of the White Devil waiting for me within the void. I have seen only his shadows since that wretched day, but feel him there. I pray not for mercy inside his wretched black hell. I pray for nothing of leniency or sympathy. I pray for every torment, every suffering. I want no doubt to remain that I was this poison thing to the world.

Sometimes I dream the nightmares of the Taxman. All of his torments and pains have been bequeathed to me. I carry his burden while I imagine he roams free with his new chance. Our fates could not be more divergent.

As a little boy I learned a secret. Through it I became this fairy tale beast. I was the corrupter of nature and time, a parasite of humanity and its history. Only death now can spring me. God or monster I wait.

Sorren and the Taxman return...

THE OTHER SONS

2012

www.ingramcontent.com/pod-product-compliance
Lightning Source LLC
Chambersburg PA
CBHW050928120626
46552CB00001B/98

9780615371238